"Four years," he muttered, almost as if he knew her thoughts. **"I haven't held my child in my arms for that long."**

When he met her gaze, she saw his pain in the starkness of his expression. "She used to call me dada," he continued, "and hold out her little arms for me to pick her up. She'd laugh when I did and that sound... Oh, that sound was pure joy." Exhaling, he shook his head. "I've pictured what it would be like when I finally found her. I have imagined that scenario a hundred times. And now... Now I realize she wouldn't even recognize me."

His voice broke. She watched as he struggled to regain his composure, unsure how to comfort him, or if she even should try.

A moment later, he straightened his shoulders, looking more like himself. "Are you ready?" he asked.

Momentarily confused, she shrugged. "Ready for what?"

"We're going to Houston. This time, we're going to find this bastard and get our daughter back."

Dear Reader,

Every once in a while, a book comes along that grabs me by the throat and won't let go. *Missing in Texas* is one of those stories. I fought it and struggled, aware I had to write it in a way that would give the tale justice. As I wrote this book, I cursed and cried, but eventually I managed to get the words right in a way that was true to these characters.

When Jake Cassin's one-year-old daughter was abducted, he never gave up searching for her. Despite losing his wife, despite being placed on leave at his job as a Houston police officer, he continued to look. Four long years have passed, and a tip leads him to the small west Texas town of Getaway and bakery owner Edie Beswick.

Edie is shocked when Jake Cassin shows up in her bakery with a photo of her adopted daughter, Laney, claiming she's his long-lost child. But that afternoon, Laney is once again abducted as she's getting off the school bus. And Edie's worst nightmare has suddenly come true.

The story is complex. The attraction between two people who could choose to be enemies is fierce. And the love for their missing child is strong. As they race against time to save Laney, can they also make something out of their tentative and growing relationship?

I hope you enjoy meeting Jake and Edie and, of course, Laney. And I truly hope you find their tale as engrossing as I did while writing it!

I appreciate you, dear reader!

Karen Whiddon

MISSING IN TEXAS

Karen Whiddon

HARLEQUIN®
ROMANTIC SUSPENSE™

Recycling programs
for this product may
not exist in your area.

ISBN-13: 978-1-335-59371-9

Missing in Texas

Copyright © 2023 by Karen Whiddon

All rights reserved. No part of this book may be used or reproduced in
any manner whatsoever without written permission except in the case of
brief quotations embodied in critical articles and reviews.

This is a work of fiction. Names, characters, places and incidents
are either the product of the author's imagination or are used fictitiously.
Any resemblance to actual persons, living or dead, businesses,
companies, events or locales is entirely coincidental.

For questions and comments about the quality of this book,
please contact us at CustomerService@Harlequin.com.

Harlequin Enterprises ULC
22 Adelaide St. West, 41st Floor
Toronto, Ontario M5H 4E3, Canada
www.Harlequin.com

Printed in U.S.A.

Karen Whiddon started weaving fanciful tales for her younger brothers at the age of eleven. Amid the gorgeous Catskill Mountains, then the majestic Rocky Mountains, she fueled her imagination with the natural beauty surrounding her. Karen now lives in north Texas, writes full-time and volunteers for a boxer dog rescue. She shares her life with her hero of a husband and four to five dogs, depending on if she is fostering. You can email Karen at kwhiddon1@aol.com. Fans can also check out her website, karenwhiddon.com.

Books by Karen Whiddon

Harlequin Romantic Suspense

The Rancher's Return
The Texan's Return
Wyoming Undercover
The Texas Soldier's Son
Texas Ranch Justice
Snowbound Targets
The Widow's Bodyguard
Texas Sheriff's Deadly Mission
Texas Rancher's Hidden Danger
Finding the Rancher's Son
The Spy Switch
Protected by the Texas Rancher
Secret Alaskan Hideaway
Saved by the Texas Cowboy
Missing in Texas

Visit the Author Profile page at Harlequin.com for more titles.

To all my faithful readers who write reviews and send me email. I appreciate you all so much! Often, you make my entire day!

Chapter 1

When the cheerful little bells over the front door of the bakery jingled, Edie Beswick looked up into the face of the most attractive man she'd ever seen. Sandy brown hair, a firm jaw and eyes the color of her special lime frosting, the most perfect shade of light green. She'd just finished baking a tray of lemon cupcakes and putting them out in the display case, but this stranger with the muscular arms and broad shoulders made her heart beat faster than a mouthful of her favorite decadent dessert. Which, since she was considered the most talented baker in an entire family of them, said a lot.

"Can I help you?" she asked sweetly, all of her insides tingling.

He smiled, revealing twin dimples on either side of his mouth, which impossibly made him even more handsome. "I think you likely can," he drawled, clearly not noticing the effect that his rich, *sexy* voice had on her. Who knew a man's voice could make all her body parts tighten?

"If you're looking for something sweet, you've come to the right place," she replied, mentally wincing at the double entendre. Now she sounded like a goof, which she basically was in most areas of her life, though not here. If anything, she was in her element in the place. This was her family's bakery, which had first opened in the small West Texas town of Getaway in 1949 and was passed down through generations of Beswicks. Here, she shone, as had all the Beswick women before her.

Her great grandmother, Irene Beswick, the original baker, had been renowned for her talent. People had come from as far away as Lubbock and Midland to buy her cakes and pies. And so it had been for Edie's grandmother, mother and now her.

Thinking of this, she stood taller, confident in her ability to find him the most delicious treat to take home.

As his smile broadened, his green eyes crinkled.

Dang it. She flushed, realizing she must sound like she was flirting with him. "I mean," she stammered, gesturing around the bakery. "I'm known for the best cakes and pies in all of West Texas." She bustled around to grab one of her specialties, a melt-in-your-mouth red velvet cupcake with sour cream frosting.

"Here." Setting it on the counter, she swallowed. "Try this. On the house."

Without taking his intense gaze from her face, he thanked her. "I'll take it with me for later," he said. "I actually came in here for something else."

For one crazy moment, she thought he meant to say

something corny and wonderful, like he'd seen her across the town square and wanted to know if she'd like to go get coffee sometime. Stuff like that only happened in books and movies, she knew. Still, she couldn't help wishing. Because men like him never walked into her bakery.

Holding her breath, she watched as he pulled a carefully folded sheet of paper from his pocket, opened it and smoothed it flat with his hand before sliding it across the counter to her.

"My name is Jake Cassin and I'm looking for my daughter," he said, his tone hopeful. "This picture is four years old, so I'm not sure what she looks like now. She was abducted when she was one, and this is all I have to go on."

Accepting the paper, Edie glanced down at it and froze. Her daughter's chubby little face smiled up at her. Edie had taken a similar photo of Laney right after she'd adopted her. Four years ago. *Crud.*

"Where…" she began. "Where did you get this?"

He cocked his head, still watching her. "What do you mean?" A frown quickly replaced his smile. "That's one of the last photos I have of my daughter. It's up on my website and was in numerous Amber Alerts, back when she first went missing. Have you seen her?"

Mouth dry, she swallowed. "No," she lied, hoping like hell she sounded normal. "I haven't. Though if this picture is four years old, there's no telling how she might have changed in that time."

Except Edie knew what that little girl looked like now at the age of five. Because she hurried home to that precious little face every single day. She tucked her in bed at night with butterfly kisses and a couple of her favorite story books and considered her the greatest blessing in her life.

"True," he allowed, taking back his paper, folding and placing it carefully back in his pocket. He pulled out a card and held it out to her. "I received a tip on my website that she might be here. I've been looking for her a long time. I'm not going to stop until I find her. Please, take this. If you hear anything, anything at all, give me a call. I'm staying at the Landshark Motel."

Somehow, she managed to smile and nod as she accepted his card. "I sure will," she said. "Is your website on here, too?"

"Yes. Give it a look, see if anything jogs your memory." He turned to go, remembering the cupcake at the last minute. "Thanks for this."

"You're welcome." Normally, she would have invited him to come again. If he'd have been any other customer, she would have. Instead, she took deep breaths, gripped her counter to keep from crumpling and watched as he climbed into a shiny black, tricked-out Ford F-150. The truck rumbled as he started it up, sunlight glinting off the custom paint as he back out and drove away.

Once he'd gone, she instinctively reached for the phone to call the sheriff but then reconsidered. She needed to hold off until she figured out what exactly was going on.

She'd adopted Laney four years ago, roughly the same time as this man claimed his daughter had gone missing. And unless Laney had a twin out there somewhere, Jake Cassin possessed her photo. Could the two be the same little girl? If so, how was such a thing possible?

Head spinning, Edie turned the Open sign to Closed, locked the front door and pulled the blinds. Everyone in Getaway knew she closed in the afternoons for a little bit so she could go pick up her daughter at the bus stop. Laney had started kindergarten this year. Edie had wanted to drive her to and from school, but Laney had insisted on riding the bus with her friends. So far, despite Edie's overprotective trepidation, her daughter's little daily bit of independent adventure appeared to be going great.

Edie slipped out the back door, taking care to lock it, and hopped into her Mazda SUV. She drove the two miles to the bus stop, aware she'd be early, and parked to wait for the bright yellow school bus. She was early, which suited her fine. Time alone in her car would be good because she needed to think.

When her parents had died in a horrific house fire in Idaho, Edie had been adopted by her aunt and uncle Marilyn and Albert Beswick of Getaway, Texas. They'd made the almost twenty-hour drive without stopping, determined to comfort a confused two-year-old who kept crying for her mommy.

Which was why when Gina, one of Edie's Idaho cousins and a single mother, had died suddenly of a brain aneurysm, leaving behind her one-year-old daughter, Edie hadn't hesitated. With her parents' blessing, she'd made her own nonstop drive from Texas to Idaho, hell-bent on rescuing her niece Laney.

Because there had been no other family, the adoption had gone without a hitch. Though Edie had zero experience raising a small child, she fell instantly and deeply in love. The moment she gathered little Laney up in her arms, she knew she'd lay down her life for this child—her daughter—from that moment on.

Shaking off the memories, Edie once again tried to figure out where this Jake Cassin came into all this. He claimed his daughter had been abducted. But as far as Edie knew, Gina had carried and birthed her child. Except now, even this might be in doubt. There were no other family members remaining in Pocatello. No one to say, yes, they'd seen Gina pregnant and she'd been as big as a house. As a matter of fact, they'd been the ones who'd taken her to the hospital when the time had come to deliver.

None of that. In fact, despite being first cousins, Edie had barely known Gina at all. Could she have— would she have somehow stolen Jake's daughter? Why? How?

Edie checked her watch. The bus should be along any moment now. She couldn't wait to see Laney's face, to kiss her cheek, to breathe in the scent of her freshly shampooed hair.

Again, she replayed Jake sliding the photograph across the counter. The instant recognition, the certainty that this was somehow, impossibly, a photo of Laney.

Several scenarios played out in her mind. Maybe Jake and Gina had been married and then divorced, and he'd gotten custody, but Gina had refused to accept that and had stolen their daughter.

Except Jake had used the word *abducted*. And he hadn't said *by her own mother*.

There, the school bus, a bright spot of yellow in the dust cloud of the dirt road. Edie pushed all worries about Jake Cassin out of her head. Putting a bright smile on her face, she got out of her SUV and stood near the area where the bus always dropped Laney off.

But this time, the bus didn't stop. Instead, it kept right on going while Edie stood in stunned disbelief. She finally gathered herself enough to jump in her vehicle and chase the school bus down.

Luckily, a few miles up the road, the bus had to stop for train tracks as required by law. This enabled Edie to catch up and be there when it made its next stop. She pulled over to the side of the road, slammed her shifter in Park and jumped out. Kids were still emerging from the bus.

Running over toward the door, Edie reached it just as the last child exited. Before the driver could close the door, Edie climbed the steps, frantically searching the bus for her daughter.

"Ma'am?" The driver, an older man who wasn't Mrs. Pope, the usual driver, stared at her. "Can I help you?"

Hyperventilating at this point, Edie tried to calm herself down enough to form coherent words. "My little girl," she managed. "Blond long hair. She was wearing a pink backpack and jeans."

He frowned at her, clearly not comprehending. "Okay?"

"She was supposed to get off at the last stop," she explained, her voice remarkably steady, considering how fast her heart was hammering in her chest. "And I don't see her on the bus. Where is she?"

Slowly, he shook his head. "I'm sorry, but I'm just a temp driver while Mrs. Pope is out sick. I was told all the children on this route knew their stops. There were several girls with blonde hair. I have no idea."

Edie stared, horrified. "You. Have. No. Idea. Are you freaking kidding me?"

"Ms. Beswick?" a young voice piped up. "I know where Laney is. She got off two stops back, with Jessica and Amanda. They were all going over Amanda's house."

This news almost made Edie's knees buckle. Only by grabbing the pole at the front of the bus was she able to continue standing.

The little girl who had spoken stared earnestly up at her. She appeared to be abut Laney's age. "They wanted me to go with them, but I knew if I did, my mommy would be mad."

"Good thinking, honey," Edie replied. "I wish Laney had thought like you."

"We need to get going, ma'am," the bus driver said, pointedly glancing toward the still open door.

"So do I." Edie turned and exited. She hurried to her vehicle, glad she'd left it running. While she wasn't exactly sure where the stop before Laney's might be, she had a pretty good idea where Amanda lived. She'd talked with her mother at the kindergarten open house.

Making a U-turn, Edie headed back the way she'd come. There was a small, older subdivision between her home and the school. The bus would make a stop right at the entrance so all the children who lived there could walk home. It wasn't too far, and maybe Edie could even catch up with the kids before they reached Amanda's house. Though she doubted that, she thought grimly. She'd wasted far too much time quizzing the bus driver.

Rounding a curve, she saw the double-sided brick entrance. There appeared to be a small group of people—

both adults and children—milling around near the exit. As she pulled up, parking on the side of the road across from the entrance, a sheriff's car came racing from the other direction, siren on and lights flashing.

Edie's stomach dropped. Jumping out of her SUV, she hurried over to the growing cluster of people, praying she wouldn't see a child on the ground. There were several children, varying in age, clinging to different adults. Edie studied all of them, looking for Laney, but she didn't see her. But for that matter, she didn't recognize any of Laney's friends either.

"What's going on?" she tried to ask, but one of the women yanked her into a tight embrace before she could get all the words out.

"I'm so, so sorry," the woman kept repeating, over and over and over.

"Sorry for what?" Edie tried to ask.

Since everyone seemed to be trying to talk at the same time, Edie couldn't make sense of the words. To her relief, the hugger released her when Rayna Coombs, the sheriff, strode over.

"I got a call about an abducted child?" Rayna looked from one adult to another. "Who can explain?"

Again, several adults began speaking at once, each one trying to talk over the others. Edie simply stood, frozen in terror, hoping against hope that this had nothing to do with Laney or her little friends.

A piercing whistle silenced everyone immediately. Rayna, despite her petite stature, didn't mess around. "Now," she ordered, pointing at the woman closest to her. "You. Tell me exactly what happened here."

"I was waiting here for my daughter, Amanda," the woman said. "She got off the school bus with two of her kindergarten friends. They were all walking toward me when a car pulled up and stopped. The man inside got out, grabbed one of the little girls, yanked her into the car and drove off. It all happened so fast." Her voice broke. "I froze. I couldn't make sense out of what was happening. That poor child."

Grim-faced, Rayna brushed back a stray wisp of her red hair. "What color and kind of car?"

"White. Four-door," the woman answered. "I think it was a Honda Accord."

"Thank you." Rayna nodded. "Where is Amanda now?"

"There." The woman pointed to a small group of children clustered around two adults.

"May I talk with her?" Rayna asked.

"Yes, certainly. Amanda. Come over here, honey. Ms. Coombs wants to talk to you."

The little girl hurried over, her pinched expression giving away her inner tension. "Yes, ma'am?"

So polite, Edie thought, trying to focus.

"I understand you saw everything," Rayna said, her voice gentle.

Amanda nodded, appearing as if she might be about to cry at any moment. "I did." She swallowed hard. "It was scary."

"The girl that the man grabbed, what was her name?" Rayna asked.

"Laney," Amanda replied, starting to cry. "He got my best friend, Laney Beswick."

Edie's knees buckled. "Noooo," she cried. As she collapsed, the woman who had hugged her earlier caught her before she hit the ground.

When Edie opened her eyes again, she found herself in Rayna's cruiser, sitting in the front seat, passenger side.

"Are you okay?" Rayna asked. "You passed out."

"No," Edie answered. "I'm not okay. I won't be until I have my little girl back in my arms." She took a deep breath, then told Rayna about the man who had stopped by the bakery earlier, searching for his own child. "I think he might have been the one who took her," she said.

"Why? What are you basing that on?"

Edie shook her head. "Long story. But keeping it short, there's a decent chance my Laney might be his kid."

To her credit, Rayna didn't ask for details. Instead, she took a moment to consider before speaking.

"I met Jake Cassin," Rayna said slowly. "He's former law enforcement and seems like a stand-up kind of guy. He stopped by my office looking for clues about his missing daughter."

Edie closed her eyes and took a deep breath before opening them. "We've got to find my Laney."

"I agree." Rayna clearly understood the need for swift action. "Follow me," she told Edie. "He's staying at the Landshark. Let's go pay him a visit."

Back in his motel room, Jake Cassin couldn't stop thinking about the woman he'd met earlier in the bakery. Not due to her beauty, though she certainly had that. But because something had changed in her expression when she'd viewed the photo of Noel. Subtle, and maybe he'd imagined it, but he'd seen the way her eyes widened and she'd swallowed hard before shaking her head and sliding the picture back to him.

All his inner alarms had gone off. She knew something.

Had she been lying? Or, like all the other wild-goose-chase leads he'd followed, might it just be wishful thinking?

In his former career in law enforcement, Jake had become quite good at sniffing out information. Following various leads, he'd tracked Noel to Pocatello, Idaho, but there the trail had gone cold. He'd learned that a woman named Gina, who'd turned out to be one of Jake's former wife's friends, had lived in an apartment there with a little girl she'd called Laney.

But Gina had died, and no one seemed to know what had happened to the little girl.

Jake had wasted a lot of time trying to find out where Noel had gone after that. Finally, he'd located a man who'd dated Gina, who swore a relative had shown up and taken the little girl to some small town in West Texas with a weird name.

Not much to go on, and Texas was huge. But at least he had a geological region, even if it was larger than many other entire states. And he'd come to learn many of the cities and towns had unique names, so he made a list and begun visiting them one at a time, staying west of Fort Worth.

Using his law enforcement connections, he'd visited sheriff's offices and police departments in small towns with names like Cut and Shoot and Gun Barrel City. He'd met a lot of good men and some not so great, but no one knew of anyone who'd suddenly acquired a little girl.

Meanwhile, time went by, both slower and faster than Jake would have liked. It had taken him the better part of a year to track Noel to Idaho, and his travels around the big state of Texas ate up even more time. He'd had to work the occasional part-time job, too, just to pay for food, gas and lodging. He'd worked as a carpenter, a painter and various other things.

Before he knew it, four years had passed. And a woman in a bakery's imperceptible reaction was all he had to show for it. He was no closer to finding Noel than he'd been when he started.

Except maybe, he might be.

Again his thoughts returned to the woman in the bakery. Despite the instant spark of attraction between them, he knew he hadn't imagined her reaction. He could spot someone who wasn't being entirely truthful a mile away.

A sharp series of knocks on the door startled him. Peering through the peephole, he spotted the sheriff of Getaway, Texas. His heart skipped a beat in his chest. Had she learned something?

Fumbling with the chain, he opened the door. "Afternoon, Sheriff," he began. And then he spotted the woman from the bakery standing behind her. She looked both furious and terrified, her gaze locking on him with a singular intensity.

"A little girl was abducted a few miles from here," Rayna informed him, her tone brusque and businesslike. "Not even thirty minutes ago. Do you mind if we take a look inside your room?"

At first, it took Jake a moment to make sense of her words. When he realized she thought *he* might have stolen a child, he shook his head and stepped aside. "Come on in."

The sheriff was quick and thorough, methodically

searching the small room without making too much of a mess. The bakery woman stayed out of her way, twisting her hands in front of her and clearly trying to keep her act together. Jake couldn't help but feel sorry for her. "Was it your daughter?" he asked.

She stared at him before slowly nodding. "I don't know what I'm going to do if we can't find her." And then she broke down, crying in loud gut-wrenching sobs that shook her entire body.

He considered doing the only thing any human being could in those circumstances. With anyone else, he would have pulled her into his arms and tried to soothe her. After all, he knew exactly how she felt.

But he knew she likely wouldn't let him touch her. He was lucky to be allowed to stay inside the room as it was.

Rayna returned from searching the small bathroom. "She's not here," she announced. The moment she spoke, the girl's mother pushed herself away from Jake and made a herculean effort to get herself together.

"Of course she's not," Jake replied, meeting Rayna's gaze and crossing his arms. "Why would either of you think I would abduct a child when I'm here searching for my own daughter?"

Both women stared at him silently. It took a second, but he suddenly understood. "This missing girl. Does she…resemble my Noel?"

Slowly, the bakery woman nodded. "That picture you showed me earlier…"

The sheriff stepped forward, looking from one to the other. "Edie, you and Mr. Cassin need to have a long talk. Meanwhile, I'll get an Amber Alert started for Laney. Mr. Cassin, if I have to leave, would you mind driving Edie home?"

"Call me Jake," he said automatically. "And no, I don't mind at all." He could hardly believe that now, after all this time, he might have a solid lead. Except if this woman's Laney turned out to actually be his Noel, then she'd just been abducted yet again.

Once the sheriff stepped outside, Edie dropped into the chair by the window air conditioner. To her credit, she appeared to be holding herself together pretty well, considering. She began to speak, telling him about her cousin Gina in Pocatello, Idaho, who'd died from a brain aneurysm. Since Edie herself had been adopted, she'd raced up there and taken immediate custody of little Laney.

"I fell in love with her the instant I saw her," Edie said. Holding his gaze, she swallowed hard. "She was the spitting image of that photograph you showed me earlier."

Her words made his chest hurt. "I tracked my daughter to Pocatello," he said. "And the only thing I could find out was that a relative had taken her to a small town in West Texas with an unusual name."

"What is your daughter's name?" Edie asked quietly.

"Noel." Just saying it out loud brought a rush of emotion. He sighed, feeling tears pricking his eyes. Blinking them away, he waited the space of two heartbeats before continuing. "She was born right before Christmas. That was actually the only name her mother and I instantly agreed upon."

"I'm sorry." She took a deep breath. "Can you tell me what happened? How'd Noel get abducted?"

He must have blanched or made some involuntary expression that had her taking a step back.

"You don't have to," she said. "I understand if you find it too painful to talk about."

"Too painful?" He gave a short bark of humorless laughter. "Reliving it feels like a knife between my ribs each and every time. Yet I've told this story so often at numerous police stations and sheriff's offices all over West Texas that you'd think I would have numbed up a little by now."

Nodding, she glanced at the door, almost as if she hoped Rayna would reappear with news that her daughter had miraculously been found. Oh, he could definitely relate to that. A day never went by that he didn't feel something similar.

When her gaze met his again, he saw both sadness and resolve. "Then tell me," she said. "I need to think about something else or I'm going to lose it."

"It was a beautiful spring day," he began. "My wife Marina decided to take Noel to a nearby park and—"

"Local to where?" she interrupted.

"The Woodlands. It's a city north of Houston." He swallowed, that old familiar ache building in him. "Everything was blooming, and Marina loved taking photos of the flowers with her phone. She said she must have gotten distracted, because when she looked up, Noel's stroller was empty."

Edie's eyes filled with tears. She covered her mouth and took a moment to get herself under control. When she spoke again, her voice came out rough. "She blamed herself, didn't she?"

All he could do was nod.

"What about you?" she asked, suddenly fierce. "Did you blame her, too?"

He hung his head, momentarily ashamed. "I'm only human," he said, admiring the way she championed a woman she'd never met. "So, in the beginning, in the awful, screaming void where we struggled with the knowledge that our child was missing, I did. Eventually, I came to realize that Marina was only human, too. She never could have imagined—*we* never could have imagined—that something like this would happen."

Now Edie began to weep in earnest. "Laney!" she wailed. "We've got to find my daughter."

"We will," he said, meaning it. After all this time, he refused to come this close and lose everything a second time.

For the first time, he realized what his appearance here would mean to this woman, to her family. Because if Edie's Laney turned out to be his Noel, he wouldn't be leaving here without her.

Chapter 2

Edie managed to get herself back together in time to answer when Rayna rapped on the door. She let the sheriff in, hoping against hope that the other woman would have good news.

Instead, Rayna's grim expression told Edie she did not.

"I got the Amber Alert issued," she said. "Even though the description of the suspect's vehicle is kind of murky. Those things are very effective. The instant someone spots her, law enforcement will be notified."

Because all she could do was remain hopeful, Edie nodded. "Let's hope this happens soon. I remember reading somewhere that it's critical to locate missing children within forty-eight hours of an abduction."

"Seventy-two hours," Rayna corrected. "I promise you, we're doing all we can."

"Thank you," Jake said. "I really appreciate that."

Rayna nodded, glancing from Jake to Edie and then back again. "I'm just going to go ahead and ask this to save time. Is Laney the same child you're looking for, Jake?"

Edie's breath caught in her chest as she glanced at Jake. He watched her quietly, clearly ready to let her reach her own determination. "It's likely," Edie finally said. "As much as I hate to think this of my cousin."

"We'll find her," Rayna promised, squeezing Edie's shoulder. She looked at Jake and made him the same promise.

"Now, do you want a ride back to your car?" Rayna asked. "Or do you and Jake here have more to discuss?"

"I think we've talked enough for now," Edie said. "I'd like to go back to my car and head home, just in case."

"Wait," Jake said just as she turned to leave. "You have my number, right?"

Slowly, she nodded.

"Do you mind giving me yours?" He lifted his phone. "Just shoot me a quick text so I can store it."

What could be the harm? After all, they definitely had something in common. She dug his card out of her pocket and typed his number in his phone, saving it as a contact before sending him a text with her own name.

Once his phone pinged, he glanced at it. "Thank you," he said.

With a jerk of her head to acknowledge, she followed Rayna outside.

Rayna stayed quiet for the entire drive. Edie appreciated that. She wasn't in the mood for small talk, and endlessly rehashing what had happened would only send her into a panic.

Back at the subdivision entrance, the crowd had already dispersed.

"Here we are." Rayna pulled over behind Edie's vehicle. "Are you going to be all right?"

Edie nodded, though she knew she wouldn't be anything close to all right until Laney was back in her arms.

"Call me if you need anything."

Of course, Edie promised she would.

Once she got into her SUV, she didn't go home. Instead, she found herself driving around town, looking for a white Honda Accord and hoping for a miracle. She called her mother and left a voicemail, only asking for a return call as soon as possible. Since her parents had handed over the bakery to Edie, they embraced retirement with gusto. They'd bought a motor home and spent nine months of the year traveling around the country. Right now, Edie thought they were somewhere in the Pacific Northwest. She knew they'd come rushing back to Getaway once they learned what had happened to their granddaughter. Honestly, she dreaded even telling them.

Four hours later, she forced herself to go home. Once she pulled into her garage and killed the engine, she sat in her vehicle a moment trying to muster up the energy to go inside.

Finally, she did. Entering the house, flicking on lights as she went, the absolute silence hit her hard. Normally, Laney would be chattering up a storm, talking about her day. She'd been begging for a pet lately, vacillating between a dog or a cat. Now Edie seriously regretted always saying no.

She knew she should make herself something to

eat, but her appetite had disappeared when her daughter did.

Wandering into Laney's room, she sat on the edge of the twin bed and fingered the purple and pink comforter decorated in unicorns. Laney had chosen that particular one herself, declaring that someday she planned to find a unicorn, even if people did say they weren't real. The closet door was open, and Laney had tossed two clean T-shirts onto the floor, discards from that morning when she'd tried to decide what she wanted to wear.

Panic made Edie hyperventilate. She pushed to her feet and forced herself to pick up the shirts and hang them in the closet. Her hands were shaking, but she managed to complete the simple task.

This couldn't be happening. It had to be a bad dream, the worst kind of nightmare. At any moment, she'd wake up and find her daughter asleep in her bed, safe and sound.

Except she knew she wouldn't and it wasn't. Laney had really been abducted. And if this Jake Cassin was telling the truth, not just this time but once before.

Around nine, Edie forced herself to drink some bone broth and to take her customary shower before bed. Since she ought to open the bakery in the morning like usual, she tended to go to sleep early and get up at 4:30 a.m. She needed to give the yeast dough time to rise and get the first batch of donuts cooking. She liked to have the front display case mostly stocked before she opened at 6:00 a.m.

For the first time since she'd taken over the bakery, she debated leaving it closed. Only the thought of how much her regulars depended on her for their morning fix of coffee and a donut had her even considering trying to open.

If her parents had been in town, she'd have gotten them to handle it. How could she even think of trying to run her business and act normally when her little girl was missing?

She didn't even bother trying to go to sleep. The instant she closed her eyes, she knew she'd only replay Laney's abduction over and over in her mind. Her baby must have been terrified. Edie could imagine her calling for her mother, which shattered her heart. She felt like she'd failed her daughter, because she should have been able to protect her. The fact that this wasn't even logical didn't escape her, but she couldn't make herself feel any other way.

Around midnight, she decided she would close the bakery tomorrow, just for one day. With a sense of relief, she typed up a note on her computer, enlarged the font and then printed it. Grabbing a roll of two-sided tape, she drove out to the bakery to tape it to the front door.

With that accomplished, she knew she should turn around, go home and try to get at least a few hours of rest. Instead, she found herself cruising up and down deserted streets, looking for a white Honda Accord and any sign of her daughter.

An hour later, exhausted and defeated, she pulled back into her driveway and parked. Instead of going in, she killed the engine and sat in the SUV.

Her phone chimed, indicating a text message. Startled, her first thought was that maybe Rayna had located Laney or at least gotten some sort of lead. Heart pounding, she fumbled to get her phone, her hands shaking.

Instead, the text was from Jake Cassin.

On the off chance that you can't sleep either, do you want to meet up somewhere for a cup of coffee?

Mind numb, Edie stared at the screen and exhaled. The crushing disappointment made her chest ache. For a moment, she felt furious with Jake for getting her hopes up, even though she understood he was only trying to be kind.

Of course she couldn't sleep. Who could, when their beloved child was who knew where with some stranger? Her mind shied away from the dark images crowding her brain. Her baby must be terrified, wondering why Mommy didn't come save her.

Tears pricking her eyes, throat closed, Edie studied the text again. This man was the only other person around who knew exactly what she was going through. His daughter had also been abducted. Even if several years had passed, she imagined the gut-wrenching horror and all-consuming sense of loss never dimmed. The very real possibility that Laney most likely was the same girl didn't change the fact that Jake Cassin knew what she was going through.

Yes, she texted back. There's a 24-hour diner in the truck stop on I-20. It's about a 30-minute drive. Let's meet there.

Without waiting for his response, she started her vehicle, backed out into the street and drove away. Even if Jake didn't show, she liked the idea of going to the truck stop. There, she would be anonymous in a way she never could be in her own small town.

Once she'd pulled into the parking lot, taking a spot close to the building, she eyed the rows of big rigs, most with their running lights on, and exhaled. Though her stomach ached, she made herself get out and make her way inside.

Bright lights, the clatter of silverware and dishes, and the strong scent of fried food felt both comforting and foreign. She slid into an empty booth, mildly surprised that even at this late hour, there were quite a few other customers.

Only then did she pull her phone out of her purse to check Jake's response.

On my way.

For whatever reason, this made her relax a little. Since she had a clear view of the entrance, she'd know the instant he arrived.

A few minutes later, he did.

He came through the door in a hurry. Her first glimpse of him—a large muscular man with a rugged kind of confidence that suggested he could fix anything—made her breath catch in her throat. Under different circumstances, she knew she'd have found him attractive, and a small, abstract part of herself still acknowledged that fact. Despite everything. Which made her feel incredibly shallow. Or human.

"I wish I had your confidence," she blurted out as he approached her booth.

Surprise flickered across his face. "Thanks?" He took a seat across from her. "Have you ordered yet?"

"No. I just got here a few minutes ago."

A waitress appeared, her long gray hair in a neat braid down her back. She slid a couple of menus across the table to them. "Coffee? Water? Or something else?"

They both ordered coffee. Why not, since clearly she wasn't going to be getting any sleep at all tonight.

"Are you going to eat?" he asked, glancing over his menu.

"I'm not sure," she said. "I haven't been able to choke down much of anything since…"

"I get it." His green eyes met hers. "But speaking as someone who's been there, you need to keep your strength up. Just in case your daughter needs you."

Gravely, she eyed him and then slowly nodded. "Thank you."

He pushed the other menu over toward her. "You're welcome. It's something I wish someone had told me when Noel first disappeared. I didn't eat for days—I couldn't. When my body finally rebelled, I collapsed. I almost had to be hospitalized. I refused, because I never would have forgiven myself if I'd been unable to function and Noel had been found."

Pretending to be engrossed in the menu, she kept sneaking glances at him doing the same. She appreciated his kindness, the way he didn't press her to admit her Laney might be his Noel, even though he definitely had the right.

The waitress reappeared with their coffees. "Are you ready to order?" she asked.

Edie looked up, momentarily confused. "I…what do you recommend?"

Appearing amused, the waitress smiled. "Are you

really hungry or just a little? In other words, do you want a huge plate of food or something smaller?"

"Like a salad?" Edie asked, even though she hadn't seen any salads on the menu.

"Chicken fried steak," Jake suggested. "You can always take half of it home if you can't eat it all."

The waitress's smile turned into a grin. "That's the best thing on our entire menu!" she said. "Most of our customers come here specifically for that."

Edie hesitated.

"We'll take two," Jake said, slapping the menu down. The waitress nodded, took their menus and bustled away. "It'll do you some good," he told Edie. "I promise."

Under ordinary circumstances, she would have taken offense at such high-handedness. But these were anything but ordinary times, so she welcomed him making the choice for her.

"Tell me about Laney," he said, leaning across the table. "Anything and everything. Her favorite color, what kind of toys she plays with, all of it."

Mentally she acknowledged his reason for asking, while appreciating the opportunity to talk about her daughter. "She loves purple and pink," she told him. "And unicorns. She even chose a comforter for her bed with all of those things. She knows all the words and can sing along to most Taylor Swift songs, and she loves when I read to her at bedtime."

Now she found herself fighting back tears. She squared her shoulders, swiped at her eyes and made herself continue. "She just started kindergarten. She's been so excited. She keeps insisting that she's a big girl now. I wanted to drive her to school and pick her up, but she insisted on riding the school bus with her friends."

She lost it then, covering her mouth with her hands. Head down, shoulders shaking, she tried to speak and failed.

"Hey." He leaned over and touched her shoulder. "This is not your fault."

"But I let her ride the bus," she wailed, loud enough to cause several heads to turn. When she realized, she tried to settle down, clenching her teeth and trying to breathe. Would he be shocked if she told him she really wanted to throw her head back and howl?

Somehow, she suspected he just might understand.

The waitress appeared just then, carrying two heaping plates of food. She pretended not to notice how distraught Edie appeared, smiling as she placed their meal on the table in front of them. "It's a lot, hon," she said, talking to them both at the same time. "But I promise it's delicious, and tastes just as wonderful heated up for lunch the next day. Enjoy!"

Instead, Edie eyed the heaping plate of food, put her hand over her mouth and ran for the restroom.

Not sure what to do, Jake eyed his chicken fried steak and took a swig of his coffee. His stomach growled, reminding him he hadn't eat anything since the cupcake in Edie's bakery. He knew basic manners decried he should wait for her to return, so he did.

Finally, eyes red and swollen, she made her way back to the table. "Sorry about that," she muttered, sliding in across from him. "Wow, that steak just about takes up the entire plate."

He nodded, picking up his fork and knife. "They left just enough room for the mashed potatoes and gravy."

She eyed the mountain of food. "I think I'll start with the green beans," she said, reaching for the small bowl that had accompanied the main plate.

Finally, he dug in. The food tasted every bit as delicious as the waitress had promised. He ate with a single-minded intensity, all the while trying to keep an eye on Edie without her noticing. The continual urge to bring up the elephant in the room—the likely possibility that her Laney was, in fact, his Noel—was something he could keep at bay, at least until Noel was found safe and unharmed.

And he had no doubt she would be soon. No way had he come all this way, devoted his entire existence to locating her, for any other kind of outcome. He'd finally located his baby girl. He refused to lose her again.

"Those weren't bad," Edie said, pushing away the empty bowl.

"This isn't either," he said, gesturing to his half-empty plate.

Gingerly, she reached for her plate and moved it closer. Then she picked up her fork and knife and cut off a slice. He watched as she popped it into her mouth, chewing slowly.

"That's amazing," she mused. She took a second bite, chewing slowly. "I've never been a fan of chicken fried steak, but this is really good."

He sat back, watching her eat with determination.

Both their phones chimed, indicating a text. Edie jumped. "Rayna!" she exclaimed at the same moment he did. The sheriff had sent a group text to both of them.

I hate to text at this hour, and I hope this didn't wake you, but I suspect right now that no one is getting any sleep.

We've had several people call in with sightings, but unfortunately none of these have panned out. I wanted to assure you that we have multiple agencies all over the state working on this. We will find her. Keep the faith. I'll be in touch later.

"Wow," Edie said, disappointment plain on her face. "I was hoping the text would be saying Laney had been found."

Jake glanced at his phone. "It's nearly two a.m. Rayna mustn't be getting any sleep either."

With a sigh, Edie picked up her fork and resumed eating. In a few minutes, she'd nearly demolished her chicken fried steak and mashed potatoes. Despite her obvious appetite, the sorrow never completely left her eyes.

"Let's work together," he blurted before he took the time to go over the ramifications of such a thing. He didn't consider himself an impulsive man, but in this instance…working with Edie to find her missing child felt right. Especially since Laney most likely was his daughter.

"Work together?" She stared. "But why? You should know up front, there's no way in hell I'm letting you take my girl away from me."

Careful, careful. "I appreciate your honesty. Don't think I haven't thought of that."

"I mean, I understand where you're coming from," she said, her fierce voice matching her expression.

"And if my Laney does turn out to be your Noel, we'll have to work something out."

Work something out. He let that statement go unchallenged for now. "How about we focus on what really matters at this moment in time? Getting her back safe and sound."

Warily, she eyed him. "I'll think about it," she finally said.

"You do that. Either way, I'm planning on going looking once the sun comes up. I doubt whoever grabbed her is still here in town, so I'm thinking of trying the next several towns over."

"Abilene," she said, surprising him. "I'm think he might have taken her there. It's not a huge city by any means, but it's larger than Getaway. Big enough to make it easier to stay hidden."

He checked his phone. "Good idea. What do you say? Do you want to go with me to look?"

Taking a sip of her coffee, she considered. Just then, the waitress reappeared, bringing a couple of to-go boxes. "Looks like you both enjoyed your meal," she said, beaming. "Would either of you like a refill on the coffee?"

"Yes, please." Edie lifted her cup.

Jake nodded also. Once their cups were full again, the waitress left the check and moved away.

"You know what? I think I will go with you," Edie said. "The most important thing is finding Laney. Maybe two heads really will be better than one."

He dug in his wallet, pulled out two twenties and left them on the table. "We've got about five hours until sunrise. We should both go home and try and get some sleep."

Though Edie shook her head, the weariness in her eyes told another story.

"I know you don't want to, but again, you have to take care of yourself if you want to help your daughter." He paused, took a deep breath and continued. "Believe me, I speak from experience. After Noel was taken, I didn't want to sleep either. I was afraid I would miss something."

Thinking back to that time, how he'd barely eaten, seldom slept yet kept up the frantic search, he shook his head. He'd tried to continue, fueled mainly by nothing more than desperation.

"I ended up in the hospital," he said. "They found me slumped over in my truck, suffering from heat stroke. I lost two entire days while they pumped me full of IV fluids and ran tests."

Expression grave, she nodded. "I can see how that might happen. I just want to keep going, keep pushing, until I get my child back."

He told himself the way she kept referencing *her* child, *her* daughter wasn't deliberate. She was out of her mind with worry.

Pushing to his feet, he waited for her to do the same. "I'll walk you out," he said.

Outside, the hum of traffic on the interstate mingled with the sound of various trucks idling. When they reached her SUV, she unlocked the doors and glanced at him. "I'll text you my address. What time are you picking me up?"

"It should be light enough by seven," he said, even though his phone claimed it would actually be a bit later than that. "We both have time to rest our eyes before we start out."

Whether or not she intended to take advantage of his suggestion, she didn't say.

He waited until she'd driven off before climbing into his truck. Back at the motel, he parked and quietly let himself into his room. Then he set his phone alarm to go off at six and undressed before crawling into bed and closing his eyes.

Instead of the alarm, the wail of an Amber Alert woke him. Checking the screen, he read about little Laney Beswick. The accompanying photo of a cute blonde girl with wavy hair made him swallow hard. *Noel*, he thought, recognizing his chin and Marina's eyes.

Seeing her at age five, knowing he had missed out on four years of her life, felt like a punch in the gut. Even worse, she was once again in danger. No one had any idea who had grabbed her or why.

Which felt awfully, terribly familiar. In fact, he had trouble believing this had happened again.

Shaking off the panic, he sat up immediately and headed for the shower. He'd mastered the art of making what little sleep he could get count. And he'd even gotten used to the bone deep weariness that dogged his steps most days.

Once he'd showered and dried off, he combed his hair and brushed his teeth before digging around in his duffle bag for a set of clean clothes.

Then he checked his phone. Sure enough, Edie had texted him her address one hour earlier. He wondered if she'd even slept at all or if she still remained determined to soldier through as if her body was invincible. Luckily for her, if she'd decided on the latter, she'd have him there to catch her when she inevitably fell apart.

After all, she'd taken care of and loved his Noel for four years. He had no doubt Noel loved her back. If Jake was going to rebuild a relationship with his child, who likely didn't even remember him, he was definitely going to need Edie's help.

Before driving over to Edie's, he stopped at a big chain gas station and got them both large coffees. Since he had no idea how she drank hers, he grabbed a handful of little creamers, some sugar and, just to be sure, artificial sweeteners, too, and plugged her address into his phone's GPS.

He pulled up in front of her house within minutes. Parking, he eyed the older brick ranch house, noting the neat landscaping and well-kept grass. He could see what looked like a child's wooden play fort, complete with swings, in the backyard.

Before he could even get out of his truck, the front door opened and Edie stepped out. He waited while she locked up. From a distance, she appeared rested. It wasn't until she opened his passenger side door and got in that he could see the weariness in her blue eyes.

"I tried to sleep but I couldn't," she told him before he could even ask. Buckling her seat belt, she accepted the coffee gratefully. "Give me a second to doctor mine up."

She added both of the creamers and a packet of the sweetener before stirring it, replacing the lid and taking a sip. "Ahhh. I feel like I could use a gallon of this stuff."

Nodding his agreement, he pulled away from the curb, glancing at her. "Did your phone send you the Amber Alert?"

She blanched. "No. I actually have those turned off.

When they sounded, it always startled me so badly, and if I was in the middle of doing something complicated, like frosting a cake, I'd mess up." With a small sigh, she pulled out her phone. "I'm not sure how to locate it now."

"Here." He handed her his cell. "Touch the screen and scroll down for alerts. It was…" He searched for the right word. "Weird for me to see what she looks like now."

Though she glanced at him, she didn't comment or question. Which likely meant she'd started to accept the idea that her Laney was his Noel. He didn't want to push, not yet, not while the five-year-old was missing.

"We have to find her," Edie said, her voice fierce.

"Yes, we do." He reached over and briefly touched her arm. He couldn't help but marvel at her soft skin. "And we will. That's a promise."

A lot of farmland lay between Getaway and Abilene, as well as the occasional small town. These places mostly had one- or two-block downtowns, eerily similar with their boarded-up vacant storefronts interspersed with cute antique shops or cafés. In his search for Noel, Jake had traveled through so many towns just like these. He didn't expect to find the white Honda Accord in any of them—there simply wasn't anywhere to hide.

"Abilene is a lot bigger," Edie said, almost as if she had read his thoughts. "Do you think it's too early to call Rayna and see if she has any news?"

"I'd give her a few."

"Okay." She took another long drink of her coffee. "What method did you use to track Noel? Do you think it would work again?"

"Yes." They'd left the small town and were once again driving past endless fields of cattle and crops. "I have a dedicated website with an email address that I check daily for tips. Now that I have a more recent photo, I can update that."

When she didn't object, he continued. "I also used to work in law enforcement, so I have contacts all around the state. If whoever took Laney is in Texas, there's a decent chance he or she will be found."

His refusal to settle on a pronoun for the abductor had her frowning. "You really think there's a possibility that a female might have taken her?"

"Anything is possible," he said, deciding not to share any grim statistics with her. Hell, he'd tortured himself enough with too much knowledge. Better if Edie remained unaware of how truly awful other human beings could be.

"True. Because if my cousin was the one who took Noel, I guess another woman could have decided she wanted Laney for her daughter. Though at five-years-old, it'll be a lot more difficult to convince Laney of that."

"Though it's been done." And quite frankly, someone wanting to pretend Laney was her daughter was the least terrifying of the various possibilities. Again, he kept those to himself.

"I'd like to see your website," she said, her phone out. "What's the web address?"

He gave it to her, keeping his eyes on the road except for occasional glances at her. She went quiet as she studied it, no doubt scrolling through all the baby pictures he'd posted.

"I'll get you more photos," she finally said. "All of these need to be updated."

"Thank you."

She took a deep breath and put her phone down. "I'm not trying to be nosy, but it's weird to me that you're out searching but your wife isn't. What's up with Noel's mom?"

For the first time in forever, he didn't feel that punch in the gut of guilty agony when he thought of Marina. For years he'd felt as if he were somehow responsible, that he should have been able to see it coming and manage to prevent it.

Except he and Marina had both been wrapped up in their own grief, neither fully present in the other's pain. He couldn't even possibly have helped his wife navigate her emotions because he'd been drowning in his own.

Blinking, he realized Edie was waiting for him to answer her question.

"She passed away in an accident a little over three months after when Noel was taken." Simple but true. He saw no need to include the gory details of the horrific car crash or the fact that he suspected Marina had intentionally driven into that tree at fifty miles an hour and taken her own life.

Since then, he'd felt like he'd failed her. She hadn't been able to live without Noel. And Jake hadn't managed to find her. Until now. Only to lose her once again.

Chapter 3

Hearing him recount his heartbreaking loss, on top of having his daughter abducted, Edie's heart squeezed. "That's awful," she said, grimacing. "I'm so sorry. That must have been like a never-ending nightmare."

"That about sums it up," he agreed. Then he changed the subject. "What about you? How'd you come to live in a small town like Getaway? Do you have family there?"

"I grew up in Getaway," she told him. "My aunt and uncle adopted me when I was two. My birth parents died in a house fire in Idaho. My cousin Gina, the one who was Laney's mom, was the last relative still living up there. She passed away from a brain aneurysm. And I carried on the family tradition of looking after our own. I drove up to Pocatello and got Laney."

His expression revealed none of his thoughts. "I'm guessing you and Gina weren't close."

"Not particularly. Why do you ask?"

"Because if you were," he said, his voice hard. "I think you might have found it a little suspicious that Gina was never pregnant, didn't send a birth announcement or have baby photos, yet managed to have a one-year-old toddler."

About to open her mouth and protest, Edie realized he was right. They'd heard nothing about Gina's daughter until she'd called to tell them she was fatally ill. Clearly aware of the seriousness of her brain aneurysm, she'd called and asked Edie specifically to look after Laney.

Of course, Edie had instantly agreed. And the second she'd laid eyes on her little blonde munchkin, she'd fallen deeply, irrevocably in love.

She said none of this to Jake. He'd fallen silent, eyes on the road, apparently lost in his thoughts.

They were coming up on the outer boundaries of Abilene, according to the sign. Was Laney here, alone with some stranger, scared to death and crying out for her mommy?

"Hell no," she muttered, managing to remain sitting upright despite wanting to double over from the pain. "We've got to find her."

"We will." Continuing to watch the road, he drummed his fingers on the steering wheel. "You need to start looking now. I will, too. If either of us spots a white four-door Honda Accord, we're stopping."

"Okay."

Now he glanced at her. "And since that's a pretty common car, we might be stopping a lot. But that's all right, because we've got to do whatever it takes."

As it turned out, they saw lots of white four-door sedans, though none of them were Honda Accords.

They had just pulled over to investigate one parked outside of a fast-food restaurant when Rayna called.

"It's Rayna." Edie's hands actually trembled when she reached for her phone.

"Put her on speaker, please," Jake said.

"Where are you?" Rayna asked. She sounded weary, as if she's been up all night. Knowing her dedication, Edie suspected she probably had.

"Jake and I are in Abilene. And I've got you on speaker," Edie replied.

"Abilene? Why?"

"Looking for Laney." Edie swallowed. "Have you gotten any leads?"

"Yes, lots of them. Unfortunately, none of them have panned out. But between law enforcement and the media blasts that are going out, everyone should be ready to alert us the instant she's spotted."

Edie's stomach twisted. "Okay. Since we don't have much to go on, we're out here hunting down white four-door Honda Accords."

"I see."

Jake spoke up for the first time. "It's better than doing nothing. Neither of us has been able to get much sleep. We decided to join forces for a bit and do what we could."

"Okay. But you need to be careful. You can't go around accusing innocent people just because of the kind of car they happen to drive."

Now Edie and Jake exchanged a look. "Surprisingly, we haven't run across a lot of those particular vehicles so far," Edie said. "It's a little bit discouraging."

"Why don't you two go on home and try to rest?" Rayna suggested. "We've got every state and local agency working on finding your daughter. She *will* be brought home safe and sound."

"When?" Edie cried out, unable to keep her anguish and fear locked inside any longer. "I can't stand to imagine how terrified she must be. She needs her mother."

"I understand." The sympathy in Rayna's voice reassured Edie. Rayna, too, was a mother. If anyone could understand how Edie felt, she could.

"Go home," Rayna repeated. "Rest. I promise that I will call you the second I learn anything."

Once again Edie exchanged a glance with Jake. Clearly understanding, he shrugged. "Up to you," he mouthed.

Though her bone-deep weariness made her thinking a bit fuzzy, Edie wasn't ready to give up yet. "Thanks, Rayna," she said. "But I won't be able to really rest until my Laney is back home."

And then she ended the call.

"I take it you want to keep looking," Jake said. "Let's go and make contact with the owner of this car."

Though they knocked on several doors and spoke to numerous people, by midafternoon it felt as if they were wasting their time. There were a couple of instances when Edie stepped out of the truck and the entire world spun and went gray around the edges, but she managed to grab onto the door handle or the tailgate and keep herself upright. So far, she didn't think Jake had noticed.

"We need to eat something," he announced after

talking to an eighty-something-year-old man who seemed perplexed they were asking about his vehicle.

"I'm not hungry," she replied, though her empty stomach chose that moment to growl, belying her words.

Ignoring that, Jake pulled into the parking lot of a small burger place. Only once he'd killed the engine did he turn and face her. "Edie, you're about to topple over. While I'm guessing that's mostly from lack of sleep, you also need to fuel your body if you want to keep going. I know it's hard to even think about food when your child is missing, but you've got to."

Tamping down the urge to argue, even though she knew he was right, she finally nodded. "Fine. Let's go grab a burger."

"And fries."

"Or a salad," she countered.

This made him laugh. "I doubt they serve salads in there, but I guess we'll see."

He was right. After they ordered, she grabbed a booth and sat while he waited for their food.

She couldn't help but notice the way other women noticed him, but she couldn't blame them. When he'd first walked into her bakery, she'd been unable to tear her gaze away, too.

Now, none of that mattered. Thinking of the very real possibility that he might have legal rights to her daughter made her wish she'd never laid eyes on him.

When he returned carrying their meal on a tray, she had to admit the food looked delicious, even if the smell made her feel slightly nauseous.

"Here you go," he said, sliding her plate over toward her.

"Thanks."

Though she had to force herself to take the first bite, once she did, she couldn't stop eating. When she finally looked up, she had one single fry left, which she quickly popped into her mouth.

"You inhaled that," he commented.

"So did you." She pointed at his equally clean plate. "I ate so fast I didn't really taste anything." She sighed. "You were right, though. I was starving."

"Me, too." He took a drink of his unsweetened tea. "Now what?"

"Do you mind if we keep looking?" she asked. "At least for a little bit longer? Then we can head back to town and maybe take a short nap."

He agreed and they grabbed their drinks and went back out to his truck. "We haven't searched the north side."

Barely stifling a yawn with her hand, she nodded. "Let's try that."

Though she tried to keep her eyes open, somehow they kept drifting closed. She'd wake herself up every time she started nodding off, but honestly, she didn't know how much longer she could stay awake. "That's the problem with getting no sleep and having a full belly," she muttered.

"Go ahead and rest," he said, encouraging her. "I promise I'll keep looking."

"No." She sat up straighter. "I'll sleep once I'm back home. For now, I want to make sure I do everything I can to help bring my daughter home."

Though she caught an almost imperceptible tightening of his jaw, he didn't comment. She'd been steadily trying to brace herself for when he finally brought up the need to talk about the likelihood that his Noel was in fact her Laney, but so far he hadn't. Probably because he understood she was already freaking out about Laney's disappearance and couldn't handle anything else at the moment.

That didn't mean she thought all of this mess would go away. She knew it wouldn't. But right now, all her focus had to be on finding her missing child.

She must have finally fallen asleep. When she opened her eyes again, they were on I-20 headed west. Her mouth felt dry and her tongue thick. She took a long drink of her tea from lunch. "How long was I out?" she asked.

His sideways smile encouraged her to smile back. "Maybe an hour. Not very long. We're on the way back to Getaway."

"I figured." Her throat felt tight. "It kind of feels like we're giving up."

"Except we're not." The fierce note in his voice made her blink. "Never think that. I've been searching nonstop for four years. I refuse to get this close and then lose her again."

The raw emotion on his face made a knot twist in her stomach. When he turned his attention back to the road, she tried to sink back into her seat, wishing she could will this entire situation away. Bad enough to have a man show up at her bakery who likely had rights to her daughter. She'd been struggling to process that when Laney had been abducted.

The entire thing qualified as a bad dream, a nightmare of epic proportions. If only she could wake up and have everything back to normal.

"Are you sure you don't know anyone who might

have a reason for snatching your Laney?" he asked, his voice tight. "An angry ex-boyfriend, or maybe your boyfriend's jealous former girl?"

Surprised, she shook her head. "No. I can't think of anyone." She didn't want to tell him she hadn't dated since before she'd adopted Laney, preferring to focus all her attention and energy on her child first, and the bakery second.

"Are you sure? Because this is really bugging me. A random perp shows up and grabs one child out of a group of three. Why her? It has to be personal. That's the only thing that makes sense."

"Maybe." Crossing her arms, she considered his words. "Or maybe this person was driving by, saw three little girls get off the bus and acted on impulse. Laney might have been the closest one, the easiest to grab."

Hearing herself, she winced. The image she'd just painted seemed too vivid, too real. "I don't really care why this person took Laney. I just want her back, safe and sound."

"I agree." He turned his attention back to the road. "Go ahead and rest if you want. We've still got awhile before we're close to Getaway."

Since she was familiar with the route, she knew he was right. Since continuing to hold a conversation felt like too much effort, she figured if she at least pretended to be asleep, she wouldn't have to talk.

Except every time she closed her eyes, all she could see were images of her little girl's terrified face.

Despite that, she managed to fall into a fitful sleep.

The ping of a text message startled her awake. Groggy, it took her a few seconds to figure out where she was and with who.

"Sorry," Jake muttered. "I'll check my phone later. We're almost at the Getaway city limits."

"And our famous sign," she murmured back. "Tourists are always stopping and taking selfies with it."

Sure enough, two different vehicles had pulled off the road. A young couple posed in front of the sign, while a small group of others waited their turn.

"You weren't kidding," Jake said as they drove past.

"Nope." She glanced back. "Everyone finds the name of our town amusing. But it could be taken two ways. Get away to beautiful Getaway, Texas. Or get away from our town." She made a small, dismissive sound. "You should have heard some of the ones we came up with as kids."

"I can imagine." Jake hesitated, and for a moment she thought he might ask her to share the childish nicknames. Instead, he looked at her. "You never wanted to leave here?"

"No, why would I?"

He shrugged. "I don't know? Broaden your horizons or something. I thought most people who grew up in tiny towns migrated to the big city."

"Is that what you did?"

"Not me," he replied. "My parents moved around a lot. We'd lived in a lot of places by the time I graduated high school. Denver, Oklahoma City, Dallas, college at UT Austin, and I finally settled down in Houston."

"A Longhorn?" she snorted. "If I'd have gone to university, I'd have been a Red Raider ."

"Texas Tech? You didn't go there?"

"Nope," she said, keeping her voice light. Any other time, she would have gladly entered into a spirited debate over the merits of the various competing state colleges, but not tonight. "I went to culinary school instead."

They'd turned on her street. The sight of her cute little house made her throat ache. She'd bought the fifties-style brick ranch with Laney in mind, wanting her daughter to have a stable place to grow up in. Her parents had helped with the down payment, and Edie had gradually repaid them.

Over the years, she'd made the house into a home, a welcoming place of refuge, full of comfort and love. Now though, knowing Laney wouldn't be there, Edie didn't even want to go inside.

But Jake pulled up to the curb and parked, leaving her no choice.

"Thanks," she said, opening her door. She hopped out with more energy than she had, and put her shoulders back as she strode toward her house. He waited, truck idling, until she'd unlocked the front door and opened it. Stepping inside, she turned and watched as he pulled away. Only then did she gather up enough courage to close the door behind her and move into her empty house, missing Laney more than anything.

After dropping Edie off, Jake didn't immediately go back to the motel. While it made sense to team up with her while they tried to find Noel, he hadn't expected to actually *like* the woman who'd been raising his daughter.

Surprisingly, so far he did. Not only because Edie clearly appeared to be a good mom, but she seemed genuine and real. She wore her heart on her sleeve. He'd rarely ever met someone so completely guileless, and while he wasn't entirely certain he trusted her lack of artifice, at the moment, he couldn't help but appreciate it.

After all, they both wanted the same thing. The return of Noel.

He must have been exhausted, too, because every time she mentioned *her daughter*, he'd had to fight the urge to correct her. But what to say instead? *His daughter* no longer seemed a hundred percent accurate, especially since Edie clearly loved the child she called Laney.

Saying *their daughter* came with another set of issues. This would imply that they shared her, which would seem impossible at this moment. Edie hadn't given him any more details about her preferences once Noel was found. Long story short, Noel would be going where she belonged. With her father.

Semantics. Pushing the thoughts from his head, he continued driving around the small town. When he found himself pulling up to the sheriff's office, he wasn't surprised. He parked and went inside.

The receptionist recognized him and waved him through without even pausing on her phone conversation. The sheriff sat behind her desk, also on the phone. Judging from her rumpled uniform and the haze of exhaustion in her eyes, she hadn't slept much either.

He waited in the doorway until she gestured him to come in and sit down. Even though he'd only met with her a couple of times, he liked Rayna Coombs. She had the kind of integrity, grit and determination that distinguished great sheriffs from mediocre ones. If anyone could find Noel, she could.

Finally, she ended her call. "Good afternoon, Mr. Cassin. What can I do for you today?"

"Call me Jake." He didn't bother exchanging any other useless pleasantries. He'd been in her position and knew her time and likely her patience were both in short supply. "I'm wondering if you've come up with any possibilities as to why the abductor might have chosen Laney."

A spark of interest lit her tired eyes. "As in, you feel she might have been specifically targeted?"

"Don't you?" he countered. "Out of a group of other children, why her?"

"It could have been random, you know. Maybe the perp grabbed whatever kid was closest to him."

"Possibly," he allowed. "Or maybe Edie Beswick has someone with a grudge against her who decided to make her pay."

Rayna sighed. "We did consider that. But Edie's a well-respected member of the community. As far as we've been able to determine, she doesn't have any enemies."

He chewed on that for a moment. "You can't tell me there's not one single person in this town who dislikes her."

"Oh, I'm sure there must be." Rayna held his gaze, her voice remaining steady. "But not enough to do something like this. Kidnapping her child. That's a pretty drastic thing."

"Ex-husband?"

"Nope." Rayna shook her head. "She's never been married. In fact, I don't believe she even dated after adopting her daughter. Edie's entire existence revolves around being Laney's mom and running the bakery. Both of which she's damn good at. Edie Beswick is a great person. I know we don't usually see a lot of those in our line of work, but she is."

Hearing the warning in the sheriff's tone, Jake slowly nodded. Now would not be the right time to remind her that Laney and his Noel were most likely one and the same. They had to get her back first.

"I'm guessing you've already run a check on local sex offenders and seen if any of them own a white Honda Accord."

"We have. Nothing turned up, at least not locally. I've reached out to the FBI to assist, and they've got someone checking records for the entire state. Which, as you know, unlike on TV, takes time."

Jake swore, not attempting to hide his frustration. "And the Amber Alert? Any realistic sightings?"

"Not yet," Rayna replied. "But all it takes is one. The right one. We'll just keep the news media blasting this out. Someone will spot them. They have to."

"They have to," he echoed. "I took Edie home so she could get some sleep. Hopefully, she will."

"I'm not trying to be rude, but you look like you could use a bit of shut-eye yourself," Rayna said, her slight smile easing any sting from the words.

"Yeah," he agreed, pushing to his feet. "I'm going to head back to the motel and try to do that. Please give me a call if anything turns up."

She gave a tired nod. "Sure will."

Once he'd gone back to his room, instead of sleeping, Jake pulled out his laptop. Instead of logging into the motel's unprotected Wi-Fi, he used his own hotspot. Despite the fact that he had been placed on unpaid leave from Houston PD, he'd managed to keep his access to several fact-finding services he'd used while on the force. He'd use those to do his own search.

Edie Beswick couldn't possibly be as perfect as everyone believed. No one was. Though he had no doubt that Rayna Coombs was good at her job, he'd look where she likely hadn't.

An hour later, he almost admitted defeat. *Almost.* So far, he hadn't been able to find anything on Edie Beswick. Not even a single traffic ticket. He now knew where she'd gone to school—Dallas Culinary Institute—and that she'd never expressed even the slightest desire to have any other occupation other than running her family's successful, if small-town, bakery.

While in DFW, she'd attended several charity events and had appeared to be in a relationship with an up-and-coming law student named Guinn Roberts. A quick search revealed Guinn was now a practicing attorney, with a gorgeous wife and three small children. Obviously, he and Edie hadn't worked out.

Next, Jake tried social media. But Edie had locked down every single one of her accounts on every platform. The only way he could hope to see anything would be by sending her a friend request and hoping she accepted. Which felt a hundred ways wrong, so he didn't bother.

Sitting back, he dragged his hand through his already disheveled hair. In searching for Edie online, he'd hoped for more than some kind of dirt on her. What he really wanted was to see photos of Noel. To note the progression over the years from age one to her current five years. He'd missed all of this, so his only way of regaining even a fraction of what he'd lost would be in pictures.

Scratch that. While he still yearned to see them, photos weren't enough. They'd never be enough. He wanted to meet his daughter in person. Get to know her. Teach her to love him again, the same way she had before. While it killed him to think she'd forgotten him, he also knew children had short memories.

All along, despite the dire predictions of previous cases, he'd refused to believe Noel to be in any danger. He'd told himself some misguided soul had stolen her to raise her as their own. She'd know love rather than fear. Turns out, he'd been right.

And now that she'd gone missing again, he struggled to keep the faith.

Since he still believed the quickest way to find her would be to figure out exactly who had taken her and why, he decided to check out the bakery next. Not only on the website but other sites where patrons might post reviews. One or two bad ones might indicate someone with a potential vendetta.

First, he checked out the website. The page looked clean and professional, with tons of photos and a price list, though he didn't see a link for online ordering. While there were customer reviews, they were clearly curated by other sites. And all of them, without exception, were positive.

Next, he went to some of the foodie apps. Again, he found nothing but good reviews. Many of them raved about the quality of Edie's baked goods. He saw nothing personal, not a single instance of anyone complaining of bad service or a subpar product.

Damn it. Sitting back in the uncomfortable motel chair, he dragged his hand across his chin. He glanced at the clock, aware he needed to try and get at least a little sleep.

Closing the laptop, he drew the blackout curtains, removed his clothes except for his boxers and crawled between the sheets.

Somehow over the last four years, Jake had trained himself to fall asleep quickly. He'd had to learn to utilize his time well, and giving his body adequate rest ranked up there at the top of his *Take Care of Yourself* list.

He put this skill to good use. Lights out, head on the pillow, close his eyes and—bam.

His phone ringing woke him. Momentarily disoriented, he fumbled in the darkness. His nightstand clock said 3:00 a.m.

"Hello?" he rasped.

"Sorry to wake you"—it was Rayna—"but I have news!"

Instantly alert, he sat up straight and clicked on the light. "Go ahead."

"Edie? Are you here?" Rayna asked.

"Yes." Judging by her husky voice, Edie apparently had also been awakened by the call.

"What's going on?" Frowning, Jake tried to contain his impatience. "Do you have news?"

"I've got you and Edie on a conference call," Rayna said, a thrum of excitement in her voice. "The Amber Alert generated a potential sighting in Cisco."

"Cisco," Jake repeated. "That sounds familiar. Where is it?"

"Cisco is a small town east of Abilene. A civilian reported seeing a man and a young girl in a four-door white Honda Civic at a gas station there."

"Finally." Heart pounding, Jake gripped his phone. "And?"

"State police have located the vehicle parked outside a motel there," Rayna replied. "They're moving in on it now."

Chapter 4

Edie opened her mouth to say something, but all that came out was a low guttural sound. Relief or worry, she wasn't sure which. Maybe a combination of both. "Is…is Laney there?"

"We don't know yet," Rayna replied. "Once they've taken the suspect into custody, they'll conduct a thorough search of his vehicle and his room. If he has Laney, they'll find her."

Suddenly dizzy, Edie sank back onto the edge of her bed. She'd tried to sleep, but despite her body's overall weariness, she hadn't been able to shut off her mind. Now, with her heart feeling as if it might pound right out of her chest, she wished she'd been able to get at least a little rest.

"I want to go to Cisco," she said, her voice stronger. "I need to be there when Laney is found. She's going to want her mother."

"I understand, but let's not get ahead of ourselves," Rayna cautioned. "We don't know for sure that this perp is the right one."

"It has to be." Jake spoke for the first time since answering the phone. "If there was a call to the Amber Alert hotline, and then the vehicle matching the description has been found, it seems like a given."

"Maybe. But you of all people should know better than to jump to rapid conclusions," Rayna said. "People can get overly excited and see things that aren't really there. Until we know more, I want the two of you to stay put."

Though Edie didn't like that, she could see the logic in the request. Sort of. Part of her wanted to rush Rayna off the phone, jump in her SUV and break every speed limit on the way to Cisco.

"Agreed," Jake finally said.

Rayna waited a moment, then prodded. "Edie?"

With a sigh, Edie also promised to stay put. "Do you promise to call the instant you have news?"

"Of course," Rayna said. "I swear. Let's all hope it's good news."

"Definitely." Blinking back sudden tears, Edie swallowed. She couldn't break down now, not when her baby girl was about to be found.

"Hang in there," Rayna said, as if she knew Edie's thoughts. "You, too, Jake."

"Edie, is it all right if I come over there?" Jake asked. "That way we can be together when Rayna calls back. We can go together when it's time."

"Sure," Edie agreed. She wasn't sure she wanted Jake to be there when she and her girl were reunited, but she had to admit he had the right. Even if she didn't really like it.

"I'll be in touch," Rayna said, ending the call.

A moment later, Jake sent Edie a text. On my way.

Instead of replying, she pushed herself to her feet and padded into the kitchen, turning on every light as she went. Three o'clock in the morning might be a weird time for coffee, but since she was up, she needed a jolt of energy.

Once she had her cup fixed the way she liked it, she carried it over to the kitchen table and took a seat. Even though she'd eaten that huge burger and fries earlier, her stomach growled, making her realize she was hungry.

"Imagine that," she muttered, talking to herself and not caring. Inside the fridge, she grabbed a small container of yogurt and ate it standing up. Protein and probiotics. The perfect combo.

A moment later, headlights swept across her front window. She got up and went to the front door, opening it and waiting for Jake on her porch. Unaccountably nervous, she put that down to anticipation over the prospect of her daughter's return.

"Hey." Jake bounded up the sidewalk, clearly as energized by the news as her. "I hope Rayna calls soon. I can't stand the suspense."

Stepping aside, she motioned him past her. Once inside the house, he followed her back to her kitchen.

"Do you want some coffee?" she offered. "I just made myself a cup."

"Sure. Black, please."

Once he had his own mug, they took seats across

from each other. Edie lasted all of thirty seconds before she pushed to her feet and started pacing.

When she glanced over at Jake, he met her gaze and nodded. "I get it," he said. "This being unable to do anything but wait is driving me up a wall, too."

She stopped and eyed him. "You don't show it. How are you staying so calm?"

He shrugged. "What choice do I have? Other than completely ignoring the sheriff, jumping in my truck, and driving as fast as I can to Cisco? It would all likely be over by the time I get there."

"You're probably right." Taking a deep breath, she figured now would be as good a time as any to speak a few truths. "She won't recognize you, you know. After all she's been through, the last thing she needs is you scaring her."

Though his jaw tightened, he didn't argue. "That's where I'm going to need your help. She trusts you, and—"

"Yes, she does," she interrupted. "Not only that, but she loves me. I'm her mother. No matter what happened before she came to me, I'm the only mother she knows."

At that, his expression shut down. "I don't think now is the time to have this discussion. We can deal with all this later. Let's make sure she's safe first."

Once again, she had to acknowledge the truth of his words. Though she knew putting things off wouldn't solve anything in the long run, there was only so much she could handle at one time. Having Laney back in her arms was the most important priority.

Her phone rang, making her jump. "Yes?" she answered.

"Put me on speaker," Rayna ordered. "Assuming Jake is there with you now?"

"He is. Just a second." Heart pounding, she pushed the speaker icon and placed her phone on the table. "Go ahead."

"First off, the tip didn't pan out. That wasn't Laney."

Somehow, Edie managed to keep from collapsing. For a second, she couldn't breathe. "What?" she croaked.

She and Jake stared at each other, both shocked.

"There was a man with a young girl who happened to be driving a white four-door, Honda Accord," Rayna said. "However, she's his daughter. His wife was waiting for them in the motel room."

"How do you know?" Edie demanded. "Are they absolutely positive the girl wasn't Laney?"

"Yes." An edge of weariness crept into Rayna's professional voice. "Not only did she not match the photograph, but an officer spoke with her separately from her parents. And they were able to provide other documentation. Turns out they're a family from Arizona passing through Texas on their way to Louisiana. Not Laney's abductor."

Numb, Edie couldn't move. Ignoring the tears streaming down her cheeks, she realized the cruelest irony was to have hope and then have it taken from you.

Across from her, Jake sat stone-faced, staring at his hands.

"The Amber Alert is still live," Rayna said. "And we've got every law enforcement agency in the state on alert. She *will* be found. I'll holler at you if I hear anything else."

With that, she ended the call.

Though she usually detested crying in front of anyone, particularly strangers, at this point Edie had gone beyond caring. In fact, the only thing that mattered was getting her little girl back, even if she had to do it herself.

The idea, once she'd had it, took root and strengthened her resolved. She got up and went into the bathroom, grabbed some tissue and wiped her eyes and blew her nose. After splashing a little cold water on her face and blotting it with a hand towel, she straightened her shoulders and went back to the kitchen.

Jake had remained motionless in the same spot, still staring at his hands.

"I've decided I'm done sitting around waiting for something to happen," she announced.

Raising his head to meet her gaze, he nodded. "What do you have in mind?"

Too energized to sit still, she took a moment to make herself another cup of coffee. "I want to go look for her," she said.

"I get that. I basically gave up my job, my home, everything to do the same thing. I've been searching for Noel the last four years, working the occasional odd job but never taking my focus off the goal of finding her. I have logic behind my search, resources that help point me in the right direction. That's how I ended up here."

"I know," she replied. "I remember. Earlier, you were telling me about your web page and your tip line. Have you updated it lately?"

"No."

"I say we do." A headache had started behind her eyes, likely from all the crying. Nonetheless, she pushed on. "We can upload more recent photos of Laney, tell the circumstances of how she was grabbed, add the latest Amber Alert and so on."

"I'd already planned to do that," he replied. "It should just take a few hours."

"I can help you," she said. "But first, once it's daylight, I need to make a few calls and see if I can find someone to work the bakery for me."

Gaze steady, he waited. When she didn't volunteer any more information, he prodded. "Why?"

"Because I can't keep it closed indefinitely. And I'm not going to go into work and make cookies and cupcakes like nothing has happened."

The sympathy in his expression told her he understood. "So what's your plan?"

"What's yours?" she countered. "Judging by the way you've kept looking before, you don't plan on sitting around town and waiting for something to turn up, do you?"

"No."

"I didn't think so." Feeling her cheeks heating, she pressed her palms against her face. "I want to go with you. You already said we should team up." She took a deep breath before she continued. "I agree. Two heads are better than one, and all that. If you'll give me your email address, I'll send you some recent photos of Laney so you can update that website."

The way he stared at her made her wonder if she sounded delirious.

"I think we both need more sleep," he finally said, getting to his feet. "My email is on the card I gave you earlier at the bakery." As he moved past her, he squeezed her shoulder. "I'll talk to you later. No one is willingly awake at this hour."

Since he clearly had no idea she'd normally have to be at the bakery in a few hours, she simply stood and followed him to the door. Once he'd gone, she locked the dead bolt and returned to the kitchen and her coffee.

The bakery. The second most important thing in her life, after Laney. For as long as Edie could remember, kolaches, cakes, cookies and pies had been part of her life. Her great grandmother, grandmother and mother had all individually kept the place running and taken great pride in turning out sublime baked goods. Each of them had developed their own specialty. Edie's was her cupcakes. She loved coming up with new flavors, with Laney's help. Since Edie figured Laney would be next in line to take over the bakery, Edie had started her early, letting her help out as often as possible.

Now, it pained her to think her daughter inheriting the family business might be in jeopardy. Despite being adopted, there had never been a question of what Edie would do once she finished school. Raised working alongside her mom and grandmother, Edie considered the bakery her destiny.

Even though she had hired help, once her mother had retired, Edie took on the brunt of the work herself. She had help, of course. Some of her employees had worked there as long as Edie, though a few had been hired more recently.

Most of her workforce was part time, since Edie preferred to open and close the place herself. Now, she'd need to call each and every one of them and see if they could come up with a schedule. She'd need them to handle running the bakery without her.

Finding Laney had to be her number one priority.

Since it was too early to disturb anyone, she carried her mug into her living room and sat down on her father's old recliner. The comfortable chair had been the one thing she'd wanted when her parents had cleaned out their house in preparation for living in an RV and traveling.

Blinking, she realized she needed to call her parents. She'd put it off, not wanting to worry them. She'd much rather be telling them the story as an anecdote after the fact, with Laney safe at her side. Unfortunately, that clearly wasn't going to be the case now.

It was 4:00 a.m. Still too early to call anyone. She headed for the shower, then changed her mind. Every part of her body ached and her mind felt muddy. Though the idea of sleeping while her daughter was missing appalled her, she knew she had to get some rest if she wanted to continue to function.

On the way to her bedroom, she passed Laney's. She almost gave in to the need to walk inside, turn on the light and curl up on her girl's bed. Instead, she forced herself to continue down the hall to her own room, peeling off her clothes as she went. Finally, she slipped underneath the sheets and put her head on her pillow.

Now she just needed to go to sleep. She closed her eyes, letting her exhaustion overtake her.

Jake blinked, staring at the dashboard clock: 4:00 a.m. *Damn it.* He must have dozed off. Good thing, since he was still sitting in his parked truck in front of Edie's house. Luckily, he hadn't started the engine. Maybe he should just try to sleep here.

He settled back in his seat to do exactly that when the porch light from the house next door to Edie came on. A man stepped out onto the stoop, peering at Jake's truck. A moment later, he went back inside, though he didn't turn off the light.

Any moment now, Jake figured Edie's neighbor would be calling the police. Since he didn't want that and Edie definitely didn't need it, he fired up the engine, buckled his seat belt and put the shifter in drive.

Luckily the Landshark Motel wasn't far—heck, nothing was in a town this size. He pulled in, parked in front of his room and went inside.

So far, he hadn't allowed himself to reflect on Rayna's disappointing news. Devastating, actually. Such things happened, he knew this, but generally when someone spotted a child from an Amber Alert, along with the actual vehicle, it turned out to be the missing kid.

Not this time. Meanwhile, whoever had Noel was in the wind.

Neither he nor Rayna had mentioned to Edie the usual reason why an adult male would grab a five-year-old child. No doubt the thought had already occurred to her, though like everyone else, she'd likely pushed it from her mind. Such things didn't bear thinking about.

There could be myriad reasons Noel had been taken. All they could do was focus on getting her back.

Right now, he needed to get some sleep. He'd pushed himself too far. Falling asleep in his truck was proof of that. And the last thing he needed was to put himself and others in danger.

He made it to the bed, pulled back the comforter and stepped out of his boots. Then, still fully clothed, he crawled under the sheets and closed his eyes.

When he woke again, he wasn't surprised to realize four hours had passed—8:00 a.m. Not enough shut-eye, but it would have to do for now. Still groggy, he padded into the small bathroom, wincing at the fluorescent lights and his image in the small mirror.

A hot shower made him feel slightly human again. As he dried off, he wondered if Edie had been able to sleep. For her sake, he hoped so. She couldn't keep going on fumes.

She wanted to work with him. Out of desperation, he knew. Actually, he didn't blame her. In the early part of his search for Noel, he would have paired with the devil himself if that would have helped find her.

Once he was sitting at the tiny desk, he opened his laptop and powered it up. Checking his email, he was surprised to see that Edie had already sent photos of her Laney, his Noel.

Heart racing, he eagerly clicked on the first one. A pretty girl, her long blonde hair fell in ringlets past her shoulders. *Marina's hair*, he thought, his throat tight.

The next picture appeared to be a school photo. A close-up, showing the child's bright blue eyes and cheerful smile. She had dimples, he saw. Just like his.

He looked at the rest of them, chest aching, then went back to the first one and studied them all again.

Damn. He hadn't expected seeing what his baby girl looked like now to hit him so hard. Four years. He'd missed out on so, so much. And Marina would never see their daughter alive and well.

Neither would he if they didn't find her, he reminded himself, pushing his maudlin thoughts away. He clicked over to his website, updating the photos and the text. A quick search allowed him to copy the Amber Alert, which he added to the home page.

Once he'd finished, he saved his work, clicked out

and then went back to take an objective look at the public view.

Clean and concise, easy to navigate. The link to his email was prominent and easy to find.

That done, he decided to go out for coffee and breakfast.

Should he try to call Edie? If she had managed to get some sleep, he hated to wake her. In the end, he decided to send her a quick text. Call me when you get a chance.

His phone rang five seconds later.

"Did you get the photos?" she asked, skipping right over any pleasantries.

"I did, and I've already updated the website. Want to take a look?"

"Yes," she responded. "I'll have to do it on my phone though. What's the web address again?"

He gave it to her and then waited while she took a look. He wondered if now would be the moment when she actually acknowledged that her Laney was his Noel.

"Nice work," she commented. "Have you thought about us partnering up for the long run? Until she's found?"

"How about we talk about that over breakfast? Where's the best place to eat that in this town?"

"The Tumbleweed Café," she replied. "Great food and their coffee is amazing."

"Good. I'll pick you up and we'll go there. How soon can you be ready?"

"How soon can you be here?" she countered. "I'm ready now."

When he pulled up to her house, she came out immediately, like she'd been watching for him. He studied her as she climbed up into his truck. She looked better. More rested and alert.

"You got some sleep?" he asked, waiting until she'd buckled her seat belt before shifting into Drive.

"I did. A couple hours. But better than nothing. How about you?"

"Same." He glanced sideways. "It's amazing how much a nap and a shower can do for you."

Following her directions, which were simple, they arrived at the Tumbleweed Café.

"People come from all around to eat here," she explained, correctly interpreting his surprise at the packed parking lot. "In addition to the excellent food, it's a gathering place for all the ranchers. You'll see."

Inside, the smell of bacon, coffee and fried potatoes made his mouth water. "I guess I'm hungrier than I thought," he said.

A smiling teenager appeared and showed them to their booth, handing them laminated menus before she left.

A quick glance at the menu, and he decided against the Rancher's Breakfast since he didn't want steak with his eggs. Instead, he chose something called the Hired Hand's Morning Meal.

The instant he closed his menu, the waitress reappeared. "Ready to order?"

Edie hadn't even opened her menu. She recited her choice from memory. Jake gave his and the waitress hurried off.

"Laney loves eating here," Edie said, her voice wistful.

Sensing she needed to talk, he nodded. "Tell me about her. What's she like?"

Edie's face lit up. "Laney is so smart, and she's funny, too. She always has an answer for everything and delivers whatever she has to say with absolute confidence, even if she's wrong."

Stunned, Jake managed to refrain from commenting. According to his entire family, what Edie had just described had been one of his own traits as a young child.

Edie continued, apparently not noticing his shock. "She's so friendly. She loves everyone, and they all love her back."

A single tear tracked down her cheek. Swiping at it, she shook her head. "And that child's hair. I've never seen hair so thick. But absolutely beautiful. She loves for me to braid it for her."

"Like yours?" he commented without thinking.

Her wistful smile looked sad. "Yes. And people always commented how we had the same blue eyes. I loved it, because no one guessed she was adopted."

Marina's eyes. Though he supposed Edie didn't need to know that. Not yet, not right now.

She sighed and then straightened her shoulders. "Have you thought about what I said? Us partnering up?" she asked, her expression intent. "I know we joined forces all along, but I want to continue searching for her together rather than go our separate ways."

The waitress brought their food right then, saving him from an immediate answer. She also topped off their coffee before telling them, "Holler if you need anything, hon."

As soon as she moved away, Jake dug in. He'd ordered breakfast platter that included eggs, hash browns, bacon and a short stack of pancakes. Edie had an egg white omelet and wheat toast, with a side of fruit.

While they were eating, Edie kept shooting him impatient looks, but she didn't ask again until they'd both pushed their plates away.

"Well?" she finally demanded, taking a sip of her coffee.

Finally, he relented. "Yes. We can work together. On one condition. If we get into any sort of sticky situation, you have to agree to do exactly as I say."

"Sticky situation?" She eyed him over her coffee cup. "What do you mean?"

He didn't want to frighten her, but it was important she understood. "Like if we do manage to find who has her, you can't just go rushing in and try to scoop her up. That's a good way to get yourself killed."

Her chin came up. "There's no way anyone is going to stop me from going to Laney if she needs me."

Time to be a little harsher. "Do you really want her to witness her mommy being shot to death?"

Edie's eyes widened. "I get that it might be dangerous, but do you really think—"

He cut her off. "Yes. You have to be prepared for anything. And if you act recklessly, not only could you endanger yourself but her as well."

"I see." Judging by her somber expression, she did.

"More coffee, folks?" the waitress appeared, coffeepot in hand.

"No thanks," Jake said. "Just the check, please."

"Sure. I'll be back with that in a moment."

Edie's phone rang. She started. "Unknown caller," she said, answering it anyway. After saying hello, she listened for a moment before ending the call and shaking her head. "Spam. I have to say, for a second there, I thought…"

"You thought what?" Jake eyed her curiously. For an instant, hope had lit up her face, until she realized who was on the other end of the line.

"I taught Laney to memorize my phone number. She knows if she's ever in trouble, she's to call me." Her voice wavered, just a little. "I couldn't help but hope maybe she'd found a phone and used it."

He must have looked skeptical, because Edie frowned. "She might be only five, but she's smart. I have no doubt if she gets the chance to call me, she'll take it."

"Let's hope she does," he replied, meaning it.

The waitress dropped off the check, and Edie reached for it.

"I've got this," Jake said, taking it from her. "You can get the next one."

"Okay." Clearly relieved, she nodded. The brightness that had illuminated her blue eyes had vanished, and her gaze had dulled.

"Are you okay?" he asked.

"No. I want my baby home safe." Drumming her fingers on the table, she glanced out the window. "We should get going. I don't want to waste any more time than we have to."

He found himself wishing he could bring back that hope he'd seen a few minutes ago. "Don't give up," he said, sounding more abrupt than he meant to. "Amber Alerts are hugely successful. This means not only every law enforcement agency is on the lookout but civilians, too."

"Wasn't there an Amber Alert when your Noel disappeared?" she asked, her voice quiet.

"There was. But one-year-olds are virtually indistinguishable from one another. Five-year-olds are not."

Her gaze swung around to find his. "You might have a point."

He put enough money for their tab and a generous tip on the table. "I do. And now that my website is updated, it should start generating some new tips. Following up on them can be tedious, but that's where I put my law enforcement connections to work."

As they got to their feet, she eyed him. "What do you mean, law enforcement connections?"

He waited until they were outside, walking to his truck. "I used to be a police officer."

She stopped so quickly he nearly stumbled into her. "Used to be? What happened?"

Since they'd reached his truck, he unlocked it and opened her door for her. Once she'd climbed in, he closed it and went around to the driver's side.

"What happened?" he repeated, starting the engine. "My daughter disappeared. I took a leave of absence to look for her."

"For four years? Did you end up losing your job?"

Slowly, he shook his head. "So far, no. I'm on unpaid leave. My supervisor was—is a good friend, and he keeps approving the extensions. All in all, Houston PD has been pretty damn understanding. Though I'm sure if I tried to go back now, I'd have to jump through a lot of hoops."

Though she nodded, she didn't comment. They drove a few minutes in silence before she spoke again.

"I'm sorry," she said. "I'm sorry this happened to

you. I promise you, I didn't know. And while I know we'll have to work out some kind of arrangement, right now I can only focus on getting Laney back safe and sound."

"Same here," he responded, his heart going out to her despite everything. "Same here."

Chapter 5

Now that Jake had finally agreed to allow her to accompany him on a permanent basis, Edie felt slightly better. Moving forward was always preferable to remaining in place. And while she knew Rayna was doing everything she could, since Laney wasn't home yet, it clearly wasn't enough.

Though she hadn't intended to apologize, the sentiment had been both spontaneous and genuine. She admired the way Jake had never given up searching for his daughter. And she meant what she'd told him about dealing with the likelihood that his Noel and her Laney were one and the same. In her heart of hearts, she knew they were. He knew, too. But for now, she simply couldn't face that. Not yet. One crisis at a time. Getting Laney home safe had to be her only priority. Once she'd done that, she'd figure out a way to manage the rest of it.

Jake dropped her off at her house, with orders to pack for a week on the road. "Pack light," he said. "Basic pieces that you can wear in different combinations. And if you take any medication, bring that. I'll pick you up in an hour."

She nodded. "I'll be ready."

After he'd gone, she found herself making a beeline to Laney's room. Before packing anything for herself, she grabbed a change of clothes for her daughter, her pajamas and her favorite stuffed bear. "Baby, I'm coming to find you," she said out loud. Then she headed into her own bedroom to get some things together for herself. That didn't take long. Glancing at the clock, she realized she had time to make the call she'd been dreading. Telling her parents what had happened.

Her mother picked up on the third ring. "Edie! How nice of you to call. We just got to Yellowstone last night and set up camp. It's so beautiful here."

"I'm glad." Edie swallowed. "Listen, I've got some bad news. Can you put the phone on speaker so Dad can hear, too?"

"Bad news? Sure." There were a few random sounds as her mom fumbled with the phone. "Here you go. You're on speaker."

"Hi, honey," her dad chimed in. "What's going on?"

"It's Laney," Edie began. As she outlined the circumstances of Laney's disappearance, her parents stayed silent. She only mentioned that, keeping quiet about the stranger showing up brandishing a photo of his missing daughter, who was a dead ringer for Laney.

As she wrapped up, she heard the heartbreaking sound of her mom trying to stifle her crying.

"Is Rayna searching for her?" her father asked. "I hope she has every deputy of hers out looking."

"There's an Amber Alert." Edie took a deep breath. "And I'm leaving with a friend to go search, too."

"Where? How on earth will you even know where to begin?" Her father sounded frustrated.

Trying to keep it simple, she outlined Jake's website. "We're going to investigate tips as the come in."

Finally, her mom spoke. "Don't you think that would be something better left to law enforcement?"

Both Edie and her dad started speaking at the same time. Clearly, her dad subscribed to the same thought process as Edie did. She let him finish before putting in her own opinion.

"Mom, there's no way I can just sit around and do nothing while my daughter is missing."

"We're going to pack up and head back to town," her dad said without waiting for her mother to argue.

"Fine," Edie replied. "But please understand that I won't be here. Not until Laney is found."

"Don't you think you should be home waiting for her?" her mom asked.

"I can't just *wait*," Edie said. "I have to look for her. But the instant she's found, I'll make my way to her, no matter what."

They ended the call the same way they always did, with lots of I-love-yous, though this time her mother made no attempt to hide her tears.

That done, Edie felt as if a small weight had been lifted. She hadn't wanted to tell her parents, though doing so had been necessary. Now she could focus on what really mattered. Bringing her baby home.

By the time Jake returned, she had her rolling duffle bag full and zipped. When his truck pulled into her driveway, she made one last sweep of the house, checking to make sure doors were locked and all the lights were out. Then she slipped out the front, using her key to use the dead bolt, and walked out to meet him.

"Good job," he said, giving her an approving look as he took her bag from her and swung it into the back seat of his club cab.

Wondering why his praise started a warm glow inside her, she nodded and kept her voice curt. "Thanks."

As they drove away, she glanced over her shoulder at her house. "You know, Laney's been bugging me for a kitten. Though right now, since I would have had to find someone to take care of it, I'm glad I didn't give in." She swallowed hard, blinking back sudden tears. "But you can be damn sure we're going to the animal shelter once she's back home."

His noncommittal sound reminded her that he likely had his own perspective on Laney's homecoming. Again, she pushed the thought away.

"Where are we going first?" she asked, figuring he had a plan.

"I've already had a few tips come in from my website," he replied, surprising her. "Of course, I've turned them over to Rayna so she could contact law enforcement in those areas, but there's no reason we can't go check them out ourselves."

"Really?" She sat up straight. "What are they? Why didn't you tell me?"

"Because I don't know which ones are credible yet. Even so, we're heading up toward Plainview now. That's in between Lubbock and Amarillo."

She nodded, taking deep breaths to try and calm

her racing heartbeat. "Okay. How reliable do these tips usually turn out to be?"

"In the past, it's been about fifty-fifty. The problem I've run into is by the time I can make it to wherever the sighting happened, the suspects are long gone."

"Okay." She thought for a moment. "But they're still worth checking out, right?"

"Right. I followed up on every single credible one." Still watching the road, he barely glanced at her and grimaced. "I should warn you. Another thing I learned is that there are a lot of heartless people out there. Some apparently have made it a hobby to give worthless tips to people searching for a loved one. It's unreal. Law enforcement still checks them out, of course."

"How do you know?" she asked. "I mean, how can you tell if they're real or not?"

"That's the thing. You can't."

Edie tried to comprehend why anyone would do such a thing but couldn't. "Can you still show me the tips, anyway?" she asked. "I can take it."

He glanced sideways at her. "Sometimes, seeing them makes it worse. I'm kind of used to this since I've been dealing with it for four years. Even so, they have a way of punching you in the gut when you least expect it. I'd kind of like to spare you that."

"Kind of high-handed there," she snapped, then instantly felt bad. "Sorry, but I don't need anyone to shield me."

"I get that," he replied, surprising her again. "But if you really want to see them, we'll go over them at night when they come in."

"Are there usually a lot?"

He shrugged. "Sometimes. Usually, there's one or

two. Days can go by without anything, and then four or five hit all at once. When you look at them, you can often spot the ones that aren't real. But then again, I've always been afraid that I'll pass up the wrong one."

"What about this one? The one in Plainview. Does it seem valid?"

"It's hard to tell." He grimaced. "But worth checking out. I've already passed it on to Rayna, and she's alerted the local authorities."

"So by the time we get there, they'll have already checked it out?"

"Yes." Again he gave her a quick glance. "But I always like to follow up after, anyway. Just in case they missed anything. They're not always as thorough as I'd like."

"Interesting."

Stuff to think about. He continued driving, and she settled back into her seat and watched the landscape go past.

Ahead, nothing but flat land. The bright blue sky stretched for miles, dotted by a few fluffy white clouds.

"There's something about West Texas…" she said, meaning it.

"That only a native could love," he said, finishing the thought.

His phone rang. Answering, he put it on speaker. "Rayna. Any news?"

"No. I contacted a state trooper friend of mine who works that area. He did me a favor and personally checked this out."

"Nothing?" Jake asked.

"Nothing," Rayna replied. "You could probably skip Plainview. It's not a big town."

Edie watched Jake to see how he'd respond, though she figured she already knew.

"We're almost there," he said. "No harm in taking a look around. Any more pings on the Amber Alert?"

"Not that I'm aware of." Exhaustion made Rayna's voice waver. "I'm going to have to head home and get a few hours of sleep. I promise you, I'll have someone overseeing this while I'm out."

"I know you will," Edie said. "And please, try and rest. I learned the hard way not to try and be a super-human."

"Yeah, I've learned that lesson once or twice my-self," Rayna responded. "Keep me posted if you find out anything."

"We will."

Thirty-five minutes later, they passed a sign wel-coming them to Plainview. As West Texas towns went, Plainview looked much the same as all of them, in-cluding Getaway. Historic buildings lined both sides of Main Street, most of them restored, a few others boarded up. A freshly painted white water tower bear-ing the town's name was one of the tallest structures on the horizon.

They drove slowly through downtown, both of them keeping an eye out for a white Honda Accord. But like back home, they saw mostly pickup trucks and SUVs, with the occasional car. None of them were what they were looking for.

"Where to now?" she asked, since he surely had some specific location in mind.

"There are two motels off the north Interstate Twenty-Seven frontage road. One of those was where the supposed sighting happened. I know Rayna's trooper friend checked it out, but I want to take a look at both motels. Just in case."

"That makes sense," she agreed.

To her surprise, both of the motels were modern impersonal chains, nothing like the Landshark in Getaway. They cruised slowly through the parking lot of the first one before stopping and parking. "Let's go in and talk to the desk clerk," Jake suggested.

She followed him inside, waiting silently while he questioned the bored young woman behind the counter. She shook her head. "Sorry. I've already talked to the cop that was here earlier. I didn't see a man with a blonde kid."

Jake thanked her for her time and they turned to go. Just before they reached the door, he stopped and turned. "Did the state trooper ask to see the surveillance footage from those cameras?"

"Yes," she replied, frowning. "And no, I'm not letting you look at them. I don't even know who you are."

"Understandable," Jake said, thanking her again.

Back in his truck, Edie shook her head. "Well, at least we know Rayna's friend was thorough."

"Yep." He started the engine. "Now let's check out the other motel."

It turned out the state trooper had looked into that one, too. "I bet he went to every motel in and around Plainview," Jake said.

Trying not to feel discouraged, Edie sighed. "If he didn't find anything, we won't either. So what do we do now?"

"We keep on going. Do you want to go back to Getaway for tonight and start out fresh in the morning?"

Surprised, she didn't even have to consider the question. "I don't want to go back home. Not until I have my Laney back. Don't we have some other tip to follow?"

"I'll have to check. I'm sure we do, and yes, I brought my laptop." He glanced at her. "I prefer to work on my computer rather than my phone, when I can. How about we go get something to eat and I'll look at it then?"

"Are you hungry again?" she asked, not bothering to hide her astonishment. "All of this stress has pretty much destroyed my appetite."

"You need to feed your body," he replied. "Hungry or not. I think we'll check out that hole-in-the-wall barbeque place right there. They usually have great food."

"Fine."

She hadn't thought she would be able to eat, but once they walked into the place, the smell of smoked meat and barbeque sauce made her mouth water. Still, she chose a brisket sandwich rather than a big platter, with a side of potato salad to go along with it.

To her surprise, once she started eating, she couldn't seem to stop. She demolished her entire meal, washing it down with sweet tea. She finished about the same time as Jake did, even though he'd gotten larger portions of everything.

"You were right," she said. "I guess I needed that."

He smiled in response before getting up and carrying their trays to a different table. Once he'd made room, he got out his laptop.

"There are a lot of anonymous ones," he said, turning the laptop around so she could see. "Most of those turn out to be crackpots or people trying to mess with me."

There were more comments than she'd thought there'd be. She read the first few, stopping about midway down the page. Her stomach twisted and she had to swallow hard before speaking. "That one," she said pointing. "This person is claiming Laney is still in Getaway."

After paying for their food, Jake walked a very subdued Edie out to his truck, chastising himself with every step he took. He shouldn't have shown her. He'd grown used to dealing with the whackos and people with bad intentions. She was not. Freshly raw with missing Laney, Edie didn't have the exterior armor necessary to understand this kind of thing yet. He actually hoped she didn't have to.

The person claiming the child had never left Getaway, he forwarded that email directly to Rayna. Her deputies had already done an impressive job canvassing the town. She would either assign someone to deal with the email sender or take care of it herself. He'd explained all this to Edie, pointing out the reasons he found such a scenario unlikely.

Though she'd looked a bit dazed, Edie had said she understood before moving on to the next comment.

There were a lot of them. Many more than when he'd first begun searching for his one-year-old daughter. From well-wishers offering prayers to clearly disturbed individuals making threats or patently awful suggestions. Edie had read through them silently, her jaw getting tighter and her shoulders tensing up, but she hadn't complained.

"Are you okay?" he finally asked, unable to help himself.

"I have no choice but to be," she replied. "Whatever it takes to find my daughter."

His daughter. Biting back the words, he'd simply nodded instead.

They *had* to find Noel quickly. Though he shied away from even the thought, he knew the more time that passed since her abduction, the less of a chance they had of finding her alive. He knew this well— after all, he had been told this over and over and over after his baby had been taken. Despite that, he'd never stopped looking. Nor would he.

Since the day was still young, they needed to keep moving and check another place out before they stopped for the night. He scanned the messages again in the hopes that one of them would stand out. None of them currently did.

"Let me check my email," he said, closing the website and opening his Gmail account. An email from Tanner Malecek, one of his FBI friends, caught his eye. He'd seen the updated website and the Amber Alert and wanted to know if Jake had time to talk. Since Jake had kept Tanner appraised each step of the way in his search, Jake took this to mean Tanner must have some new information.

Though Jake had Tanner's number and wanted to call, the last line in the email let him know he couldn't. Tanner wanted to meet in person.

Jake typed a quick response—On the way now. Should be there in time for dinner.—and hit send. He looked up to find Edie watching him.

"We're heading out," he said.

Her eyes lit up. "A good tip?"

"Not this time. We're heading up to Oklahoma City."

"That's a bit of a drive," she commented. "Do you really think whoever grabbed Laney has left the state?"

"I don't know. It's a possibility, but that's not why we're going. I'm meeting a buddy of mine who now works for the Bureau up in Oklahoma City. He's helped me a lot in my search."

"And you think he can help us now?" she asked. "How?"

"That I'm not sure. But one thing I do know is when an FBI agent offers to help, you don't turn it down. Ever."

"What exactly does he do for the FBI?"

He grinned. "He's a profiler. Pretty cool, right? I'm hoping he can help us narrow down a little bit what we should be looking for."

She thought about this for a second. "That makes sense."

"Until a better tip or two comes in, right now we have nothing to go on."

The storm clouds started to gather before they even reached Wichita Falls or crossed the Red River. Dark and ominous, the air turned heavy, with a green cast to the sky. A native Texan, Jake knew what that meant. Likely Edie did, too. He glanced at her, finding her sitting up straight and scanning the horizon.

"Looks like there's a severe thunderstorm coming. With hail," she said, echoing his thoughts. Pulling out her phone, she swallowed hard. "I can't help thinking of Laney. She's terrified of thunderstorms. She always climbed into bed with me and insisted on being held." Her voice broke, but she continued. "The thought of Laney going through storms alone makes my chest hurt."

Since there were no words to make this better, he did the only thing he could think of. Reached over and squeezed her shoulder. "We'll find her," he promised, having no choice but to believe he spoke the truth.

"I know we will. Let me..." She cleared her throat. "Let me check the radar on my weather app."

While she did that, he kept driving, keeping his eye on the sky ahead.

"What I'm seeing on my phone isn't good," she said. "It's weird, but despite growing up with the ever-present threat of tornados and severe storms every spring and summer, I still get worried whenever conditions became ripe for one."

"I think we all do," he replied. "Some people just hide it better than others. What kind of warnings are you seeing?"

"I see a severe thunderstorm warning. What's worse is there's even a tornado warning for an area up ahead of us, in Oklahoma." She glanced at him quickly, then back at her phone. "Looks like we have to drive through this, so we'd better keep our eyes open."

He glanced at the darkening sky. "How close?"

"Right now, it's all north of us, moving east. Like right above Lawton."

"Damn it," he cursed. This earned a semi-alarmed look from her.

"I don't like this," she said.

"You know it's not really tornado season," he commented, more of a distraction than anything else.

This made her shake her head. "I know. But you know how unpredictable our weather can be."

"True," he said. "Right now, I'm not worried. If there's a tornado, we should be able to see it long before it reaches us."

"As long as it's not blowing rain in sideways sheets,"

she said. She reached for the radio knob. "I'm going to try and find an Oklahoma station so we can stay on top of this."

"Great idea."

As they crossed the Red River, leaving Texas and going into Oklahoma, the sky continued to grow darker and the wind picked up. Ahead, flashes of lightning lit up the dark greenish-gray horizon.

"No rain yet," Jake commented, keeping his voice level, though the tightness of his double-handed grip on the steering wheel was a dead giveaway if she happened to notice. As ominous skies went, this one was a doozy. And the air had that particular kind of electrified feeling; a kind of warning that things were about to get rough. He knew Edie felt it, too.

"Maybe we should pull off into the next town until the storm passes," she suggested.

"Maybe." He cracked a smile, trying to downplay things. "I definitely don't want to get hail damage on my truck."

He'd barely finished speaking when rain began to fall, big fat drops at first. He turned his windshield wipers on. Then it was like the sky split open, dumping a torrential rainfall so heavy that visibility shrank down to a few feet.

Ahead of them, several vehicles had pulled over and parked under the overpass, flashers on. "That's never a good idea," Jake said, continuing on slowly past them. Despite the television news anchors regularly warning people not to do this, lots of people still did. He got it though. No one liked to have hail turn their vehicle into a pitted mess. Right now though, he suspected hail was the least of their worries.

"I think we'll keep going," Jake said, squinting to try and see, even with his windshield wipers on high. "I feel like our chances are better if we stay moving."

"Except if a tornado does come at us, with this rain, we'll never see it," she said.

"Are you worried?" He hated to put her through even one more thing, but this couldn't be helped.

"I'm slightly nervous," she said. "More for the lack of visibility than anything else. We aren't yet in the area of the tornado warning on the radar. And I'd like to keep it that way."

"Check the radar," he asked. "Just so you can see what's out there."

"Okay." She pulled out her phone again, opened the app and swore. "It's gotten a lot bigger. And we're heading right into the worse part of it. I can't help but think we shouldn't drive too much further north until this storm has passed."

Concentrating on trying to see the road, Jake nodded. "Agreed. We'll stop in the next town we come to and find some sort of shelter."

"Thank you," she said, relief plain in her voice.

She'd barely gotten the words out when as a car appeared out of nowhere behind them, moving way too fast for the road conditions.

"Damn fool," he said, changing lanes with a quick turn of the wheel as the other vehicle barreled past, sending plumes of water into the air. The truck tried to hydroplane, but he managed to keep it under control, pulling over to the shoulder and coming to a stop.

Ahead, the car that had been passing them spun around, swerving toward the other side of the road. They both watched in horror as the vehicle almost hit a passenger van head on. Somehow, it managed to continue on, eventually disappearing from view.

"If they keep going like that, they're going to cause a bad accident," Jake said, his jaw tight. "Who the hell drives like that in a storm like this?"

As if it heard his words, the storm intensified even more, wind pushing sheets of rain sideways, shaking the truck.

Jake swore, slowing to a crawl, his knuckles white on the steering wheel. "I can't see."

Just then, alarms went off on both their cell phones.

"Tornado warning. Seek shelter immediately." For the first time, panic edged her voice. "I don't like this."

"Me neither. But there's nowhere to go except forward."

Slow as that may be. Inching ahead, several other hapless vehicles ahead and behind them, he really regretted his earlier decision to press on.

A growling, rumbling sound joined the shrieking of the wind.

"Do you hear that?" Edie sat straight up. "I sure hope that's not what I think it is."

Tornado. Struggling to hold on to the steering wheel, he couldn't even get the word out. The truck shook as the storm battered them. He felt a moment of pure terror as the truck shimmied sideways. Left, right, and then it felt like a giant hand plucked them from the road and tossed them skyward.

Edie screamed, the sound warring with the howling of the storm. Blind instinct kept him hanging onto the steering wheel, though there was no way to steer as the wind pitched them around and around.

It felt like an eternity, though it likely had only been a few seconds. The seat belt kept him in his seat.

As abruptly as it had picked them up, the wind dropped them. Hard. On all four wheels. As the truck pitched left and then right, he thought they might roll, but miraculously they didn't. At some point, he must have instinctively shifted into Park. Which was a really good thing.

Neither he nor Edie moved or spoke. Dazed, he sat there trying to figure out what the hell had just happened. Next to him, Edie sat ramrod straight, staring straight ahead, equally silent.

Breathe in, breathe out.

"Are you okay?" he asked, eyeing her. As far as he could tell, neither of them were bleeding. His entire body ached, which he supposed was to be expected after what he'd just been through.

Slowly, she turned her head toward him and rolled her neck, then her shoulders. "Yes, I think so. How about you?"

"I'm good."

"Look," she said toward the passenger side window. "It's moved away past us. You can actually see the tornado tearing up stuff in the distance."

"Debris field," he commented absently, still slightly dazed. Had he hit his head? He didn't think so.

"Maybe we should go somewhere. Just not that way. No sense in chasing that twister."

"The truck's still running," he heard himself say. Since he didn't know how badly smashed up the body might be, he had no idea if it would move. Guess there was only one way to find out. Try.

Slowly, he put his foot on the brake and shifted into

Drive. The instant he touched the gas pedal, the truck lurched forward. Surprised, he stepped on the brake and shifted back into Park.

"We need to make sure no one else got hurt," he said. "There were other vehicles all around us. Since no one's come running up to check on us, we've got to assume there are some injuries."

"Good thinking." Clearly more energetic than he, she jumped out. "Are you coming?"

Every part of his body aching, he followed her. Looking back the way they'd come, he saw one other vehicle sitting on the shoulder of the road and another upside down in the ditch. He and Edie were the only ones outside.

"Call 911," he told her, but before he'd finished getting the words out, they heard the sound of sirens in the distance.

"I think they already know," she said.

As they approached the car sitting on the shoulder, an older man got out. "You two are lucky to be alive," he declared. "That tornado picked you up and spat you out."

They all turned to look at the car on its roof. "Those folks weren't so lucky."

Chapter 6

After the paramedics had freed the two inhabitants of the wrecked vehicle and transported them to the hospital, Edie and Jake gave brief statements to the police and got back into his truck to continue on. She checked the weather app and saw that the bulk of the storm had moved east and the tornado was no longer on the ground.

"It's safe to continue toward Oklahoma City," Jake said.

She simply nodded and averted her gaze, faced the side window and struggled to get a grip on her emotions without making Jake aware of her inner turmoil.

Ten minutes in, she gave up the effort. Despite her best efforts, tears filled her eyes and rolled down her cheeks. Throat aching, nose clogged, she couldn't make herself stop crying.

Worse, she wasn't sure why not. They were safe.

They'd made it through. The people in the upside-down car were going to survive. But it felt like the trauma caused by the tornado and the storm combined with not knowing if her little girl was safe had been the last straw.

She kept her head averted and tried to keep quiet, hoping Jake wouldn't notice her shoulders shaking. But she felt his gaze on her right before he pulled off the interstate into a motel parking lot.

"We're stopping for the night," he declared, his tone leaving no room for argument. "You need a hot shower and a glass of wine, in that order."

Nodding, she didn't protest. How could she, when she felt as if she'd broken into a thousand tiny pieces?

"Wait here," he said, pulling up under the portico. Before he opened his door to get out, he turned to her. "Are you okay with sharing a room? Separate beds, but one room?"

"Sure," she replied, wondering if he simply wanted to keep an eye on her or if cost was a factor. The last, she understood. They hadn't actually had any kind of discussion over sharing the expenses, but she didn't have a lot of discretionary cash lying around. And if he was on an unpaid leave from his job as a peace officer, she doubted he did either.

They'd need to talk about that, too, she supposed. If they ended up being on the road awhile. She couldn't help but keep hoping Rayna would call with the news Laney had been found, safe and unharmed. But until that actually happened, she'd need to see about paying her half of the costs.

She located some tissue in the glove box and got busy mopping at her eyes and face. She'd managed

---

to forget her makeup. She'd need to pick up some at some point.

Jake returned a moment later, got in and pulled around to the side of the building. "We can go in this door to get to our room," he said. "No need to go through the lobby."

"Do I look that bad?" she asked, her tone rueful.

"Not bad. Just like you've been crying. Which is completely understandable," he hastened to add.

"That's putting it mildly," she said. "You know what? For the very first time since this ordeal began, I was actually glad Laney wasn't with me." Her voice shook, but she made herself continue. "I could imagine how absolutely terrified she would have been. It was all I could think about as the tornado lifted your truck up off the pavement and we began to roll."

He eyed her. "What about yourself?" he asked quietly. "Weren't you afraid for yourself?"

"Yes, I was. But while I worried about how badly you and I might get hurt, I refused to even think about getting killed. I can't leave this world, not now, not yet. Laney needs her mother."

At her words, something changed in his face, almost imperceptibly, reminding her yet again that he, too, had a claim to her daughter. His daughter, too. She could hardly bear to even think of that. She got out, grabbed her duffle bag from the back seat and followed Jake to the side door.

Once they reached their hotel room, she waited while he unlocked the door. The room, while small, seemed clean and pleasantly decorated. There were two full-sized beds separated by a generic end table with a lamp and a small alarm clock. It looked like every other modern budget motel room in Texas, she thought.

"Which bed do you want?" he asked. Once she'd pointed to the one closest to the bathroom, he hefted his bag onto the other.

At a loss as to what to do next, she settled for dropping onto the edge of her bed. "What now?"

"Why don't you go ahead and take a hot shower, and I'll go out and pick up some food and a bottle of wine. Do you prefer white or red?"

She shrugged, appreciating that he seemed to realize she needed some time alone. "I like both. Pinot Grigio or Pinot Noir are my favs. The red would probably be easier since we don't have any way to chill the white."

"Got it." On his way to the door, he turned and handed her a room key. "I got two. I'll see you in maybe half an hour."

Thanking him, she stayed seated until she heard the sound of his truck starting up and driving away. Then she got up and opened up her duffle. After getting clean comfortable clothes and her toiletries, she headed for the bathroom and a shower as hot as she could stand.

By the time Jake returned, she felt a hundred times better. The hot water had helped lessen the ache in her muscles, and a clean body and clean hair made her feel much more human and closer to normal. As normal as she could be with her daughter still missing.

She'd even turned on the television, watching the local news. They had devoted an entire segment to the tornado damage, showing the car upside down in the ditch as well as several destroyed buildings in a nearby town. When the door opened, she tensed up a little because she'd been so engrossed in the coverage that she hadn't heard his truck return.

"I hope you like Chinese food," he said, brandishing a couple of large paper bags. "I got an assortment of things for us to try. It smells amazing."

"That sounds good," she told him. "Did you remember the most important thing?"

"The wine? Of course." Settling the bags down on the small desk, he pulled out a bottle and two plastic cups. "Best I could do as far as wine glasses," he said, smiling.

"Good. Because I definitely feel like we need to celebrate surviving that tornado. You just missed seeing the news coverage. The tornado went on to wreck several buildings in a nearby town."

The scent from the food reached her, making her inhale appreciatively. "Laney loves Chinese food," she told him. "Particularly the egg rolls."

He nodded, not sure exactly how to respond.

"When was Noel's birthday?" Edie asked, her gaze intent. "I always celebrated it the day my cousin told me Laney was born. October first."

Throat aching, he grimaced. "She was actually born pretty close to that date. September twenty-ninth."

Though Edie smiled, she didn't immediately respond. When she finally did, her expression was thoughtful. "I adopted her right around that date. September twenty-eighth, when she was one-year-old."

The sorrow in her voice nearly undid him.

"Come and eat," he said, taking out all the boxes on the desk. "I got a couple of paper plates with the order. I can eat in that armchair there and you can have the desk chair."

The Edie she'd been before would have teased him about letting her sit so close to the food. Instead, she got up and moved. "I just realized how hungry I am," she announced. "Which makes me feel strangely guilty. How can I even think about eating when my daughter is likely hungry?"

"You can't think like that," he told her. "Not if you want to keep on going. You've got to keep your body strong, which means eating and sleeping."

"I know," she said, slightly annoyed. "You've mentioned that several times now. I promise I won't forget." To prove her point, she opened the first carton, grabbed a plate and began loading it up with food. He'd gotten all of her favorite things, she realized. Sweet and sour chicken, fried rice and the best part, egg rolls.

Once she'd taken all she wanted, she sat down and waited for him to get his dinner so she could start eating.

"No need to wait on me," he said, smiling. "I can practically see your mouth watering."

She laughed, again surprised. But instead of digging in, she watched him. He was, to use one of her father's phrases, good people.

Finally, Jake took his seat and lifted his fork to his mouth. Halfway there, he stopped and eyed her, one brow raised. "What are you waiting for? Dig in."

Needing no second urging, she did. She'd finished everything and was debating going back for more when her phone rang, making her jump.

Heart pounding, she scrambled to reach it, grimacing when she saw her mother's name on the caller ID instead of Rayna. Jake, too, had gone on full alert.

"Hi, Mom," she said when she answered, noting

the way Jake instantly relaxed. "We don't have any news yet."

"We?" Her mother immediately picked up on that. "Who's we?"

Luckily, in the way her mother had of answering her own questions, she didn't give Edie a chance to react. "I suppose you mean you and that friend you mentioned. Do I know her?"

"No." Edie didn't bother to correct the pronoun. "You don't. What's going on, Mom?"

"Your father and I have stopped for the night in New Mexico," her mother replied. "I just wanted to check in with you and see if there had been any developments."

"Not yet. But I plan on calling Rayna soon. I promise I'll keep you posted."

"I know you will, dear." Her mother sighed. "It's all just so hard to believe. Sweet Laney, she must be so frightened."

Tears immediately pricked Edie's eyes. "I've got to let you go," she said, not wanting to break down crying. "I love you both. Drive safely." She ended the call without waiting for her mom to respond.

When she looked up, Jake met her gaze. "Are you all right?" he asked, his voice quiet.

She wasn't, but she nodded anyway. "I kind of have to be, don't I?" Then, her appetite gone, she carried her plate over to the trash.

Jake went back for seconds, asking her if she was sure she didn't want anything else. "Since we don't have a refrigerator, anything that doesn't get eaten will have to go in the trash."

"I'm full," she said. "But knock yourself out."

Still she couldn't help but smile when he brought

the last egg roll over to her, along with the plastic container of sweet and sour sauce. "Thank you."

"I kind of figured you might be able to make room for that," he said, his rakish grin making her ache in a way she'd nearly forgotten.

She wanted him, she realized, shocked.

Pushing to her feet, she shook her head, as if by doing so, she could shake off the unwanted feeling. How could she even think about something like that at a time like this? What kind of awful person must she be?

"It's going to be okay," he said, making her wonder how he'd known her thoughts. *Dang.* She hoped not.

"Thanks." She wondered if he could tell her cheeks were burning. "I have to believe there will be light at the end of the tunnel."

"Yes," he agreed. "That's the only way you can keep moving forward."

Still feeling a bit nonplussed, she made a show of checking her fitness watch. "Do you think Rayna would mind if I check in with her one last time before going to bed?"

"She said she'd contact us the minute she heard anything," he reminded her, his voice gentle.

When she looked up, the softness in his gaze matched his tone. Her insides melted a little before she shored herself up and took a deep breath. "You're right. I don't want to bother her, but the radio silence is frustrating. You'd think they'd have something by now."

He nodded. "I haven't ever been a sheriff, but speaking from a law enforcement perspective, I can guess she's likely doing everything she can to weed out the flakes. That last tip, the one everyone thought was it, turned out to be a gut-wrenching disaster. I'm sure she doesn't want to put either of us through that again."

Once more, the quiet reminder that he, too, had a stake in this. As if she could ever forget. Just because she didn't allow herself to dwell on his claim to her daughter didn't mean it wasn't always there in the back of her mind.

Shaking off the melancholy these thoughts brought, she sighed. "You're right. I'll wait until the morning and call her then."

His quick bark of laughter had her hiding an answering smile. "I think I'm going to turn in early," she said. "If that's okay with you. It's been a really long day."

"It has," he agreed.

"I don't mind if you want to watch TV or something. I can just pull the covers over my head."

"It's all good. I think I might just see if this place has an in-house gym. I could use a workout after that heavy meal."

Of all the things he might have said, for some reason, she found this funny. Once she started, she couldn't seem to stop. She laughed until no sound came out of her mouth, until she doubled over, tears streaming down her face. Horrifyingly out of control, on the verge of a total meltdown, but she couldn't get herself together.

"Edie." He wrapped his strong arms around her and held on, his very presence solid and comforting. To her embarrassment, she clung to him, attempting to draw strength from his embrace. He let her, no doubt aware how close to the edge she'd been standing.

Finally, she pulled herself together long enough to step away. Avoiding looking at him, she gathered her night things and hurried toward the bathroom. "Have fun looking for a gym," she said.

"I'm not going anywhere," he said. These were the last words she heard as she closed the bathroom door. And the kindest thing he could have possibly said.

Of all the scenarios Jake might have expected when meeting the woman who'd lived with his daughter for the last four years, the one thing he had never expected was having to battle such a fierce attraction. Luckily, he hid it well and he believed Edie herself had no idea. Usually, he was great at keeping the desire under control. But right now, his body throbbed as she got ready to sleep in the other bed next to him, and he wondered how he'd make it through the night.

Part of him felt horrible about the entire thing. How could he want Edie, freaking crave her this way, when his little girl was still missing? He told himself repeatedly that he was only human, which helped a little. Also, Edie Beswick just might be the sexiest woman he'd ever met, even more so since she didn't seem to have any idea of her own beauty.

Honestly, everything about her appealed to him. Her physical appearance, from her long, blonde hair and blue eyes to her lithe curves and fluid movements. But more than that, he liked the way she laughed, the timber of her voice when she got excited, and even the way she tried so damn hard to be strong. In this situation, he suspected any other woman would have broken long before now.

He admired the hell out of her. Her steadfast, unwavering devotion, the fierceness of her love for her daughter. Not for the first time, he wondered how he could ever even consider taking Noel away from her. That, he suspected, would be the one thing that would break her.

Not to mention doing what would be best for the child. Noel no doubt loved Edie, the only mother she remembered. He couldn't just swoop in and snatch her away just because he was related by blood. Even if the law would be on his side, he no longer felt sure it was the ethical or right thing to do.

"Good night," Edie murmured softly, cutting into his thoughts. She smiled at him as she reached for the lamp and switched it off, plunging the room into darkness. Her lazy, sexy smile sent his pulse into overdrive.

"Good night," he replied, glad the sheets hid his growing arousal.

For the first few minutes he lay still, scarcely daring to breathe. Though she wasn't in his bed with him, she might as well have been. Every movement she made, each rustle of sheets, her soft sighs as she struggled to get comfortable, became a unique form of torture. Finally, her breathing evened out as she drifted to sleep.

Maybe now he could relax. He tried, damned if he didn't, but he couldn't keep from imagining how good it would feel to hold her in his arms. And more, though he quickly shut that thought down. Otherwise, he'd be in real trouble.

Finally, he managed to sleep, though with that annoying kind of restlessness that had him waking every hour or so. He'd check the clock on the nightstand between them, listen to make sure Edie was still okay, and then turn over and close his eyes. By the time the sunrise colored along the edges of the motel's blackout curtains, he felt more exhausted than he had when he'd first gone to bed.

As the darkness lightened, he sat up and looked over at Edie, who still had the covers pulled up to her chin. His morning arousal instantly got worse. He grabbed his pillow and put it in front of him. Then, moving slowly and carefully, he made his way into the bathroom. Stepping into the shower and turning the water on, he soaped his hands up and took care of himself. Feeling much better, he finished his shower, dried off and, after brushing his teeth, put on the same clothes he'd worn the day before.

When he finally emerged from the bathroom, he saw that Edie had turned all the lights on. Sitting cross-legged on her bed, she watched him as he made his way toward his bag.

He glanced at her and nearly stopped short.

Damned if she didn't look pretty first thing in the morning, with her tousled hair and drowsy, heavy-lidded gaze. And by pretty, he also meant sexy as hell. He managed to smile blandly at her, inwardly cursing the way his body went on instant alert.

"Good morning," he said, his voice raspy.

If she noticed anything unusual in his demeanor, she didn't show it. "Morning," she said. "It won't actually be good until Laney is found."

"You're right," he agreed. Glad she was unaware of his desire for her, he gestured toward the bathroom. "All yours."

"Thanks."

A few minutes later, he heard the shower start up. He allowed himself a minute or two fantasizing about joining her, but then found himself rock hard again. *Damn it.*

Grabbing his laptop, he powered it on and logged in. But he couldn't focus on anything except Edie naked in the shower. Talk about a one-track mind.

The shower cut off. A moment or two later, the door opened. Edie emerged, her damp hair combed, wearing only a towel. She stood framed in the doorway, clearly uncertain. Then, evidently reaching some sort of decision, she moved across the room toward him.

"Jake?"

Harder than he'd ever been, heartbeat thundering in his ears, he stared up at her. "What do you need, Edie?"

"You," she replied, and dropped the towel.

He couldn't move, couldn't think, but he sure as hell wasn't going to turn down what he'd been fantasizing about ever since the moment he'd laid eyes on her behind the bakery counter.

Another woman might have taken his silence for a refusal. Not Edie. "Make me stop thinking," she ordered. "Help me get out of my head for a while."

Needing no second urging, he hurriedly stripped off his clothes.

When she saw the strength and size of his arousal, she laughed. "You're as ready as I am."

To prove her words, she guided his hand to her, letting him feel her warmth and wetness. He hadn't thought it possible for him to grow any more aroused, but stroking between her soft folds drove him wild.

"Come." Taking his hand, she led him to the bed. "Do you have a condom?"

It took a minute for her question to register. Since he always kept at least one condom with him at all times, he nodded. "Do you mind grabbing it for me?" he rasped. "It's in my jeans pocket."

She immediately retrieved the wrapper. Instead of handing it to him, she opened it herself. "I want to do this."

Since he couldn't speak, he nodded instead. As swollen as he was, the moment she wrapped her small hand around him, he groaned.

Somehow, she managed to get the condom on him. Each touch and tug only aroused him more. Body throbbing, he struggled to keep himself under control.

Once she'd finished, she pushed him back and climbed on top of him. Lowering her body, she took him all the way inside of her, sheathing him tightly.

He almost lost it again, right then and there. "Wait." Using his hands, he held her around the waist to keep her from moving. "Wait," he repeated, his jaw clenched. "I just need…"

Instead, she threw back her head and gave a throaty laugh. "I don't want to wait," she said, and began riding him with a wanton sort of passion that made him lose his mind.

A goddess, with her long throat and blonde hair swirling around her shoulders. Still moving, she bent over and kissed him open-mouthed. Her full breasts pressed into his chest, sexier than even his wildest imaginings.

Body bucking against hers, he abandoned any attempt to rein himself in. He met her thrust for thrust, his blood on fire, roaring in his ears. She was everything he'd ever wanted in a woman and somehow more.

Burning up, he couldn't seem to get enough. More. He wanted more.

With one quick move, he rolled them over so that now he straddled her. Instead of protesting, she flashed him another sexy grin and pulled him back to her for another long, deep, kiss.

Now it was his turn to drive her crazy. Kissing her, letting his fingers explore her smooth skin and every curve and hollow of her body, he moved with agonizing slowness. She made sexy little moans of protest, thrashing against him, urging him on to go faster, deeper.

Unable to resist, he began to move faster, though he managed to keep a tenuous grip on his rapidly shredding self-control.

"Jake!" she cried out, her entire body shuddering. As she convulsed around him, he let loose, pounding himself into her, intent on possessing her with every rock-hard inch of him.

She climaxed and he joined her, holding her close, their bodies joined in mutual earth-shattering ecstasy.

Even after the tremors ceased and their breathing slowed and he'd rolled over onto his side to keep from crushing her, they stayed close. Forehead to forehead, his gaze settled on hers in a kind of intimacy he'd never experienced.

Wrong. Immediately, he chided himself. This entire situation was intense. Which would explain a lot of the feelings he knew couldn't possibly be true.

Surreal. And more wonderful than the bad timing said it should be. Still, he needed to make sure there were no misconceptions on her part.

"About what just happened…" he began.

"No." She placed her finger against his lips. "We don't need to talk about that. We're both adults. There won't be any misunderstandings or false promises. We each took what we needed. End of story."

End of story. Cut and dried. Pretty damn close to what he'd been about to try and express, though maybe not so bluntly. Unsure how to react, he simply looked at her.

"This has to just be a physical thing. I can't mentally or emotionally deal with any more right now," she told him.

"And you won't have to," he promised. "I'm in agreement with you. We need to keep our focus where it belongs. Getting Laney back safe."

"Agreed."

After cleaning up, they dressed and packed their things away. Making one last sweep around the room to make sure nothing had been left behind, he loaded their bags in the back seat and headed toward the office to check out.

She got into his truck and waited for him. Once they were both buckled in, he started the ignition. As he pulled away from the motel, he couldn't shake the feeling that there was something he was missing.

"I know we've been over this, but are you absolutely sure you don't know someone who might have a reason to grab Laney? I still can't dismiss the possibility that this was personal."

"I almost wish that you're right," she murmured. "Because if taking her was a personal thing, then they'd have more of a reason not to harm her."

The words neither of them had said out loud. As long as he'd been searching for his daughter, he'd avoided putting any kind of awfulness out into the universe. Sure, he'd encountered more than one insensitive cop and had to listen to a nauseating account of their personal worst investigation involving an abducted child. Somehow, he'd kept from decking the guy. And in his own mind, where it mattered, he'd refused to accept anything but the belief that Noel was safe somewhere. Maybe even loved.

Turned out he'd been right.

"No other relatives up there in Pocatello?" he asked.

She shook her head. "No. We've already been over this."

"I know, but bear with me."

They pulled onto the interstate. Relieved to see both lanes were clear and free of debris, he accelerated. The skies were blue, dotted with fluffy white clouds, like the horrible storm the day before had never existed.

"How well did you know your cousin?" Not too well, he figured. Especially since Edie hadn't known this other woman had stolen a child.

"We played together when I was small," she said. "But mostly we kept in touch through social media."

Since he'd checked out Edie's online profile and spent time scrolling through all her friends, he had to ask. "Is her profile page still active?"

She frowned and then got out her phone. "I don't think so. Let me check."

A moment later, she shook her head. "I'm not finding anything. Shortly after she died, someone took it down."

"Someone?" He zeroed in on that. "Who?"

"I don't know," she said. "I'm guessing one of her friends."

Her friends. "Were you close with any of Gina's friends? Maybe stayed in touch over the years?"

Considering his words for a moment, she finally got out her phone and started scrolling. "I'm looking at my online friends list. I mean, I met several at the funeral, so it's possible."

But after a few minutes, she shook her head. "I'm not finding anyone who looks suspicious."

"Don't worry," he said. "We'll figure it out."

He only hoped he might be right.

Chapter 7

Edie wasn't sure why she couldn't stop thinking about the amazing sex she'd just had with Jake. Maybe because dwelling on that felt a million times better than picturing what awfulness might be happening to her daughter.

They'd nearly reached Oklahoma City when her phone rang, startling her out of her thoughts.

"It's Rayna!" she exclaimed, her heart rate going into overdrive.

"Please put her on speaker," Jake asked.

Edie nodded and then answered. "Hey, Rayna. Any news?"

"Please forgive me for skipping the basic pleasantries," Rayna said, her voice clipped, "but a very unusual voicemail was left on the tip line, and I need to know if you recognize the voice or have any idea what this man is talking about."

Every instinct on full alert, Edie swallowed. "Play it."

"Here we go."

Call off the Amber Alert. The child you call Laney Beswick is not in danger. She's safe and where she belongs. Leave us alone.

Trying to digest the words, Edie glanced at Jake.

"Play it again, please," he asked, his jaw tight.

Rayna did. Once she'd finished, they all sat in silence for a few seconds.

"Well?" Rayna finally asked. "Do either of you have something to say?"

"I do. I want to know what the hell all of that means," Edie said, close to tears.

"Are you absolutely certain you don't recognize that man's voice?" Jake asked, staring at Edie.

Perplexed, she shook her head. "No, I don't."

"No old boyfriend or ex?" He continued to press. "Because he sounded like he definitely had an axe to grind."

A flash of anger had her sitting up straight. "I might ask you the same question. How do you know that person doesn't have a problem with *you*?"

"People, people," Rayna said, interrupting. "Bicker on your own time. I'm going to play it again. Maybe the third time will be the charm."

And she did. Once it finished, she spoke again. "Anything? From either of you? We really need your help. While there's always the possibility that this guy is a crackpot, he might actually be the one who took Laney."

Edie's blood froze. "He said she's where she belongs," she whispered, now struggling to get words past the lump in her throat. Her earlier spurt of anger had been replaced with terror. "Do you really think he has my daughter?"

"It's a distinct possibility," Rayna replied, her voice dry.

"Should we turn around and head back to Getaway?" Edie asked, struggling to throttle her panic.

"Not unless you want to. We have no idea where that call originated. He could be anywhere."

Edie opened her mouth to speak again, but Jake put his hand on her arm, forestalling her.

"Rayna, let us talk about this and we'll get back to you," Jake said. "And please let us know if you get any more leads."

"Will do."

After Rayna ended the call, Edie exhaled. Letting her phone fall into her lap, she struggled with the urge to cover her face with her hands and cry. "This is unreal," she told Jake. "Honestly, I don't understand what all of this means."

Jake took the next exit, pulling into the parking lot of a barbeque restaurant. Once there, he pulled into a space under a large tree and turned to face Edie.

"This is what I was talking about earlier," he said, his earnest expression matching his voice. "That guy, whoever he is, definitely makes it sound like Laney's abduction was not random. He chose her for a reason. We just have to figure out what that reason is."

Feeling lost, Edie nodded.

"Now tell me," Jake said. "Though I know you don't like the idea, it's necessary. Let's go over all your old boyfriends. Were any of your exes messed up enough to do something like this?"

"I don't have any exes," she said, suddenly so exhausted she couldn't even feel angry. Then, noting his skeptical expression and raised brow, she shook her head, refusing to allow his disbelief to make her defensive. "I haven't really dated anyone since college, and even then, nothing was serious."

"But…" His frown deepened. "You're telling me you haven't dated anyone in *years*? What's wrong with the men in your town?"

Was that a compliment? Deciding it didn't matter. She met his gaze. "That's my choice. After I adopted Laney, I devoted my life to her. I didn't want to bring different men around her, so I just…stopped dating."

"Do you ever intend to take it back up?" he asked.

"I don't know. Maybe someday." Frustrated, she sighed. "What does any of that matter?"

"Because we're trying to figure out the identity of that guy who left the message, who likely has Laney. If we can help the police find out who he is, we can get her back."

"But I don't know who he is," she said. "Believe me, I wish I did. What if this person isn't connected to me? What then?"

"I'd say he's definitely connected, somehow. Whether to you or to Laney, there's some sort of a tie. Otherwise, he wouldn't have made the statement that she's where she belongs."

"Like I said before, what about you?" she asked. "Maybe that's where the connection is. You've been searching for your missing child for four years."

He dragged his hand through his hair. "Believe me, I looked into that. I checked out every possible scenario. I still don't know why my Noel was taken, though after hearing your story, I'm guessing it was more of a crime of opportunity than anything else. Your cousin must have simply been in the right place at the wrong time."

Her sweet older cousin, who'd been so overjoyed to finally become a mother. Edie's heart had broken when she'd learned about Gina's brain aneurysm. Her death had left her beloved daughter motherless. Edie hadn't hesitated, not even once, in her decision to take Laney in.

Like Gina had always said, having Laney completed her and filled her life with a joy she hadn't even realized she'd been missing. Now, with Laney missing, all the light had left the world.

"I still find it hard to believe Gina would do something like that," she said. "She had lots of issues, but stealing someone else's child? I don't see it."

"Yet she had Noel." His quiet statement once again served to remind her that this man had a valid claim to her daughter. "Maybe her husband or boyfriend was the one who grabbed her."

"She wasn't married. She did have a live-in partner though. And while it seems clear one of them took your child all those years ago, when Gina died, her boyfriend was the one who called me and asked me if I would come get her daughter." She exhaled. "It seems unlikely he'd have come for her now, four years later."

"Her boyfriend?" A spark of interest lit his gaze. "What was his name?"

"Derek something or other. He was a drug addict and seemed pretty strung out the one time I met him. But before you start thinking he might have had something to do with this, not only did he ask me to take Laney, but he went to prison shortly after I brought Laney home. As far as I know, he's still there."

"He might not be. Maybe after all this time, he's re-thought things and decided he wants her back."

"But why not ask me?" she countered. "Despite all his obvious shortcomings, he cared enough about Laney to reach out to someone he knew would love her and provide a stable home."

"Because he knew you'd tell him no? I mean, you do have legal custody. With his track record, there's no way he'd have much of a chance in court against you."

She nodded. "True. I wonder if he ever got out of prison."

"There's a way to find that out," he said. "But you'll need his full name. Once you have that, text Rayna and ask her to check on that."

"Easier said than done." She went through her contacts. "I have him listed with his old phone number, but I only show his first name. Maybe I never knew his last."

"Try to remember," he urged her. "Any connection could be the one. Please."

"Let me check my old text messages and IMs," she said. "I don't ever delete them." Scrolling, she went back to four years ago, when she'd learned of her cousin's untimely passing.

Finally, she found one from Derek. The last thing he'd sent had been to give her the address where he and Gina had been living so she could get there to pick up Laney. Before that, he'd mentioned having warrants and how he was terrified the police would come for him and put Gina's daughter in foster care. This statement had made Edie drive straight through from Texas to Idaho, wired on energy drinks and prayers.

Luckily, she'd made it before Derek had been arrested. In fact, after he knew Laney would be safe, he'd turned himself in. Closing her eyes, she struggled to remember if she'd ever known his last name.

"Lambert." The instant she spoke out loud, she knew she was right. "His name is Derek Lambert. Let me text Rayna and ask her to check and see if he's still in prison."

Once she'd done that, she slid her phone back into her purse. "Is your buddy in Oklahoma City expecting you?"

"He is. We're meeting him for lunch." Jake checked the dashboard clock. "And we're going to be way too early. We'll need to figure out a way to kill an hour or so."

"Could we stop at a drugstore?" she asked. "I need to buy some makeup. I forgot to grab my makeup bag when I packed."

"You don't need makeup."

Though his reply had been automatic, he sounded as if he meant every word. *Men.*

Her eyes widened. "Thanks, I guess. But I'd like to look my best when meeting with law enforcement or talking with media. Since we have a little time to kill, I'd appreciate it if we could make a stop."

"No problem."

Ahead she saw a Walgreens. "Let's stop there."

It didn't take her long to pick out some basic makeup. Foundation, powder, blush, eye shadow, mascara and lipstick. She carried them all to the counter and waited while the cashier rang them up.

While she shopped, Jake snagged a few snacks. Nuts, candy and chips. Edie walked up to join him, unable to help but notice the way his cashier eyed him like he was a particularly delectable kind of treat.

Edie got it.

Though she'd be ashamed if she actually allowed herself to think about it, she planned to have sex with Jake again. That very night, in fact. She wasn't sure if it was because she'd gone so long without any form of physical pleasure or if surviving the tornado had made her want to reaffirm life, but whatever the reason, she craved his touch.

A distraction from the worried, frantic terror that constantly threatened to engulf her, letting loose and getting lost in the passion she felt for him couldn't be beat.

Selfish? Maybe. But if so, he'd appeared to share equally in the respite of pleasure they'd had. She doubted he'd turn her down if she initiated sex again.

While Jake drove, she carefully applied the makeup, using the visor mirror. Once she'd finished, she felt pretty good about the end result. Since she really couldn't do much about her hair, she debated putting it into a long braid and then decided to leave it hanging loose down her back.

"We're still too early," Jake said. "How about we find the restaurant, park and then I can check the website for any additional tips that might have come in?"

"Fine with me."

Jake asked her to put the name of the place into her phone. Normally, she would have been thrilled to eat at a Mexican restaurant, since that was her favorite. Laney's, too, which sobered her right up. Taking pleasure in tacos and enchiladas without her daughter felt wrong, so she tamped down any hint of enthusiasm and let her phone GPS give Jake directions.

When they reached the restaurant, he pulled in and chose a parking space under a large tree. The building had been painted in cheerful colors—yellow, orange, purple, green, pink and a particularly bright shade of turquoise. Though it was barely eleven, people had already started arriving for lunch.

Noticing her watching them, Jake touched her arm. "After I do this, we can go in and make sure we grab a table if you want. I can text Tanner and let him know where to find us."

She nodded. "I think that'll be a good idea. I have a feeling this place fills up fast."

He grabbed his laptop from the back seat and opened it. "I know I can do this on my phone, but it's a lot easier on the computer."

A moment later, he let out a low whistle. "I'll be damned. The person who called the Amber Alert tip line left a note here as well."

"What's it say?"

"Pretty much the same thing as before, though with slightly different wording. 'This child is safe and back where she belongs. Stop looking for her. She's safe and well loved.'"

"Back where she belongs," Edie repeated. "I'm thinking that means Houston, where you're from. Maybe it's time you start taking a look at some of your and your wife's relatives instead of some mythical enemy of mine."

"You might be right," he said, surprising her. "Though I checked into all of them after Noel went missing the first time, the circumstances are different now. Since I haven't kept anything about my search secret, I guess there's a possibility one of them might have followed me here and figured things out before me."

Put that way, it did sound like a long shot. "Let's just ask your FBI friend about it and see what he thinks."

With twenty minutes to spare before they were supposed to meet Tanner, Jake figured they could wait inside. From what he remembered, Tanner had always been early anyway, so they shouldn't have to wait too long.

After instructing the hostess to send Tanner their way when he arrived, they were given a nice booth in an area close to the kitchen. It hadn't filled up yet, so it wasn't as crowded or as noisy as the rest of the restaurant.

Once they'd been seated, a large bowl of chips along with several smaller ones filled with salsa were placed on their table. Edie smiled. "My favorite part," she said, and then her smile dimmed. "Laney's, too," she added. "She loves Tex-Mex."

Though she reached for a chip and dipped it into the salsa, her earlier spark of enthusiasm was gone. Jake found himself wishing there was something he could say to make it better, to bring back her smile, but he knew there truly wasn't.

Their waitress brought menus and asked them if they'd like something to drink. He and Edie both ordered iced tea, and he let their server know another party would be joining them.

She went to get their drinks. A moment later, Jake glanced toward the entrance and saw Tanner striding toward them. He wore his usual navy blue suit, white cotton dress shirt and a tie.

Jake pushed to his feet. "Tanner!" he said, holding out his hand. "You haven't changed at all."

"Right back at you." Tanner's easy smile included Edie.

Jake introduced them, unable to keep from noticing the way his friend's gaze lingered on her. Since he'd filled Tanner in on the basics of the case, including the likelihood that Edie's missing daughter and Jake's were one and the same, he figured it had to be mostly curiosity.

After they'd placed their food order, Jake filled Tanner in on both the voice message and the written one that had been left in the comments section on his website.

"Definitely sounds like this was personal," Tanner agreed, his gaze again drifting toward Edie. "I'm assuming you both have already gone over relatives and past relationships, looking for someone who might have done this?"

"We have," Jake replied. "And I'm aware there's not a whole lot to go on, but is there any possibility you could work on coming up with a profile?"

Tanner laughed. Then, as he realized no one else shared his amusement, he stopped. "You're serious? Usually when I profile someone, I study a pattern of behavior. There is no pattern here."

"Please," Edie asked. "Just try."

Slowly, Tanner nodded. "Okay. From what I can see, this is someone with a twisted notion of righting a wrong. He or she feels this child was not meant to be where she was—with you, Edie."

Slowly, she nodded. "I adopted her when my cousin Gina died from a brain aneurysm. It was pretty sudden."

Their food arrived, and it got quiet at first as they ate. Tanner spread his attention evenly between his plate and Edie, throwing in an occasional glance at Jake. It might have been humorous if Jake hadn't felt protective of her. He didn't even want to analyze why he felt his way all of a sudden.

As the food began to disappear, they talked a little more, going over possibilities just like Jake had, from Gina's boyfriend Derek to any of her girlfriends.

When they'd finished discussing her past, Tanner turned and looked at Jake. "Now you," he said. "I know Marina was killed, but what about her parents? Or siblings? Any of Marina's family members or friends who might feel they have a right to raise this child?"

Instead of immediately discounting the idea, Jake promised to look into it. "I still communicate with Marina's parents and sister," he said. "We're on friendly terms. When Noel was first taken, I went over every possibility with a fine-toothed comb and came up with nothing."

"Check again," Tanner advised, just as the waitress arrived with the bill. "I'll take this," he said, waving away Jake's protests and tossing cash onto the table. "It's been too long since I've seen you."

Since the check had been settled, they all stood and made their way toward the door.

Once in the parking lot, Tanner looked from one to the other and smiled. "Kudos to the two of you," he said. "Both of you have clearly opposing stakes in this, yet you've come together, combining resources, to help find this child. Most other people would be fighting, backstabbing and blaming each other. I really respect what you're doing."

"Thanks," Jake replied. "Please give us a holler if you think of anything that might assist us."

"Will do," Tanner said, his voice cheerful. "And please call me and keep me posted if you get any new leads."

"We will," Jake said.

"Thanks. I really hope you find her." With that, he walked away and got into a dark blue sedan and drove off.

"Well, that was awkward." Clearly trying to inject humor into the moment, Edie shook her head. They made their way to his truck and got in. "Now what?" she asked.

"I'm going to try and engage whoever wrote that comment on the website," he said. "I've done that before in the past. Sometimes they respond, other times they don't. I think it really depends on how big the commenter's ego might be."

"And if you're successful in opening a dialogue? What do you hope to gain?"

"Hints." He started the engine, mainly to get the AC running. "If I goad him or her, ask the right questions, they might give something away. Like where to find them. Or even who they are."

"That would be awesome, but it almost sounds too easy."

"I know." He grinned approvingly at her. "Most times, the commenter doesn't even respond. When they do, it often turns out to be some crackpot looking for attention. It's discouraging, but who knows? It just might work."

"True. And at the very least, I'm thinking you can weed out the fakers."

"It's worth a shot." He got out his laptop. "Let me do this and then we can head back to Texas."

After taking a few minutes to type up a response, he posted and closed the computer. When he looked up, Edie sat quietly watching him, her expression pensive.

"Penny for your thoughts," he said, grabbing one from the console and handing it to her, along with a tissue. Though she accepted it, she turned it over and over in her hand like she wasn't sure what to do next.

When she didn't respond, he touched her arm gently. "I'm not trying to be intrusive. I'm just wondering what is going through your head."

She shook her head, still twisting the tissue in her hands. "I'm just wondering how things got so messed up. It's shocking how one minute, life can be chugging merrily along with the sun shining and birds singing, and the next…"

"I get it," he said. "I know exactly how you feel. First, I lost my daughter, then a few weeks later, my wife." And his job as a police officer, the only career he'd ever wanted, had become a third casualty. While it mattered, he wouldn't do anything differently. How could any father ever stop searching for his baby girl?

She honored his words with silence before turning to face him. "We should be enemies, you know."

Her earnest comment momentarily surprised him. But what she said was only truth. "Maybe," he responded. "Though I think the choice we made to team up is better than that."

"I hope so. Honestly, the only thing I care about is getting Laney back safe and sound."

"Me, too," he answered, meaning it. No matter what came after, like always, his daughter came first.

After leaving Oklahoma City, Jake wasn't sure where to go next. When this had happened previously, he would simply stop at the next small town and hole up for a few days in the first clean motel he found. But that had been when he was traveling on his own. Now he had Edie.

And finding Noel felt increasingly urgent. Despite the email seeming to indicate whoever had her had taken her for misguided beliefs that they were her family, he knew better than to trust that. The unstable mental workings of an individual who'd snatch a child off the street were too complicated. He didn't dare allow himself to become even the tiniest bit complacent.

"I'm thinking about stopping in McAlester," he said. "We need to regroup and see if we can figure out what to do next."

"What?" Frowning, she half turned in her seat. "Why stop now? We've got half the day ahead of us."

"Because we don't have another destination planned."

She stared at him while she digested this. "I'd rather cross back into Texas first," she said. "If that's okay with you."

"Of course."

"Thanks." She heaved a sigh. "I don't know why, but I didn't think this would be so slow going. I remember hearing the more time that passes, the worse the chance is of finding a missing child."

Alive. The unspoken word hung in the air between them.

"Normally, that's true." He kept his voice calm to diffuse any potential panic. "But we've already been contacted by whoever took her. There were no ransom demands, no threats—nothing but a vague assertion that she's where she belongs."

"Which is a good thing," she said, as if hoping to reassure herself.

They pulled into the first motel he saw when he exited the interstate. Three stories tall, it appeared to have been built fairly recently. As a bonus, there was a Country Kitchen Restaurant right next door.

"Food and lodging," he said. "Can't beat that combo."

"Isn't it a bit early to stop?" she asked. "We've still got quite a bit of daylight left."

He shrugged, pulling under the portico and parking. "It would be if we had somewhere we needed to go." Looking at her, he cocked his head. "Do you want to go back to Getaway? I think we could easily make it before dark."

Immediately, she shook her head. "No, thank you. My parents are there now. And I'm sure everyone in town is well aware of the situation. I don't want to deal with the questions, the pitying looks—any of that. Plus, if I go back home, I'll feel like I've given up and admitted defeat."

The sun lit her hair to gold, highlighting her cheekbones and her bright blue eyes. Beautiful, he thought, his body aching. Once, in the early days of his search, he would have hated himself for being attracted to her. Now, older and wiser, he understood this didn't make him any less of a good father. He'd been a widower for years now and had come to understand that needing another woman wasn't a betrayal of anything.

But this, what he'd begun to feel for Edie was different.

"I refuse to give up," she reiterated.

"You haven't," he reminded her. "But I understand. That's one of the motivating factors that kept me on the road. If I kept moving, I was searching. So I get it, believe me."

They walked into the motel together and checked in. For now, he reserved only one night, just in case some news came in that meant they'd have to hit the road. He figured he could always extend it as needed.

As soon as they got to the room, she turned to face him. "I don't like this," she said, arms crossed.

Puzzled, he eyed her. "Don't like what? The room?"

"The room is fine. But I don't like even stopping." She shook her head, her expression militant. "There's got to be *something* else we can do rather than holing up in some motel room."

Chapter 8

Edie wanted to stomp her feet and raise her voice. In essence, pick a fight. Part of her hoped Jake would oblige. The other part of her hoped he wouldn't.

His mild expression seemed to indicate it would be the latter. "Do something?" he asked. "Like what?"

Since he had a valid point, she considered ignoring his question. Instead, she decided to throw out a few suggestions. "Follow leads, for one thing."

"Which we will, when we get them. Right now, we have nothing but a few crackpots trying to yank our chains."

"But how do we know that?" Frustrated, she took a step toward him. "Who decides what is a valid lead? What if we miss one?"

"Come here." Expression compassionate, he held out his arms. "You don't want to do this right now."

"Don't tell me what I want." Nonetheless, she took a step toward him. "I just want my baby back."

He wrapped his arms around her and held on tightly, offering only comfort. As she clung to his muscular, strong body, she realized she wanted more. Distraction and pleasure, violence and tenderness—all of it.

When she raised her head, the fierceness that she saw in his eyes told her that he wanted the same. He slanted his mouth over hers, and she met him in kind. She felt the swell of his arousal, even through his jeans. Too impatient for the niceties, she practically tore her clothing off. He did the same. They fell on each other as if they were starving. In a way, she supposed they were.

That night, they slept in the same bed. The lovemaking had given her a tentative sort of peace, and she hoped it had done the same for him. It had been years since she'd gone to sleep wrapped in a man's embrace, and she supposed she should get up and move over to the other bed, but she couldn't seem to make herself move. As she drifted off to sleep, for the first time since Laney had vanished, she felt a little bit calm.

Once during the night, she woke to find herself still snuggling in his arms. Despite the dark, the nightstand clock provided enough illumination for her to see his chiseled features. He was, she thought as she drifted back to sleep, the most handsome man she'd ever met.

Then came the dream. She dreamt of fire consuming everything in its path. The heat seared her, singeing her hair and her skin as she turned this way and that, searching for an escape. Just when she thought all was lost, a rush of water came. A deluge, a muddy swirling flood sweeping over the flames and extinguishing them. On the other side of the raging rapids, she saw her Laney, standing forlorn on a tiny piece of scorched earth. She screamed Laney's name over and over, but Laney couldn't hear her. Her baby stood crying, shivering and scared and calling for her mother.

Then she saw it. A boat of some sort battling the waves. At the helm, Jake. Heading toward her at first, but then he turned and went after Laney. "Thank you," she called out, even though she doubted he could hear. He'd save her daughter, then come back for her.

Except he didn't. Anticipation and fear had her trembling as he pulled Laney to safety. Once he had her onboard the boat, he wrapped her in a pink fluffy blanket before returning to the wheel. And then, instead of motoring over to where Edie waited, her patch of earth getting smaller and smaller as the waves claimed more ground, he turned the boat around and went back the way he'd come.

"No!" Edie shouted again and again as the water lapped over her feet. "No!"

"Edie." Jake's voice. Smoothing her hair away from her face, he lightly shook her. "Wake up. You're having some sort of bad dream."

It took a moment to adjust, to pull herself out of that place, that horror. As she opened her eyes, she realized she lay under the sheets in a lumpy motel bed. And Jake sat beside her, solid and real, his bare chest and tousled hair reminding her that he'd been sleeping right next to her. He'd switched on the lamp, no doubt to help wake her.

"Thank goodness," she said, sitting up and filling him in on the details. "Talk about symbolism. That was pretty damn textbook."

Unsmiling, he nodded. "Is that really what you think

of me?" he asked, his voice rough, making her realize she'd offended him. "Good to know."

"No, of course not. It was only a dream," she said. "I have no control over that."

"Subconsciously, you do." He dragged his hand through his hair, mussing it even more. "Edie, I want to save her as much as you do. But I would never leave you to drown once I had her. Dream or not, that's a terrible thing to believe."

She stared at him, unable to believe what she'd just heard. That was as close to a declaration of peace as he could get. Did he truly understand what he'd just promised? Did she dare ask him, or would it be best to let it go for now?

Deciding to err on the side of caution, she looked away. "I'm sorry. I meant no harm. I shouldn't have told you."

"I almost wish you hadn't," he replied. "But I'm kind of glad you did."

"What time is it?"

"Nearly five," he answered, his voice remote. "Since we're both awake, do you want to get an early start on the day?"

"Yes. I'll take the first shower." She slid out from under the sheets and hurried toward the bathroom, managing to avoid meeting his gaze.

Under the hot spray of water, she tried to clear her mind. Despite what Jake might think, at no point had she ever considered him a bad guy. In fact, the longer they were around each other, the more she saw him as a loving father, determined to reunite with his missing child.

How could she deny him that?

Yet even the thought of giving up Laney felt as if her heart had been ripped from her chest. The same way she now felt constantly, ever since her daughter had disappeared.

Her mother called just as Jake had gotten into the shower.

"We're home," she said. "Your father has taken over running the bakery. I'll help out there, too, as much as I can."

"I made sure it will be staffed," Edie said. "The bakery will be just fine."

Ignoring that, her mom continued. "Though we just got in town last night, we've already met with Rayna. Why didn't you tell us about the guy showing up claiming to be Laney's birth father?"

Edie winced. "I don't know. With everything else that's going on, it didn't seem important."

"Not important?" her mom screeched. "Edie, you need to hire an attorney."

Funny how even the idea made her stomach churn. "No, Mom. What I need is to get my daughter back. Then I can deal with the rest."

"Maybe so, but it never hurts to be prepared. This man, this Jeff or whatever his name is—"

"Jake," Edie interrupted. "His name is Jake."

"Fine. He could be some kind of scam artist, you know. He should have to take a DNA test. You need proof to back up his claims."

Edie understood why her mother had fixated on this aspect of things. Distraction. "Look, Mom, I get it. But honestly, the only thing I can focus on at this moment is finding Laney. The rest will sort itself out after that."

"But—"

"Please. Enough about that. I'm barely holding my-self together as it is." Edie sighed, figuring she might as well tell her mother the rest of it before she found out from someone else, like Rayna. "And Jake really isn't a bad guy. As a matter of fact, he and I have teamed up to search for Laney. He used to be a police officer, so he has quite a few connections in law enforcement. He's got a website going where people can send in tips, too."

Realizing she'd started babbling, Edie went quiet. Her mom had also gone silent, no doubt attempting to process this new information.

"Edie?" When she spoke again, a thread of worry colored her mother's voice. "None of that sounds like you. Are you sure you're all right?"

"No, Mom, I'm not all right," Edie snapped. Im-mediately, she felt awful. Taking several deep breaths, she tried for calm. "Obviously, I'm not. How could I be? I don't know who has my baby and if she's okay."

Suddenly on the verge of tears, Edie struggled to keep from losing control. "I'm sorry, Mom," she said. "I'm going to let you go now. I promise to keep you posted if there's any news."

"Sounds good." Now clearly trying to be cheerful, her mom didn't argue. "I love you, honey. Your father does, too."

"Love you, too," Edie replied and then ended the call.

That shouldn't have been so difficult, she thought. Her mother only wanted the best for her and for Laney. She couldn't possibly understand the complicated emo-tions and feelings Edie experienced around Jake.

Laney was his daughter, too. Just because Edie had adopted her, raised her and loved her for the past four years, that didn't erase his claim to her. No matter how much that knowledge hurt. She could only hope and pray they could come to some sort of agreement.

But first, Laney had to be found and brought home safe. Covering her face with her hands, she gave in and allowed herself to cry.

She'd just started wiping at her eyes and pulling herself back together when the bathroom door opened and Jake emerged. He took one look at her face and hurried over.

Crouching down in front of her, he took both her hands in his. "We're going to find her," he said, his fierce expression matching his voice.

"I know we are," she replied, choosing what she said with care. She'd always believed words held power, and she only wanted to speak positive things.

Both their cell phones rang, almost simultaneously. He glanced at her, she him, and they both answered.

"This is Lauren Wakefield from *Nightly News*," a cheerful woman's voice. "We've recently learned about your missing daughter, Laney. We'd like to interview you for a story we're planning to run on our broadcast."

"Why do you need an interview?" Edie asked. "All of the details are already public knowledge."

"Are they, though?" Lauren responded. "We understand that there is a possibility that your Laney might be the same missing child as one Noel Cassin. We've reached out to her father as well. Would you care to comment on that?"

Stunned, it took Edie a second to gather her thoughts. "No, thank you," she replied, and ended the call without another word.

Judging by Jake's thunderous expression, he was

also listening to someone from the network. "That's not going to happen," he finally said, also ending the call.

"They want to make our story into a prime-time circus," she said, more hurt that she probably should be. "Not because they care about Laney, but because they think sensationalizing this will garner viewers."

"Yeah." Jake dragged his hand through his hair. "I wonder if they'd be shocked to learn we're working together as a team."

Thinking of her mother's reaction, Edie suspected they would. "We should talk to Rayna," she suggested. "She could tell us if she thinks something like that might help. I mean, it is a national news show. So a lot of people would see it."

"True." He considered her words. "I suspect they won't want us if they know we're not at each other's throats."

She shrugged. "Then we don't tell them."

"Let's see what Rayna thinks." Pulling his phone back out, he put it on speaker before calling the sheriff.

Rayna picked up immediately. She listened as Jake outlined the situation. "It might be a good thing," she said once he'd finished. "We haven't heard anything else from that person claiming to have Laney. I'd prefer to keep him or her engaged in a dialogue. Going on the national news might help provoke that."

Edie and Jake exchanged a look.

"If you think we should do it, we will," Edie said. "We each pretty much declined, but I bet we could call them back and say we'd reconsidered."

"Hold off for a day or two," Rayna suggested. "We're still broadcasting the Amber Alert to various law enforcement and news agencies around the country. I'm hoping we get some sort of hit soon."

"We do, too," Edie replied. "Did you find out if Derek Lambert is still in prison?"

"He is," Rayna answered immediately. "Which means we can eliminate him from our list of subjects."

"Thanks." Edie sighed. "I never really suspected him, anyway. He made sure Laney was safe with me before surrendering to the authorities."

Jake spoke up then. "Wait, that can't be all. Were you able to speak with him? Did he say anything about Gina? Laney? He has to know something about what happened."

"I was getting to that," Rayna replied softly. "We did talk to him. He wouldn't admit to knowing about the kidnapping, but he conceded that it was possible in retrospect. He wasn't around much during the time Gina would have been pregnant, but he came back when Gina said she'd had a baby. He wanted to be around for his daughter. In lieu of that, he wanted her to be cared for by family. That's why he called you, Edie."

Edie's gaze flickered over to Jake. She felt a pang of guilt, seeing the dulled grief behind his eyes.

"I think it's safe to assume that Gina was responsible for the first abduction," Rayna continued. "Whether or not that case and this case is related somehow, I don't know. I don't think we'll get much more out of Derek without an immunity agreement for his cooperation. I imagine he doesn't want to add digits to his sentence."

Jake's jaw hardened. "Right."

"Where are you two off to next?" Rayna asked. "Any new tips from your website or social media feeds?"

Jake sighed. "Not so far. It can get frustrating, how slow this can go sometimes."

"Yeah, but we have about as good a scenario as one can hope for with a child abduction," Rayna said. "It sounds like whoever took her doesn't intend to harm her."

"True," Jake agreed. "It could definitely be a lot worse."

While Edie tried to process that, Rayna ended the call.

Something of her inner turmoil must have shown in her face.

"Edie? What's wrong?" Jake asked.

"What Rayna said." She swallowed. "I haven't looked at it that way. I never considered that we might be lucky."

"I have. Since day one. It's hard not to dwell on the horrible possibilities."

"How'd you do it?" she asked. "You've been searching for her a long time. Four years. Yet you never lost faith. That's some kind of strength."

Expression bleak, he simply stared at her. "I believe you would do the same. And as far as how? One foot in front of the other. You wake up every morning and keep on looking."

All she could do in response was nod. What he'd said might be true, but she sincerely hoped she didn't have to. She wanted Laney back now. The sooner, the better.

Though Jake didn't recognize the number on his caller ID, he went ahead and answered anyway. He braced himself in case it was another reporter. "Jake," a deep voice drawled. "This is Bob Eager. I'm not sure if you remember me, but we attended police academy in Houston."

Jake did remember him and said so.

"I wanted to let you know that some reporter has been digging around here," Bob said. "Asking a lot of questions about your wife and your missing child. I'm not sure what's going on, but I thought you might like to know."

"I appreciate that." Without volunteering any additional information, Jake ended the call.

"Was that a tip?" Edie asked.

"I wish." After explaining what Bob had told him, Jake shook his head. "They're exploring every possible angle for a story. I bet they air it with or without speaking to us. Has that reporter called you again?"

"No. What about you?"

"Not yet." He couldn't help but wonder what they'd report on Marina's death. While the coroner had ruled it a horrible accident, most of her friends and family considered it otherwise. In his heart, Jake also suspected it had been no accident. Whether or not she'd intended to take her own life, she'd gotten behind the wheel when she shouldn't have. Marina hadn't been able to cope with the abduction of their baby. Instead of joining forces with Jake to help search, she'd retreated into alcohol and drugs, attempting to blot her pain.

Her blood alcohol reading had been three times the legal limit when she'd crashed.

For too long, he'd suffered from a crippling guilt, believing he'd somehow failed her. Though he continued the dogged search for Noel, he'd found a good therapist. He'd attended virtual therapy twice a week, well aware he needed to get his head right if he wanted to find his daughter and be half the father he wanted to be.

"Those reporters." She shook her head, her expression worried. "I've always hated the way some of them take advantage of people's heartaches to get their story. I'm not sure what to do about them."

"I'm thinking we should talk to them," he blurted out. "I don't like the possibility of them putting their own false spin on things. At least if they interview us, we can set the record straight. Then they have no option but to go with the truth rather than sensationalize things."

Edie frowned. "Sensationalize how?"

"Pit us against each other," he said, "just to make the story more interesting."

"You mean make it look as if you and I are at each other's throats? I don't care what people think. You and I know the truth. What would that even matter?"

"It might matter to whoever has Laney," he replied. "If he or she thinks we are two separate warring factions, that would give them even more reason not to want to give her back."

And days could turn into weeks and months and years. After all, it had taken Jake four long years to finally locate his daughter only to have her snatched away by someone else before he could even see her.

What bitter irony.

He didn't want that to happen to Edie, he realized. To lose years of Laney's life and face the prospect of her child not remembering her if she were to ever see her again.

Naturally, he said none of that out loud. Edie had enough to worry about without considering such an awful possibility. There was only one thing that would be worse, and he refused to even speak that into existence.

"There's got to be a way to goad whoever has Laney into communicating with us," Edie said. "If a major network news story would do it, then I'm in. If you can think of something else, then we need to look into that."

Slowly, he nodded. "Let's talk with Rayna and get her thoughts."

"Okay." She looked down at her hands, which she'd begun twisting in her lap. "I should let you know my mom called while you were in the shower. Somehow she found out about you and is convinced you're mistaken about Laney actually being your missing daughter."

"I see." Though he'd gone very still, he kept his gaze on her. "I can understand why she might feel that way. It's a natural reaction to a possibility someone doesn't want to face."

"Is it?" The hint of bitterness in her tone didn't sound like the Edie he'd started to get to know. "But then again, my mother hasn't seen the photograph you were showing around. If she had, she might understand a little better."

His phone rang. "Rayna," he said. "Maybe she's got news." And if she didn't, it would be a good time to ask her about the reporters and their proposed story.

"Rayna," he answered. "I'm putting you on speaker."

"We have a sighting!" The excitement in Rayna's voice vibrated through the phone. "Several tips, all from different people, have come in. Law enforcement has been notified and is on the way."

Jake's heart skipped several beats. He and Edie exchanged a quick look.

"Where?" Jake demanded.

"Conroe. North of Houston," Rayna replied. "A private residence."

"I know it well. I grew up in Spring, which is close to there. And I used to live in the Woodlands." He glanced at Edie again, brow raised. When she nodded, he told Rayna that they were going to pack up and head that way now.

"Where are you?" Rayna asked.

"Archer City, just south of Wichita Falls."

"Damn." Rayna whistled. "You've got a hell of a drive ahead of you."

"We do," Jake agreed. "Please keep us posted on what's happening. Hopefully, they'll have apprehended the perp by the time we get there."

"Let me give you the address. Do you have something to write with?"

Jake grabbed the motel pad of paper and cheap pen. "Go."

Rayna rattled off the number and street. "Conroe, Texas," she reiterated. "If I hear anything else, I'll give you a call. And you do the same, will you?"

"Of course," Jake said and ended the call.

"We need to hurry." Blue eyes glowing with excitement, Edie began cramming things back into her bag. "The sooner we can get on the road, the better."

Since he had a lot more practice living out of a duffle, he hadn't really even unpacked. All he had to do was zip his bag closed.

Once she'd finished, he grabbed both bags and carried them out to his truck, stowing them in the back seat. She followed him out, climbing into the passenger seat.

"I've got to go check us out," he said, tossing her the key fob. "Press the button to start the ignition. I'll be right back."

He'd turned the room keys into the completely disinterested front desk clerk and hurried out to the truck. Edie had not only gotten it running, but she'd also put in the address Rayna had given them into the GPS on her phone.

"Nice work," he told her, climbing into the driver's seat and buckling up. "And we're on the way."

Unable to sit still and practically thrumming with impatience, Edie eyed the road ahead of them. "What's the fastest route?" she asked, turning down the metallic voice of his GPS. "And is that thing right? I'm hoping not. How long do you think the drive is going to take us?"

"Five and a half to six hours, depending on traffic," he replied, which was exactly what the dashboard screen showed. "And we need to get over to I-45, which is complicated but where I'm heading now." He reached over and turned the GPS volume back up. "I need to hear this to find the quickest way to get there."

She nodded, turning away to look out the window. Since clearly she wasn't in the mood to talk, he focused on the drive. And his thoughts. He hadn't allowed himself to spend too much time considering what it would be like when he finally caught up with his daughter. Noel wouldn't even recognize him. She'd been too young, and four years had gone by. She'd want the woman she knew as her mother and no one else. And while it would break his heart to watch from the background, he didn't see how he would have any other choice.

Once Noel got over the trauma from this ordeal, she likely would need counseling, because who knew how bad that would be. She'd have to be given time and space and a lot of love. Once again, Jake would remain in the background. No matter how much he wanted her little face to light up when she saw him, he understood he was a stranger to her these days.

He'd need Edie's help to get to know his own baby girl, now hers. Slow introductions, visits with Edie present, and a lot of time. He could only hope Edie would be willing to give it.

Other people might have barged in with their attorney on speed dial and swept the young child away from the only home she'd ever known, ripping her out of the arms of the woman she called mama and loved. Even without going through the terrors of this abduction, he suspected such an awful stunt would leave lasting scars on her psyche.

Because he loved his daughter, he would never do such a thing. He wanted what was best for her, even if he had to wait a bit longer to hold her in his arms. He'd waited so long already, he'd survive waiting a little longer.

Oblivious to his thoughts, Edie continued to stare out the window, drumming her fingers on her jeans leg.

They made one stop for lunch and a quick potty break in Waxahachie, which had a surprising amount of traffic on the main thoroughfare. There, they chose fast food, deciding eating in the truck would be quicker than going in somewhere.

Near Corsicana, on 287 South, they finally reached I-45. Eventually, the landscape changed from flat farmland, becoming hillier and populated with thick groves of tall trees.

Edie kept taking out her phone and checking it, as if by doing so she could make something happen faster. "No texts from Rayna," she told Jake.

He nodded. "She won't text. She'll call."

"You're right." Her expression stretched tight, she eyed the passing landscape. "I can't help but wish we could somehow make the truck fly."

"Me, too," he replied, which almost made her smile. Almost. For some reason, he really wished he'd succeeded.

"I can't wait to see my Laney again." She closed her eyes, lips moving as if saying a silent prayer. "I'm choosing to be positive. I have to believe that this is it. We're going to find her."

Unable to help himself, he reached out and squeezed her shoulder. "I like the way you think," he said. "By the way, have you ever driven this way before?"

"No, why?"

"We're coming up on Huntsville. In just a few minutes, you'll see a giant statue of Sam Houston on your left."

"Giant?" she asked. "Like how giant?"

"I think I read that it's something like sixty-five feet tall," he said. "I've seen it a bunch of times, but if you haven't, it's really something."

Curious, she pulled out her phone and did a quick internet search. "Sixty-seven feet."

"Here it comes," he said, pointing.

The statue truly was huge, looming over I-45 like an unearthly stone giant. As they drove past, Jake noted there were several tourists gathered near the base, taking pictures.

"That is really tall," she commented. She even

turned around in her seat and watched as it faded into the distance.

He nodded. "I love watching when someone sees it for the first time. I've always thought it was pretty random. You're driving along and then—bam."

Settling back into her seat, once again facing forward, she sighed.

"Don't you think we should have heard something by now?" she asked. "Maybe I'll call Rayna and see if there's any kind of update."

Since he'd been feeling as jumpy as she, though he thought he hid it better, he agreed. "It wouldn't hurt to check in."

Swallowing hard, she hit the contact to call Rayna and then put the call on speaker.

It went straight to voicemail. Instead of leaving a message, she hung up. "That's weird. I'll try again later."

"She's probably just busy," he said, hoping that was the case. "She does have a lot of other stuff to do as well."

"True," she said. "And I know as soon as she hears anything, she'll fill us in."

They hit traffic in Conroe, which slowed them down quite a bit. Edie kept taking out her phone, scrolling through social media and putting it down again. He suspected she was just hoping Rayna would call.

He didn't blame her. He wished Rayna would call, too, and tell them Noel was safe.

Chapter 9

Edie had always considered patience to be one of her strengths. Dealing with a small child required a lot of it, as did working at the bakery with the general public. But right now, wishing she could magically transport Jake's truck up and over the I-45 traffic, any coolness or composure she might once have possessed had definitely vanished.

Her rapid heartbeat played like a drum in her ears, saying her little girl's name over and over. *Laney. Laney. Laney.*

She didn't know how much more of a delay she could take.

"Are you all right?" Jake asked, glancing at her. "You seem a bit jumpy."

"That's a nice way to describe it," she replied, shifting in her seat. "I feel like a little kid who wants to keep asking if we're there yet. This traffic is driving me up a wall."

"I get it," he said. "Believe me. Even if we were in a police car with lights and sirens on, I doubt we'd make any faster headway in the gridlock."

She groaned. "I feel like every minute that ticks by is giving him some sort of advantage."

"I hope not. On the bright side, at least we don't have to go into Houston itself. Traffic is definitely worse there." He glanced at the dashboard clock. "But I'm with you. Too much time has passed. They've got to know something. Why don't you try Rayna again?"

Her gut twisted. She knew he was right. No news at this point almost certainly was a bad thing. Hand shaking, she grabbed her phone and tried Rayna again.

This time, the sheriff answered. "Edie, put me on speaker," she said.

Instantly, Edie complied. "Done. Go ahead."

"It's not good," Rayna said.

A sick feeling in her stomach, Edie almost dropped her phone. "What do you mean?" she asked, her mouth dry. "Did you find Laney?"

"No, and that's the only good thing at this point." The grimness in Rayna's tone spoke to the gravity of the situation. "When Conroe PD pulled up to the address, the house exploded. One officer has been transported to the hospital with serious injuries. The other fared a bit better. The fire department is on the scene trying to extinguish the blaze. The house is a total loss."

Next to her, she heard Jake's sharp intake of breath.

"Was…" Edie could hardly force the words out. "Do you…" Her voice broke. "Do you know if Laney was inside?"

"Not yet. As of right now, I'm being told they're thinking the house was empty. I hope like hell it was."

Edie closed her eyes, feeling dizzy. She struggled to breathe, to keep from bursting into tears. Laney had to be safe. She had to be. Edie couldn't bear to think of anything else.

Jake touched her arm lightly, apparently understanding her struggle.

"Look." He pointed toward a plume of black smoke on the horizon. "That must be it."

"The fire captain is there and he's expecting you," Rayna said as if Jake hadn't spoken. "Call me as soon as you learn something concrete."

"We will," Edie rasped, blinking back tears.

"And keep your chin up." Sounding as if she might cry herself, Rayna abruptly ended the call.

Damn.

"How far?" Edie demanded, swiping at her eyes with the back of her hand.

"We're almost to Conroe now." Jake cut from the left lane into the middle, trying to pass a couple of vehicles that should have moved over. "I'm trying to get there as quickly as I can."

As if to prove his point, the metallic GPS voice that had been advising them all along announced they had 3.7 miles until their exit.

"See," Jake said, reassuring her. "We're nearly there."

"Good." She kept her eyes on the smoke, telling herself over and over that her baby hadn't been in there. Couldn't have been. What kind of monster would burn a house down with a child inside? Surely not someone who'd sent a message saying the girl was exactly where she belonged.

"I agree," Jake said, making her realize she'd spoken her thoughts out loud. He touched her hand. "We have to believe she wasn't there."

"We have to," she repeated.

They took the exit when the GPS told them to and kept following the directions toward an older residential neighborhood that sat behind a shopping center. Even if Jake had turned the GPS off, the cloud of thick smoke would have led them to it.

As they turned onto the street, two police cars blocked them from going any further. "Let me talk to them," Jake said, parking and getting out.

"No way I'm waiting here," Edie replied, following him.

To her surprise, once Jake explained, the policemen seemed to have been expecting them. "Follow me," one of them said. "And please stay on this side of the curb. The fire is still pretty intense."

Two fire trucks were parked in front of the blaze, both of them spraying water from powerful hoses. Fully suited firefighters bustled around, all intent on helping to extinguish the fire. Neighbors stood watching individually and in small groups in front of older wood-frame houses.

A tall man noticed Jake and Edie, removed his helmet and moved to intercept them. "I'm Captain Mc-Neely," he said, holding out a gloved hand.

Jake took it and performed the introductions. Intent on the burning structure, Edie barely acknowledged any of it.

"So far, there's no indication that anyone was inside," the captain said. "We've talked to several of the neighbors and a couple of them claim to have seen a man and a little girl get into a car and drive away."

Edie's focus sharpened. "Was it a white four-door Honda Accord?" she asked. "Because that's what kind of vehicle witnesses reported abducted my daughter."

The captain looked toward the police officer. "You'll have to discuss that with him. Now please excuse me, I've got to get back to this fire."

"Come with me," their police escort said. "I haven't seen the report, but I can take you to who has."

He led them over to where two other uniformed officers stood talking to neighbors.

"No, not a white car at all," one of the neighbors said, hearing Edie ask. An elderly woman with sharp features and oversized glasses who appeared eager to relay what she knew.

"It was a dark blue minivan with tinted windows," she said. "I noticed it parked in the driveway. That house has been empty for a good three months, if not more. So when someone shows up, we all pay attention."

Disheartened, Edie nodded. "Did you see a little girl?" she asked.

"Yes, I did. Same one from the Amber Alert. I'm the one who called the police," she said proudly. "I waited outside so I could keep my eye on them. But they left maybe five minutes after I called." She held up her cane. "And I couldn't exactly chase them down."

"Who was with the little girl?" Jake asked. "Eyewitnesses told us that a man grabbed her, but we don't have a good description."

"I already told the police all this, young man." She

looked him up and down, her lips pressed tightly together. "What's it to you?"

"She's my daughter," Jake answered without missing
a beat. "And we're trying to figure out who took her."

"Ahh, I see." The old woman's expression softened.
"I apologize. I thought you were another one of those
nosy reporters the police chased off earlier."

Edie and Jake exchanged a quick glance. *Reporters.*

"I'm her mother," Edie interjected. "Please tell us
who you saw with our daughter."

"Of course, honey. But the person who was with
her wore one of those hooded sweatshirts, so I can't
help too much with a description. He was really tall
and lanky, that's for sure."

"Did she look...scared?" Edie asked, her heart aching. "My little girl? How'd she seem to you?"

This time the older woman's gaze was compassionate. "I think she was all right. He wasn't holding on to
her, if you know what I mean. She didn't look scared,
at least as far as I can tell."

Edie exhaled. "Thank you for that," she said quietly.
"As you can guess, I'm very worried."

"I would be, too, honey." The old woman patted
her shoulder.

The policeman cleared his throat, drawing everyone's attention. "Thank you, ma'am." He inclined his
head toward the neighbor before shepherding Edie and
Jake away.

"We've got an APB out on the blue van," he told
them. "Though without a license plate, it's unlikely
we'll get any hits."

Numb, Edie nodded. She felt exhausted, wrung dry.

In the space of several hours, she'd gone through a gamut of intense emotions.

"Do you know who owns this house?" Jake asked, gesturing toward the now smoldering pile of rubble. "Once we know that, we can see if there are any ties to either of us."

"Check the Montgomery County appraisal district's web page," the officer replied. "It's accessible to anyone and will give you that information." He glanced back toward the other officers, clearly wanting to rejoin them.

Jake thanked him and took Edie's arm to lead her away. She went willingly, hoping her legs wouldn't give out. Only once she'd gotten back inside the truck did she heave a sigh of relief that she'd made it.

"Now what?" she asked Jake, leaning back in the seat and closing her eyes. "It feels like we're right back where we started."

"Except we're not. We've had a bona fide sighting," he said. "That's huge. And while we don't know for sure which way they're going, I think we can rule out west. That's the direction they came from."

Sitting up straighter, she opened her eyes. "Where do you think they'll go?"

"My money's on Houston." Buckling his seat belt, he pushed the button to start the ignition. He sounded certain.

"Why?" she asked, genuinely curious.

"It's a huge city, to begin with. Easier to disappear. Have you ever been there?"

Slowly, she shook her head. "I have not."

"Not even on your way to the coast?"

She grimaced. "I've never been there either. I'm more of a vacation-in-the-mountains type."

"We need to call Rayna," he said.

"I'll do it. And yes, I'll put her on speaker."

Rayna answered immediately. "Did you get her?" she asked.

"No," Edie replied, her voice breaking. She gestured at Jake to talk while she got her emotions under control.

Voice terse, Jake took over, explaining everything that had happened.

"What caused the explosion and fire?" Rayna wanted to know. "I'm assuming it was deliberate?"

"We didn't ask," Jake replied. "But I'm sure the fire captain can tell you. He was there and we met him."

"I'll touch base, for sure." Rayna paused. "I know you said no one got a good description of the guy, but any leads on where he might be heading next?"

Jake told her what the policeman had said and his own theory. "I'm betting on Houston."

"That would make sense," Rayna said. "It's easier to get lost in a place that size." She sighed. "I'm hoping someone else spots them."

"Me, too." Finally able to speak again, Edie glanced at Jake. "The good thing is that Laney is alive and appears unharmed."

"We'll take all the good things we can get," Rayna agreed. "Did you get a chance to look up who owned that house?" In the background, they could hear the sound of her typing on a keyboard. "I'm guessing not, so I'll do that real quick."

Exchanging glances, they waited.

"It's owned by a Myrna Mosely," Rayna finally said.

"I'll get to work to see what I can dig up on her. Does that name ring any bells with either of y'all?"

"No." Edie and Jake answered in unison.

"Too bad." Rayna sighed. "It's never that simple. Let me touch base with my contact down there and see what he can tell me. I'll keep you posted."

"We'll do the same," Jake said. He reached over and ended the call. For one brief second, his rigid expression appeared to crumple, though he rapidly regained his composure.

Edie's heart went out to him. While she understood on some level he also worried about Laney, she'd been so focused on her own desperate terror that she hadn't given much thought as to what he must be going through.

"Four years," he muttered, almost as if he knew her thoughts. "I haven't held my child in my arms for that long."

When he met her gaze, she saw his pain in the starkness of his expression. "She used to call me Dada," he said, "and hold out her little arms for me to pick her up. She'd laugh when I did, and that sound…oh, that sound was pure joy."

Exhaling, he shook his head. "I've pictured what it would be like when I finally found her. I have imagined that scenario a hundred times. And now… Now I realize she wouldn't even recognize me."

His voice broke. She watched as he struggled to regain his composure, unsure how to comfort him or if she should even try.

A moment later, he straightened his shoulders, looking more like himself. "Are you ready?" he asked.

Momentarily confused, she shrugged. "Ready for what?"

"We're going to Houston. This time, we're going to find this bastard and get our daughter back."

Our daughter. Jake waited for Edie's reaction, too tired to worry about how she felt about him staking a claim. He'd always had one, and she'd known it, though he'd never disputed or challenged her when she spoke about *her* daughter. Her love for her Laney shone through in every gesture, every word—hell— every breath Edie took. She'd do anything to protect and save her child.

He got this. Because quite honestly, he felt exactly the same.

Four years might have gone by, but time did not diminish the bone-deep love a father felt for his daughter.

Still, he hadn't meant to reveal so much of his inner torment to Edie. They'd shared a bed, true. And their common goal as well as the intense amount of pressure they were under had brought them close very quickly. But he'd needed to stay strong, keep his emotions under wraps the way he always did. No more letting her see even the slightest chink in his armor.

Keeping his jaw tight, he concentrated on the road.

"I'm disappointed, too," she said softly.

"Yeah. I should have known better than to get my hopes up." He couldn't conceal the bitterness in his voice. In four years of searching, it had never been that simple or easy. But an Amber Alert for a five-year-old was bound to generate more hits than one for a twelve-month-old.

And there'd been that email. Just one, so far.

"I think he'll reach out again," he said. "Especially since we didn't stop looking like he asked."

"Oh, I hope you're right." Turning in her seat to eye him, he saw a spark of hope had come back into her expression.

"I bet it's soon. He's bound to be pissed about being sighted at that house in Conroe."

She nodded. "And that we know he ditched the Honda and got a van."

"Yeah. I imagine he'll have to switch vehicles again."

Edie's phone rang.

"It's Rayna." Answering, Edie immediately put the call on speaker.

"We got another email." A thread of excitement ran through the sheriff's tired voice. "I've forwarded it to you. It's too long to relay over the phone, but the gist of it is that he wants us to back off."

"No threats?" Jake asked, holding his breath.

"Surprisingly, no. At least, not yet."

"Threats?" Edie asked, her brow furrowed. "What do you mean?"

"Well, usually the next step would be to warn us if we don't back off, he'll hurt the child," Rayna replied. "But he hasn't said anything like that, thank goodness."

"Even if he eventually does," Jake said, "he won't mean it. So far he genuinely appears convinced he's doing the best thing for the child."

"I agree." Rayna shuffled through some papers. "He does mention you by name."

"Who?" Edie asked. "Me or Jake?"

"Jake. Read it and see if it jogs any memories."

"Will do," Jake said. "Anything else new?"

"Not yet. I've had people working to see if they

could locate a connection between the owner of that house in Conroe and either of you. So far, I've come up with nothing."

"Myrna Mosely," Jake said. "I'll do some searching of my own once we stop for the night."

"Keep me posted," Rayna replied. "And as usual, I'll do the same. I've got people trying to trace where the email originated from. Though he's probably using a mobile hot spot, it doesn't hurt to look."

After Rayna ended the call, Edie sat and turned her phone over and over in her hands. "I hope she's wrong. I won't do well if he starts threatening her."

"I won't either." He dug in his pocket and handed her his phone. "Check my email, if you don't mind. You can read us this guy's latest message."

"Sure." It took her a couple of seconds to locate Rayna's email. "Here we are. Let me open it."

He moved into the slow lane from the middle, briefly considering pulling over, but they were already in the thick of Houston traffic. He figured he'd keep driving south until he figured out where they should stop.

"Are you ready?" Edie glanced at him. Determination had replaced fear in her bright blue eyes.

"Yes. Let's hear it."

I told you to leave us alone. But you didn't. Don't you understand? This angel, this child, is with someone who will love her and care for her for her entire life? She's mine. Not yours, by virtue of either birth or adoption, but mine. By fate.

Edie paused, taking a moment to process the words. "He seems well educated."

"I agree. The rhythm of the words is almost lyrical. Definitely poetic."

This comment made Edie snort. "I'll show him poetic. This is my daughter he's talking about. Fate, my ass."

"My daughter, too," he reminded her. He was done staying quiet.

To his pleased surprise, Edie nodded, her blue eyes solemn. "Your daughter, too."

For a moment, their gazes locked and held. Then, because he was driving and needed to watch the road, he looked away.

Edie cleared her throat. "Let me continue."

Go away. Leave us alone. In time, she will forget you and whatever pitiful life you hoped to give her. With me, she will want for nothing. I promise you, she will have the best possible existence on this entire planet. As she grows, I'll make sure she receives an excellent, top-notch education. Better than anything she could get in a backwater West Texas town.

"Backwater?" Edie snorted. "Obviously, he's not from around Getaway. We might be small, but we're a tight-knit community. We look out for each other. I went to school there and then went on to culinary school in Dallas. Most people go to college at Texas Tech, which isn't too far away. It might not be Harvard or Yale, but I can assure you they do just fine."

"I went to A&M," he said, surprising her. "I get it."

"You're an Aggie?"

"Through and through," he replied. "And I got a

hell of a good education. I suspect he's talking about private school or something."

"It shouldn't matter. This guy doesn't get to decide Laney's future."

The pain in her voice wretched at his heart. "I agree," he replied. "But as abhorrent as it may seem, the fact that he's still communicating with us is a good thing. We need to figure out a way to get him to keep it up."

"I just want my baby back," she said.

"I know." He covered her hand with his, caressing her smooth skin with his thumb. "And we'll get her back, I have no doubt. The more we can keep him talking, the more clues he'll inadvertently reveal."

Slowly, she nodded. "Do you think he has money?" she asked. "It sounds like he might. That could be another clue toward his identity."

"Possibly. It definitely sounds like he's bragging about material things. That's another potential characteristic we need to mention to Rayna, if she hasn't already picked up on it."

Edie sighed. She'd begun absently playing with her long blonde hair, twirling it around her finger. "No doubt she has. Our sheriff is really good at her job," she said. "Do you want me to keep reading? There are a few more paragraphs in this guy's email. Mostly reiterating how good he is for Laney and how bad we are. It's awful."

"Tell me, please. Even if it's hard to swallow, I need to hear it."

"I don't blame you." She took a deep breath and continued on.

Everyone thinks they want what's best for this little girl, but I'm the only one able to give it. She was always supposed to live with me, from the moment she took her first breath. I have searched for her, too, for far longer than the man who considers himself her father.

"What the…" Jack grimaced. "That really pisses me off."

"Me, too," Edie agreed. "There's more."

And to the woman who raised her, thank you. But it's time to let go now. You've done your part. In time, she will forget you.

Edie's voice thickened.

He glanced at her, noticing the way she blinked back tears. One sparkled on the end of her long eyelashes, until she brushed away. She saw him looking and exhaled before lifting her chin and forcing herself to continue.

Now go away and leave us alone. This is your final warning. Especially you, Jake Cassin. You aren't what you think you are. And if you keep up your pointless search, I'll have to make you pay.

As she read the final sentence, her voice caught. "He knows your name."

Jaw clenched so tightly it ached, he bit back a few choice curse words. "That might not mean anything. It's entirely possible he got that from my website."

"True. Either way, he has Laney. And for whatever reason, it sounds like he has a bone to pick with you."

"Yes, it does." He just didn't know why. Or have any idea who this person might be.

Still staring at him, Edie glanced down at the phone. "Ironic, though. All along, when you said it had to be something personal, it turns out it is. Only it involves you, not me."

"Apparently so." He wouldn't blame her for being angry. After all, he'd insinuated one of her old boyfriends might have been the one to grab Laney. "Though I don't have a clue who he is."

"I see." She glanced at him then. He saw frustration and compassion in her gaze, but no anger. "Why can't this ever be easy?"

"I know. But at least he's giving us clues with these letters. That's more than I had for four long years."

Downtown Houston came into view. She gestured at the tall buildings. "I have an idea. What's the wealthiest part of Houston?"

"River Oaks? Galleria-Uptown? Those two come to mind right off the bat, but I'm sure there are more. Houston has a lot of expensive neighborhoods."

"That's where we need to go," she said. "At least it's a starting place."

He didn't tell her what would likely happen if the residents of those neighborhoods took exception to an unfamiliar vehicle driving slowly up and down their streets. Most of those neighborhoods were probably gated, anyway.

"One thing," he said. "If this guy is rich, wouldn't he have hired someone to do his dirty work? Why would he risk grabbing the child himself?"

"Good point," she agreed. "And why drive a four-door Honda Accord? Unless he was looking for something that blends in. They are a popular car."

Jake nodded. Mentally, he was still trying to process the fact that Noel's abductor had called him out by name. He had no idea who might be holding a grudge against him and, even more importantly, who would feel as if they had a right to his child.

Traffic had slowed to a crawl. Jake put his blinker on and hoped someone would be kind enough to let him change lanes so he could exit. "The Galleria is coming up. I need to get in the right lane."

Finally, someone stopped their vehicle and gave him a small opening to move over. He did and then lifted his hand in a quick thank-you. "We're exiting as soon as we can," he said. "I want to find someplace to park and see if we can figure this out."

They'd just pulled into the mall's covered parking when his phone rang. He pulled into a spot before answering. "Hello?"

Nothing but silence on the other end. He realized he should have checked the caller ID.

"Hello?" he repeated. Still nothing, so he ended the call. "Must have been a wrong number." Caller ID said Private Number. "Or spam."

Eyes wide, Edie stared at him. "Or it might have been whoever has Laney."

Briefly, he considered telling her they couldn't be jumping to conclusions.

A text came through. "It's from Rayna," Edie said. She read it out loud. "Sorry, can't call. But the IP address is close to Galleria-Uptown. My IT guy is trying to pinpoint a more exact location."

He gave a tired laugh. "Coincidence? Or blind luck?"

The hope he'd refused to allow himself to feel made her blue eyes sparkle. "How about just good detective skills? We're going to find them. I just know it."

Chapter 10

Though Jake didn't appear to share her optimism, Edie refused to allow herself to sink back into the black pit of despair she'd been teetering on the edge of.

They were close. She could feel it. Soon, she'd be holding her precious Laney in her arms.

The hotel they chose for that night appeared to be several levels above any of their prior hotels.

"Proximate to the Galleria," Jake said, correctly interpreting her quiet gasp when they entered the spacious well-appointed room.

"I'm sure the price reflects that, too," she said, dropping her duffle on the bed nearest to the bathroom. "But it's worth it just to have a place to stay close by where the email came from."

Jake nodded, his expression closed off. She suspected he refused to allow himself to be optimistic, and she got it. He'd spent four long years searching, only to have her abducted before he even got to see her. She couldn't even begin to imagine how he must feel.

He tossed his bag on the bed closest toward the door. When he looked up and met her gaze, the vulnerability she briefly glimpsed in his eyes made her heart ache. She almost went to him, well aware of the way they could take comfort in losing themselves in each other's embrace. When the worry and stress threatened to overwhelm her, Jake and his lovemaking helped diffuse the ticking time bomb of her emotions.

Except after the day they'd had, she felt icky. Uncomfortable in her own skin. As if some of the soot and smoke from the house fire had embedded itself into her pores.

Body-to-body contact would definitely have to wait. As much as she craved his touch, she wanted a hot shower more.

Something flickered in his gaze, letting her know the same thought had occurred to him.

"Edie?" he asked, his voice thick.

Though she hated to leave him so clearly in need, she had to scrub herself clean before anything else.

"I've got to shower and change into some comfy clothes first," she told him. "I won't be long." Giving him her best, hopefully smoldering look, she turned and hurried into the bathroom.

Closing the door, she looked around in satisfaction. Marble counters and a huge whirlpool tub, as well as a shower with rimless glass door that also appeared to be made of the same gray-and-white marble. The modern pewter fixtures and the glittering chandelier hanging from the ceiling made this a beautiful and upscale bathroom.

Not for the first time, she wondered what the nightly rate was in this place. She and Jake had agreed to split expenses, so while one night here would be a definite treat, she suspected they'd need to find less expensive lodgings if this turned into a longer stay.

Which, hopefully, it would not. She wanted to have Laney back by tomorrow. *Positive thinking*, she told herself. She *would* have Laney back tomorrow.

She turned the water as hot as she could stand it. Once under the spray—another deluxe feature—she soaped up and simply let it pummel the stress from her aching body until she was clean.

By the time she'd finished, she felt like a new person. A lot better. She decided she'd suggest Jake use it, too. He had to be exhausted as well. Once she opened the door, the steam should clear from the large mirror.

When she emerged, her hair wrapped in a towel, he'd turned the TV on. Looking up, he shook his head when he saw her. "How you managed to look sexy all the time, I'll never know."

A warmth spread slowly through her, heating her blood. In the shower, once she'd felt better, all she'd been able think about was getting skin-to-skin with him.

Renewed and smelling like soap and shampoo, she debated untying her bathrobe, but she thought he'd welcome the shower first, too.

About to suggest it, something the news anchor said caught her attention. "Look." She pointed at the TV. She and Jake both watched silently as the camera panned to a reporter wearing a windbreaker with the network logo on it, who stand in front of the rubble of the house in Conroe.

And now to some new developments in a story that's caught everyone's attention. Police are still on the lookout for five-year-old Laney Beswick, abducted in a small town near Abilene. The Amber Alert is still active. They've received tips, which led them to a house in Conroe earlier today. That house exploded shortly after the child's captor escaped with her. We'll go live to Alex Trainer at the scene.

While Edie gaped at the screen, Jake came to stand silently beside her. They both watched as the reporter gestured to the charred remains of the house before interviewing the same neighbor woman who'd spoken to them earlier.

Once Alex had finished with her, he faced the camera once again. *Police have said they're following up on another tip that the abductor, along with little Laney, are in the Houston area. They've asked us to show the Amber Alert again, and to remind you if you see her, to immediately call the police.*

The Amber Alert, along with Laney's photo, flashed on the screen.

Any tips will be welcome. And now, to Sally with the weather.

Jake hit the remote and turned the TV off. "Wow," he said. "They sure jumped on that story fast." He dragged his hand through his hair. "At least they stuck to the facts."

"Is that a good thing or bad?" she asked. "I mean, obviously, it's good that the people of Houston know to be on the lookout for them. But do you think that might scare him off and make him keep running?"

He grimaced. "It's hard to tell. If his home is here, I think he'll likely stay put. Maybe hole up until things calm down." Jake began to pace. "He might even try to disguise Laney. Maybe cut or color her hair."

Though she hated that idea, it made sense. Suddenly restless, she went to her duffle bag and began to rummage inside for clothes. "Let's go drive around," she said. "Why don't you jump in the shower, and we can get out of here. I just need to get dressed."

"Wait." He held up his hand. "Not tonight. It's been a long day, and we need to rest up for tomorrow. After that news story, he's going to be careful not to make any mistakes. How about we order a pizza and maybe watch a movie?"

With her roller-coaster emotions, at first his suggestion outraged her. Which made zero sense. She forced herself to take several deep breaths and think objectively. "You're probably right," she finally said, shoving the clothes she'd grabbed back into her bag. "This constant tension is getting to me."

He slung an arm across her shoulders and pulled her in for a quick, casual hug. "I get it, believe me."

"You smell like smoke," she said, wrinkling her nose. "I promise you'll feel so much better after a shower."

Though he nodded, he didn't move.

"Go." She gave him a gentle shove. "The bathroom is amazing. And that hot water makes a world of difference."

"Yes, ma'am." His mock salute made her smile.

But once he'd disappeared into the bathroom, she sank down into the chair. She hadn't been kidding about the emotional mood swings. One minute up, the next so low she could barely make herself move. Hope, terror, despair. Through it all, she kept imagining Laney crying out for her, afraid and lost. This tore out her heart.

The one constant was Jake. She appreciated that he understood exactly what she was going through. After all, he'd experienced similar emotions for the exact same reasons.

They both loved Laney. She didn't doubt his devotion for one minute. Though she'd shied away from a confrontation over what might happen once their little girl was found, in the back of her mind she knew it would happen.

Blood trumped paper. While her adoption four years ago had been legal, she imagined the fact that the child she'd made her own had been stolen from her birth father negated that.

She could only hope she was right about Jake's kind heart. Surely he wouldn't tear Laney away from the only mother she remembered, especially after an ordeal like this.

The shower started. For whatever reason, she found the sound comforting. Tonight, she hoped Jake might be able to figure out who from his past might think his daughter belonged with him and why.

Somehow, she must have dozed off sitting up. The sound of the bathroom door opening woke her. Dazed and groggy, she sat up straight, blinking as Jake sauntered over toward her with only a towel wrapped around his waist.

"You were right," he said, one corner of his mouth curling into the beginnings of a smile. "That shower was a great idea."

Her body responded to that smile immediately. He was, she thought, a beautiful man, in a rugged, masculine kind of way. She stood, untying her bathrobe and shrugging it off, letting it fall in a puddle at her feet.

Jake's green eyes darkened, though he kept his towel in place.

Impatient, she reached for it, intending to yank it off him. But he grabbed her hand, preventing her. "Maybe this isn't a good idea," he said, though his body gave him away.

"You need this distraction as badly as I do," she told him. "If I'm sure of anything, I'm certain of this."

He nodded, the intensity in his gaze taking her breath away. "You're using me." The matter-of-fact statement contained no rancor.

"We're using each other," she countered. "To take the edge off. Nothing more, nothing less."

He claimed her mouth then, the press of his lips hard and possessive. "Definitely something more," he growled, before giving himself over to her embrace.

Later, as they lay together while their breathing slowed, she wondered about his words. Yet another thing she didn't have the emotional bandwidth to deal with now.

In fact, she should get up. This spooning together after sex probably wasn't a good or necessary thing. Yet she couldn't seem to force herself to move. *Not now, but soon*, she told herself.

Her phone rang, making the decision for her. She sat up, reaching for her phone on the nightstand and checking the caller ID. "It's Rayna," she said, her heart skipping a beat. "Maybe she has news."

Jake sat up, too, his gaze locked on her.

Answering, she put the call on speaker as usual. "Hi, Rayna. What's new?"

"Where are you?" Rayna asked. "Are you driving or in your hotel room for the night?"

"A hotel. Why?"

"Turn on your TV," Rayna ordered. "Find that show called *One Hour*. It's about to come on. I just saw a teaser, and it appears they're doing a story on the two of you and Laney. Now I know why that reporter was snooping around Getaway, asking everyone and their brother questions."

Edie and Jake exchanged a look. He grabbed the remote and began searching for the right channel.

"Earlier we saw a brief segment on the Houston news," Edie said. "It featured Laney's disappearance. I thought they did a good job. Very matter-of-fact and to the point."

"I take it they didn't touch on the drama or try to pit the adoptive mother against the birth father?" Rayna asked, her tone dry.

"No, thank goodness." Edie sighed. "Honestly, this entire situation is rough enough without them trying to stir up stuff."

"Better brace yourselves, both of you. Judging by the teaser I saw, that's exactly what *One Hour* intends to do. I've got to go," Rayna said. "I'll let you know if I hear anything else."

"Thank you."

"One more thing. Y'all hang in there." Rayna ended the call without waiting for a response.

"Here it is," Jake said, turning up the volume. "I hope Rayna's wrong. If she isn't, let's hope at least whatever they include in this piece helps us find Laney."

"Me, too." Propping up the pillows against the headboard, Edie sat back in the bed to watch. A second later, Jake joined her, the mattress dipping for a moment from his weight.

Despite everything, her chest felt tight as she glanced at him. He'd come to mean a lot to her in a short time. A bond had formed due to their close proximity and shared love for one little girl.

The back of her eyes stung. She cleared her throat, returning her attention back to the TV, where a commercial currently played. "Two news stories in one day. That's unreal."

"I know." He hesitated, then continued. "But from what Rayna hinted at, I'm not sure this is going to be either fair or impartial."

The familiar introduction came on. As usual, they were splitting the show into four distinct segments, each featuring a unique story.

"Looks like they're leading with us," Jake said. "Damn, I hope they treat us fairly."

Of course, in the way of sensationalism, the story focused on garnering public interest. Since drama made people watch, the focus of the *One Hour* piece appeared to be pitting Edie against Jake, as well as the poor abducted child. They'd even somehow managed to obtain copies of the emails the man who'd take Laney had sent.

Is there a third party with a legal interest in Laney Beswick? the reporter asked. *We will have to follow this case to find out.*

A commercial came on. Both Edie and Jake sat silent, stunned.

"They want us to hate each other," Jake finally said, his voice flat.

"I see that." Edie made herself look at him. "Maybe we should," she said softly. "But we both love Laney—Noel."

Still silent, he nodded.

"Maybe we need to talk," she heard herself say.

He glanced up, appearing wary. "In my experience, it's never good when a woman says that." Getting up from the bed in one swift motion, he glanced toward the door, as if he really wanted to leave.

"I've been putting it off." The more she thought about it, the more she realized this was the right time. "I didn't know you well enough before."

"You still don't," he countered, arms crossed. "We don't need to do this now."

"I think we do." She patted the spot next to her that he'd just vacated. "Sit back down. Please."

Instead, he shook his head. "I'd rather stand. Edie, we've got to continue to work together, at least until she's found. Don't drive a wedge into our relationship."

His word choice startled her. "Is that what we have? A relationship?"

Now he looked away. "I don't know," he finally said. "But we get along. I actually like you, and I think you like me."

She nodded. "I do. But in the end, when Laney is found, she's coming home with me."

There. She'd said it. Heart pounding, blood roaring in her ears, she waited for his reaction. Part of her wondered if he'd storm out and leave her there, in a hotel room in an unfamiliar city, with no transportation. She wouldn't actually blame him, but the Jake she'd come to know would never do such a thing.

Jaw tight, he didn't speak. He simply stared at her, his expression shuttered. "I am not going to discuss this with you now."

He walked to the door, turning as he opened it. "I'm going to go get us something to eat. I saw a Whata-burger down the street, so I'll get that. I have my phone, so call me if you need me for anything."

After he'd left, she refused to give in to the urge to cry. Seeing their very private story on a national television program had been brutal.

And she didn't know why she'd wanted to pick a fight with Jake, other than to nail down what exactly he planned to do.

According to the *One Hour* segment, he could take her to court. Fight her for custody. And, since he had first rights due to blood relationship, he could legally take Laney away from her.

Like her abductor had. She'd be getting her baby back only to lose her again. The thought was damn near unbearable.

Pacing, she told herself to calm down. She went back into the bathroom and blow-dried her hair. By the time she'd finished, Jake had returned with their dinner.

When Jake got into his truck and started the engine, he sat for a moment in silence, Edie's declaration playing over and over again inside his head.

Laney is coming home with me.

Of course she was. As if he would subject that little

girl to any more trauma. She'd already been through enough.

It hadn't been a shock or even a surprise to hear what Edie planned. He'd been expecting that, ever since he'd come to realize how much she loved and adored her daughter.

He just couldn't believe she'd chosen this moment to say it. Not sure how he was supposed to react, he scratched his head. Eventually, once Laney was safe and at home with her mother, he knew he and Edie would need to have a serious discussion.

But for now, he'd simply pretend she hadn't said anything.

Decision made, he shifted into Reverse and backed out from his parking spot. Once he reached the service road, he fought his first impulse—to keep on driving—and pulled into line at the Whataburger drive-through. He got them both a burger and fries and soft drinks and pulled back into the hotel parking lot less than fifteen minutes later.

The food smelled delicious. Somehow, he resisted the urge to eat a fry or two out of the bag. He hurried inside, took the elevator to their room and juggled the bags, the drinks, and the room key before Edie heard him and let him in.

He only hoped she didn't pursue the earlier subject. After the disturbing television show, he simply wanted to eat in peace.

"Here, let me help you," she said, taking the drinks from him and carrying them over to the desk. She sounded friendly, and a quick glance at her face revealed nothing.

Maybe she'd decided to let sleeping dogs lie. The

tension that had begun gathering in his shoulders dissipated a little.

"It's been a long time since I've had one of these," she said, setting out both their meals, along with the handful of ketchup packets that had been tossed inside the bag.

Settling on a casual smile, he grabbed his and dropped into the armchair, letting her have the one that went with the desk. With the television on in the background—a sitcom, he noticed—they made short work of their dinner.

The first attorney called his phone exactly forty-five minutes after the *One Hour* segment ended. How they'd gotten his number, he had no idea.

"This is Stan Leander with the law firm of Leander, Ponca and Hellum," the caller said. "We'd like to represent you in your custody battle against Ms. Beswick."

Startled, it took Jake a moment to gather his thoughts. "With all due respect, I'm not interested." He'd barely ended the call when his phone rang again.

"Who was that?" Edie asked. Before she even finished the sentence, her phone rang, too. She answered, and judging by the shocked look on her face, another attorney had reached out to her.

She hung up without even saying a word. "Did you just get a call from—"

"Yes." Gesturing at his phone, he shook his head. "I'm thinking that *One Hour* news story generated this."

It kept up continuously. One call would go to voicemail and another would come in.

"I'm muting the sound on my phone," Edie said, her voice shaky.

Jake did the same. "If not for needing to be available to Rayna, I'd say turn them off."

"Where did these people get our numbers?" she asked. "I always thought cell phone numbers were kind of unlisted."

"Where there's a will, there's a way," he said, grim. "I'm thinking these people see lots of dollar signs, or they wouldn't be knocking themselves out to contact us."

"Either that or notoriety," she said. "They might feel this is their chance to get their name mentioned on a national program like *One Hour*."

Turning away, he almost gave in to the urge to cover his face with his hands. But he couldn't, not in front of Edie. He had to remain strong for Noel and for the woman she called her mother.

"I don't know how much more of this I can take," Edie commented.

"It's not like we have a choice," he shot back. "At least not until we find her. Then we can tell them all to go to hell."

Or hire them. The thought hung in the air between them.

She met his gaze, her mouth slightly open. He wondered if she'd had the same thought, and then instantly chided himself. He'd never been a fanciful type of person and damned if he intended to start now.

Thunder shook the walls, startling him out of his thoughts. "Springtime in Houston," he said, going to the window and pulling aside the blackout curtain to peer out.

More rumbles of thunder, then the flash of lightning.

"I'm glad we're in for the night," she commented.

"After that tornado in Oklahoma, I'm not a fan of driving in a storm."

"Me neither," he agreed. "Why don't you see if you can find an old movie, something familiar that we can watch until we doze off?"

His suggestion made her smile. Even though it was a slight smile, wan even, he loved the way it transformed her face. "*Sleepless in Seattle* is coming on in a couple of minutes. How about that?"

"Sure." He shrugged, deciding not to tell her that he'd never seen it.

He climbed up in the bed beside her to watch, unable to keep the warm feeling from spreading through him. *Cozy* wasn't a word he'd ever thought would apply to himself again, yet here he sat. He could easily drape his arm around her slender shoulder and pull her closer. Refusing to give in to the temptation, he didn't.

The continual buzzing of one phone and then another annoyed him. He caught Edie glancing at her phone, too, frowning. "I'm going to text Rayna and tell her to text first if she needs us," she said. "At least these ambulance chasers aren't texting."

"Yet," he said, only half kidding.

Just like clockwork, his phone vibrated. Since it had been going off constantly with attorney calls, he almost didn't look at it. He was glad he did.

"Hold off texting. It's Rayna," he said. As usual, when he answered, he put her on speaker so Edie could also hear.

"There's been another sighting." Rayna kept her tone even, though he could hear an undercurrent of excitement in her voice.

"Where?"

"At the Galleria itself," she replied. "This is where it gets tricky."

Jake immediately understood. He glanced at Edie. "Crowd control," he told her. "I'll explain more later."

"Exactly," Rayna said. "They've got one plain-clothes officer following him and are stationing men at every exit door. The hope is that they can grab him and Laney when he leaves the mall. Since we don't know if he's armed, every precaution is being taken."

"It's storming here, too," Jake said. "Flash flooding and all that."

Rayna swore. "Great. Just great."

"Why?" Edie wanted to know. "What's the weather got to do with any of this?"

"Torrential downpours and flash floods means anyone already inside the mall is likely to stay there, at least until it passes."

The lights flickered off and back on.

"You'd better hope there's not a massive power outage," he said. "Because if there is, it'll be damn near impossible to keep tabs on this guy."

Another loud boom of thunder shook the room, followed almost immediately by a flash of lightning.

"Wow," Rayna said. "I heard that. And yes, you're right about the power. And the rain. All of it makes this way more difficult than it should be. No way are they going to station officers outside the doors in a rainstorm. They'll either have to be just inside or in cars parked near the exit."

Neither one was ideal, though Jake kept that information to himself. A man inside ran the risk of being spotted. And stationing someone inside a vehicle, no matter how close to the exit, increased the chance of the perp escaping.

Again, the lights flickered off. This time, a few seconds passed before they came on. "It's looking more and more like we might lose power," Jake said. "Not sure if what happens here at the motel would happen at the mall or not."

If it did, it would be a cluster.

"I want to go there. Now," Edie declared, jumping to her feet.

"No!" Both Jake and Rayna spoke at once.

"You being there would only jeopardize the entire operation," Rayna continued.

"He'd likely recognize you," Jake said. "And for sure, Laney would. As difficult as it is, we need to stay back and let the professionals do their jobs."

Edie glared at him, her expression mutinous. "I want to be there for Laney."

"And so you will be," Rayna said. "As soon as the man who grabbed her is safely in custody."

Finally, Edie nodded, her gaze still locked on Jake. "Can we go sit in the parking lot inside Jake's truck?"

"Will you stay inside the vehicle?" Rayna shot back. "I'm going to need you to give me your word, Edie Beswick."

"For how long?" Edie asked.

"Until law enforcement has the suspect in custody. And by 'in custody,' I mean cuffed and in the back of a squad car."

Watching her, Jake waited to see how she would respond.

"I will," Edie finally said. "I give you my word. But what about Jake? Why are you not worried about him?"

"Because he's a trained law enforcement officer," Rayna answered, her tone brisk. "He knows better. Now, Edie, I need to ask you again. Do you swear to stay inside the vehicle until Jake tells you it's okay to leave?"

"Yes. I already told you I would."

"Okay. But, Jake?" Rayna asked. "Will you restrain her if her excitement somehow gets the best of her?"

"Seriously?" Edie interjected, her expression as wounded as her voice. "You doubt my word?"

"Of course not," Rayna soothed. "But I also know how worried you are about your daughter. I can't help but think the moment you actually see her, you'll forget any promises you might have made."

Jake agreed, though he knew better than to say so.

After considering for a moment, Edie agreed. "You're probably right. Jake, that means you have my permission to hold me back if necessary."

"Just don't interfere," Rayna reiterated. "Either of you. I've got to go. I'll call you back if I hear anything else."

Once she'd ended the call, Jake looked at Edie and sighed. "Houston is known for flooding during storms."

He'd barely gotten the words out when they heard a loud bang outside and the hotel went dark.

"What was that?" Edie asked.

"It sounded like a transformer blew." Crossing to the window, he opened the drapes. The weather had gone from bad to worse. "Come look," he said. "The wind is crazy. The rain is coming down in sheets."

Clearly humoring him, she took a quick peek outside. Side by side, they watched the fury of the storm wreak havoc. Illuminated by frequent flashes of lightning, trees bent in the wind, shaking from side to side. The sheer force of the driving rain made it difficult to see even as far as the parking lot.

Only a fool would go out in weather like this. He turned to suggest they stay put, but before he could speak, she laid her hand on his arm.

"We have to go," she said. "We can't let this chance to get Laney back slip out of our hands."

Chapter 11

Edie didn't want to let hope light a fire inside her bloodstream, setting every nerve ending ablaze. After all, she'd allowed herself to believe twice before, and both times, the end result had been nothing but crushing disappointment.

But this would be different. She *knew* it. Felt it, on a molecular level. At the end of this day, she'd have her little girl safe and sound, wrapped up tightly in her arms.

The electricity in the air made the tiny hairs on her arms stand up. Grabbing hotel towels and putting them over their heads, she and Jake ran across the parking lot, getting drenched despite their precautions. Once inside Jake's truck, they did their best to use the sodden towels to try and blot some of the wetness.

After starting the truck, he turned the wipers on high and put on the defroster to clear the windshield.

He eyed the river of water rushing down the street. "This is going to be touch and go."

Damp and chilled, she shivered. "It doesn't matter," she replied. "You know as well as I do that we have to try." And this time, their efforts would be rewarded. She just knew it.

With a nod, he shifted into reverse. "Hang on, Edie. This is the kind of storm where the weather people always urge you to stay home."

"Turn around, don't drown," she echoed, repeating what they always said. "But I have faith in you."

The look he gave her told her maybe she shouldn't. "I can only do the best I can. This is really bad. If the truck floods and loses power, I sure hope you can swim."

His grim expression told her he was dead serious. "I can," she replied. "But please, just get us to that mall."

"I intend to do my damnedest." He pulled out onto the road, both hands gripping the steering wheel in a white-knuckled grip.

"Thank you." Straightening in the truck seat, she glanced over at him. He stared ahead with a single-minded focus, concentrating on trying to see the road.

Even with the windshield wipers on fast, they could barely keep up with the rain. The dark skies were full of roiling clouds, and the wind not only bent the trees over but sent the rain whipping sideways. The streets were deserted. Traffic had vanished, most drivers apparently deterred by the storm and the rising water.

Luckily, Jake's truck sat up higher than most vehicles. Even so, it felt like they were trying to forge an actual angry river instead of the feeder road of a busy downtown interstate.

"First a tornado, now a flood," she commented, her nerves warring with her overwhelming desire to see her child.

"I know, right," he replied. "I'd almost say, 'What else can possibly be thrown at us?' but I don't want to tempt fate."

"I agree." She kept her phone clutched in her left hand, ready for Rayna's text or call or in case she needed to contact emergency services to rescue them. "You used to live here," she said. "Do they often get storms like this?"

"In the spring, yes. Houston floods a lot when it gets this much rain. Hold on." Wind buffeted them, and Jake fought to keep them from going sideways. Water splashed up, great waves of it despite their low speed, some of it seeping in at the bottom of the doors.

Jake cursed, letting her know how really bad their situation had become.

"Turn around, don't drown," she muttered, once again repeating the slogan of every Texas meteorologist under her breath.

"Now you tell me," he said, only half joking. They crept along, the rising water battering the truck and trying to sweep them off the road. Somehow, he managed to keep them going forward. "We're okay as long as water doesn't flood the engine. We're lucky we aren't staying too far away."

Frustrated and scared, she tried once again to focus on the fact that her daughter had been sighted.

She nodded. "Do you think they're still at the mall?"

"Why wouldn't they stay there? It's the safest place to be until this storm blows over."

Hoping he was right, she gripped the door armrest

and prayed. When she finally saw the parking garage through the rain, she leaned forward to make sure and then pointed. "Look! There it is."

Too busy concentrating on driving to immediately reply, he managed to navigate a move from the middle of the road toward the right. When he managed to make the turn into what now appeared to be a small lake, he headed immediately for the covered parking.

"Wait," she protested. "What are you doing? Don't we need to go somewhere closer to an exit?"

"There are exits to the garage," he said. "And since we don't have any idea which exit to park near, this makes the most sense. We can't go driving from door to door, around and around the mall in weather like this."

Though she didn't like it, she had to concede his point. "So that means we still have to wait until someone notifies us."

"If we want to find out what's happening, yes."

Thunder boomed, underscoring his statement. At least once they pulled into the garage, they were no longer pummeled by rain.

"Second level?" he asked, since the first had almost as much standing water as the road.

"That's fine, as long as there's an entrance there," she replied. But as they approached the ramp leading to the second level, she changed her mind. "Wait. Let's stay on the ground floor. It'll be much easier to get somewhere else in a hurry."

He didn't comment or argue, just drove as close to the door as he could get, searching for a spot with the least amount of water.

Thunder, lightning and the never-ending rain driven by a wind so strong it made the pickup truck shake.

"Does Houston get tornados?" she asked. "This is too much like what happened to us in Oklahoma."

He grimaced. "I actually looked it up one time. Believe it or not, Houston has more tornados than any other city in Texas."

"Seriously? I always thought it would be somewhere like Wichita Falls." Even more nervous now, she kept her gaze on Nordstrom while twisting her hands in her lap.

"The worst outbreak was in May of 1983," Jake said, clearly trying to distract her. "Something like forty tornados ripped through the area. I remember my parents talking about it. In fact, they brought it up every spring."

Spring in the Lone Star State. She shook her head. "Since we just went through a tornado, the odds of us going through another must be astronomical, right?"

"I guess." He patted her shoulder. "I checked the weather app on my phone. Tornado watch, not warning."

Since every Texan knew the difference between the two, his statement helped her relax somewhat. "Yeah, I haven't heard any tornado sirens."

"Exactly," he replied. "For now, I think we're okay."

Her phone chimed, indicating a text: South entrance by Nordstrom.

She told Jake, glad he'd kept the truck running. "It's right there!" She pointed.

He nodded, shifted into drive and headed that way. The instant they left the covered parking, visibility returned to next to nothing. Though there were still numerous cars in the lot, she didn't see a single person brave enough to risk the storm.

Have they spotted them? She texted back.

Rayna didn't reply.

"Look." Jake pointed to a man hunched against the storm, wearing a trench coat and struggling with a large umbrella. "I bet that's a plainclothes officer on his way to intercept them."

"I'm joining him," she declared.

As she reached for the door handle, Jake grabbed her arm. "We promised to stay in the vehicle," he reminded her.

Jaw tight, she forced herself to nod and let go. "I know. But all bets are off once I have eyes on my daughter."

Jake didn't reply, which she took to mean he wouldn't try to stop her.

Refusing to look away from the hapless man still battling with the umbrella near the door, she didn't even want to think about what might happen to him if a tornado hit. The lightning was bad enough. She remembered watching a video of a man walking two dogs when he was struck. He'd been lucky to survive.

Even so, she knew she'd brave the storm's fury, lightning and all, if it meant she could save her daughter.

The wind increased, buffeting the truck with renewed force. "Still no tornado warnings?" she asked, without tearing her gaze away from the exit.

"Severe thunderstorm warning," Jake replied. "Tornado watch. High wind warning. That's it, so far."

The police officer, if that's what he was, apparently decided his position had become too dangerous and headed inside. Edie shifted in her seat, finally breaking her focus on the exit to look at Jake. "Should we go in?" she asked, feeling helpless.

Frowning, he sighed. "I don't know. It might be safer. These winds are starting to feel dangerous."

Since straight-line wind bursts could cause almost as much damage as a tornado, she supposed he was right. Still, she hesitated. "If we go in, do you think we could jeopardize the operation getting Laney back?"

A particularly strong gust rocked the truck, reminding her of how the tornado had picked them up and set them back down.

"Fifty-fifty," he finally said.

The loud wail of a tornado siren decided for them. Right away, they both checked their phone.

Tornado warning! Take immediate shelter!

"Inside the mall," Jake ordered. "It's the safest place for us right now. We'll make a run for it. Are you ready?"

Hand on the door, she nodded.

"One, two, three…go!"

The instant they left the truck, they were drenched. Rain and wind pummeled them, so strong Edie had to run bent over to keep from getting blown away.

When they reached the mall entrance, Jake struggled to get the door open but finally managed, holding it open long enough for her and then him to make it through.

Inside, they stood shell-shocked, dripping water onto the porcelain floor. Looking into Nordstrom, not another customer was in sight.

"At least they still have power," Jake said.

"Definitely no sign of Laney," Edie muttered.

"Or the guy with the umbrella," he said.

Another boom of thunder rattled the building.

"Let's get away from the doors." Taking her arm, Jake led her deeper into the store. "We need to stay away from glass. Come on."

As they approached the exit from the store into the mall itself, Edie balked. "If she was seen around here, this is where I want to stay."

His tight jaw revealed his frustration. "Look around. If they were here, they aren't now. Like everyone else, they've probably taken shelter somewhere in the mall."

"Away from windows," she said, capitulating. "Though I don't feel like anywhere in here is safe."

"We're going to find an interior bathroom or a storage room," he told her. "I'm sure that's where everyone is hunkering down."

The deserted inside of the mall felt eerie. Hurrying along with Jake past the brightly lit but empty kiosks and stores, she noticed the sounds of the storm were now muffled. Oddly enough, this made her feel safer.

Until the entire mall went dark.

Jake cursed. "Take my hand."

Immediately, she stuck her hand out until she connected with his. "I don't like this."

"It's going to be all right," he promised.

"That's not it. How will we ever find Laney in the darkness? How will we find anyone?"

Instead of answering, he squeezed her hand.

"I mean it," she said, persisting. "How are we going to locate them?"

"Your guess is as good as mine." He didn't sound

worried. "Look at the bright side. No one is going anywhere in this weather."

Since that made sense, she found it comforting. "Where do we go now?" she asked.

"Now, that, I don't know." He tugged her closer. "But let's keep moving. All of the other people had to go somewhere."

Another valid point. Except she worried they might trip over something trying to navigate the unfamiliar space in nearly total darkness.

"We have flashlights on our phones," Jake said, demonstrating. "I can't believe I forgot that."

"Me, too." She felt sheepish. "Too much going on, I think."

"I'll use mine for now, and we can use yours if my battery runs low."

She nodded, still clutching his hand. "Let's go see if we can find where everyone went. Maybe, just maybe, Laney will be there."

They'd gotten as far the food court area when the power came back on. Since there were restrooms nearby, Edie wasn't surprised when a large group of people came around the corner.

"The tornado warning is over," a man wearing a mall security uniform told them. "Everyone is safe to go back to work and or shopping now."

Edie barely heard him. She was too busy scanning the crowd looking for Laney.

As the last of the group filtered past, Edie sagged in disappointment. "She's not here," she told Jake.

"Are you looking for someone in particular, ma'am?" the security guard asked. "There are several other places where people are directed to take shelter.

"Several?" Trying not to panic, Edie clutched onto Jake's hand like it was her lifeline.

"Where are they?" Jake asked.

The guard pulled out a pamphlet. Using a Sharpie, he circled two other areas before handing it to Jake. "Here you go," he said. "If you go that way, you should run into the next group of people. Hopefully, your friend will be with them."

Not bothering to correct the man, Jake thanked him.

Edie yanked her hand free and started running in the direction the man had pointed, with Jake right behind her.

By the time they encountered the people who'd been sheltering together, most of them had dispersed. Seven or eight walked in Edie and Jake's direction. Laney wasn't among them.

"Excuse me," Edie asked a middle-aged woman with a pleasant face. "When you were waiting out the tornado warning, did you happen to see a little blonde girl? About five years old?"

The woman frowned. "There were no children with us, other than a couple of babies. Have you lost your child? Maybe you should notify mall security. Or better yet, call the police."

"She's with an adult," Edie replied, not wanting to go into a detailed explanation, for obvious reasons.

Jake, having caught up with her, grabbed her hand. "Come on. We've got one more area we can check. It's on the other side of the mall, so we need to hurry."

Even though she figured they'd likely be too late, she nodded. "Let's go."

They encountered more and more people on the way.

This time there were a couple of children, but none of them was Laney. Even so, she refused to give up hope.

It wasn't until they'd made a complete circle of the bottom level of the mall that she had to acknowledge possible defeat. Only possible, she told herself grimly. How could they have come this far, gotten this close, only to not find her.

Her phone rang. She knew before she even looked that it would be Rayna.

"We've swept the entire ground floor of the mall," Rayna said. "They've even sent a couple officers to check the upper areas. No luck so far. I don't know how, but if they were ever here, it looks like Laney and her abductor managed to get away."

Though Laney didn't put the call on speaker, Jake could tell by her expression that it wasn't good news. When she punched the button to end the call and shoved the phone into her back pocket, he grabbed her hand. The dejection in her eyes told him more than words,

"Rayna?" he asked.

Slowly, she nodded. "Yes. And she says if they were ever here, they're gone now."

Words failing him, he pulled her into his arms without saying a word. She allowed this, holding herself stiffly, but after a moment she stepped away.

"I can't," she said, not meeting his gaze. "If I do that, I'm going to fall apart."

Since he understood all too well, he simply nodded.

Another crushing disappointment. He didn't know how many more he could take. But worse than his own sorrow was watching beautiful, brave Edie try so hard to stay strong.

Her mouth trembled and tears shone in her eyes, but she squared her shoulders, lifted her chin and swallowed before meeting his gaze. "We are going to get that bastard," she said. "We are. Obviously not today, but his time is coming. He can't keep Laney from me. Whatever I have to do, I'll hunt him down and get her back."

He knew he should agree and then do the manly thing: chin up and soldier on. And he would in a minute. As soon as he got his own messed up emotions under control. This seemingly endless cycle of ups and downs had gotten to him, too. But watching the strongest woman he'd ever met try so hard not to crumble affected him more than he'd ever thought possible.

For so long, his focus had been narrow and well defined. Find his daughter. Nothing more, certainly nothing less. Finding Noel had been his reason for breathing, and sometimes he suspected it had become his only reason to live.

He'd never expected the search to become so…complicated. And he admittedly hadn't given a thought to how the passing of so many years would affect his and his daughter's relationship.

Noel wouldn't remember what she'd been named at birth. Laney had become her identity, the same way Edie was the only mother she remembered and loved. Then, if all of that wasn't enough, it would seem he'd developed *feelings* for the woman who'd been raising his child. The woman from who, until he'd gotten to know her, he'd intended on taking his daughter away from.

Complicated didn't even begin to describe this.

"Let's go," he told her, his voice hard. Without

waiting to see if she would follow him, he turned and strode away.

Because she must have also understood, she didn't even have to hurry to catch up. She was right there with him, moving back toward Nordstrom without another word.

Outside, rain still fell, though the worst of the storm had moved past them. The gray sogginess matched Jake's mood. Not caring, he splashed through the flooded parking lot until they reached his truck.

Once inside, he waited a moment before starting the ignition. Glancing at him, she shivered.

"Are you okay?" he asked her, aware it was a pointless question.

Instead of answering, she shook her head and heaved a heavy sigh, wrapping her arms around herself to try and get warm. "Are you?"

"You've caught a chill." Ignoring the bitterness in her voice, he reached for her. "Come here. Let's get you warm. No one can see us."

"Warmth doesn't matter."

For whatever reason, he decided to argue. "No sense in getting sick. Come here. Please." Realizing he'd come close to begging, he wondered if he needed her comfort more than she needed his.

"Not yet." Expression bleak, she met his gaze. "Jake, I need you to take us back to the hotel."

Though her refusal felt like a punch to the chest, he kept his act together, nodded and shifted into Drive. Hopefully, the roads would be better heading back. No, scratch that. He needed one hell of a distraction to keep from falling apart in front of Edie.

No surprise, but the still flooded streets provided

that. Since the rain had tapered off and the wind had let up, it wasn't nearly as bad. Challenging instead of downright dangerous. Even so, he kept all of his attention on the road, gripping the steering wheel so hard his knuckles showed white. Due to the improved conditions, they made it back to the hotel in much less time than the trip out had taken.

Edie didn't say another word the entire trip. To be fair, he didn't either.

The second they parked, Edie jumped out. She made a beeline toward the entrance, leaving him to catch her. Not sure if he should give her space or be there to catch her when she fell apart, he went after her. To his surprise, she held the elevator for him.

"Thanks," he said.

"You're welcome." Voice still devoid of emotion, she punched the button to their floor. When they arrived and the doors opened, she shot out like the hounds of hell were fast on her heels. She rushed down the hall, disappearing around the corner before he'd even taken more than a few steps.

Not sure what to expect, he wondered if he should go somewhere else for a few hours and give her some space. Maybe he could use some alone time himself.

Deciding he'd ask her if that's what she wanted, he made it to their room and used the key card to open the door. He wasn't sure what to expect, but at least she'd turned on the lights.

Inside the room, she sat on the edge of the bed. As he entered, she met his gaze. The panicked look in her eyes made his chest hurt.

"Edie," he began.

She shook her head. "This feels like it's never ending. Like we're trapped in a horror movie or something."

Staying close to the door, he nodded. "Do you need me to give you some space? I can leave you alone for an hour or so, if you want."

"Why?" she asked, cocking her head. "Do I look like I'm about to have a meltdown?"

"To be honest, yes." Then he braced himself. In the past, he'd often been told he was guilty of being too direct. "But then, I am, too."

She stared at him for a moment, then sighed. "You don't have to pretend for me. I appreciate your strength. You're actually the only person who understands what this is like."

"Strength?" His voice broke on the word. "Edie, I'm not pretending. I'm about to lose it, too."

Instead of appearing horrified as he'd half expected, she jumped to her feet and wrapped her arms around him. "I'm sorry," she murmured, holding on tight. "I should have been there for you, too. You've been great with me, and meanwhile, I've done literally zero for you."

Alternating between permitting himself to be comforted and feeling foolish, he allowed himself to relax and breathe in the scent of her hair. As long as he lived, he'd never forget this moment. He'd let his guard down, revealed his inner turmoil, and she'd offered him her embrace. Without judgment.

He felt pretty sure she had no idea how big of a gift she'd given him.

They clung together like two lost souls. Which, in a way, they were. They hadn't even known of each other's existence a short time ago, and now more than a shared love for a child bound them.

At least as far as he was concerned. He doubted she felt the same way.

Giving himself a mental shake, he moved out of her arms.

Maybe he should thank her, maybe not. He decided to pretend nothing unusual had happened. He figured she'd do the same.

"I'm going to call Rayna," he said. "I need to find out if anyone knows how this guy was able to escape. We've got news coverage, every cop in the city is looking for him, and we tracked him to a specific location in the middle of a severe thunderstorm. Maybe the mall has security footage that can give us some answers. It shouldn't have been that easy for him to slip away."

"I agree." Edie fumbled around in her bag and then began to brush her long, blonde hair.

Mesmerized for the space of one heartbeat or two, Jake couldn't look away. How such an ordinary act become something beautiful and sexy, damned if he knew. Then he looked down at the phone in his hand and remembered what he'd been about to do. Call the sheriff.

But Rayna didn't answer.

And Edie continued brushing her hair, her gaze unfocused, her thoughts clearly far, far away.

He watched her for another moment, loathe to interrupt. But she must have sensed his gaze on her, because she stopped and then looked at him. "No luck?"

"No. She didn't pick up."

"She must be busy," Edie said.

"Or sleeping." He glanced at the clock. "Even

though it's still afternoon, I have a feeling she hasn't gotten much sleep lately."

"Rayna is dedicated," she agreed. "That's why everyone in town loves her so much. She really cares."

The comment made him feel a bit wistful. He'd often wondered what it would be like to live in a small town. "Getaway must be really close-knit."

"It is." Her blue eyes lit up when she smiled. "Even though I went away to culinary school, I can't imagine wanting to live anywhere else. I came back as soon as I graduated." Her smile faded. "I wanted my daughter raised there, just like I was."

"I get that," he said. "It seems a totally different way of life than growing up in a larger city. For me, College Station was the smallest place I'd ever lived."

Distracted, she cocked her head. "College Station isn't all that small. I've been there."

"It's smaller than anywhere else I lived in," he replied. More than anything, he wanted to keep her engaged so the sadness stayed out of her gaze. "Oh, you have? When?"

"A couple of my friends and I went after high school. We made the rounds—Tech, UT and A&M. By then, we'd all committed to where we were going to college but wanted to make sure we'd made the right choice."

"You wanted to see who had the best party atmosphere," he said, grinning.

"That may or may not be true." She smiled back. "But I sure had a lot of fun."

Then, as she realized what she'd just said, her smile vanished. "Try Rayna again," she ordered. "Please."

"Of course." This time, the call went directly to voicemail.

"No luck?" Edie asked.

"No. I'm sure she's just really busy."

Edie nodded. "What you said about security footage. Is there someone else we could ask?"

Stunned, he stared at her. "I can't believe I didn't think of that. Most malls have security footage. Let me make a few calls and see what I can find out."

He called the mall management office first. No one would even talk to him since he wasn't actual law enforcement. Next, he called Houston PD. After identifying himself, he was actually put through to a detective who seemed slightly sympathetic. "I can't discuss an open case," the man finally said. "But I can tell you this. There is no security footage. The storm knocked their cameras off line."

When Jake relayed this information, Edie's face fell. "Figures," she muttered. "It's like we can never catch a break."

Chapter 12

Edie saw the way Jake's jaw tensed and wished she'd kept her mouth shut. None of this was his fault. Yet sometimes it seemed as if he took every setback personally.

But then, she did, too.

She just wanted Laney back, safe and sound.

"We haven't talked much more about who the abductor could be," she said. "Like why this person thinks he has a valid claim to Laney. He has to be someone from your past."

"Or your cousin's past," he said. "Honestly, I've been wracking my brain trying to think of something, anything. And I haven't come up with a single suspect."

Needing something to do, she grabbed the hotel stationery and pen from the small desk. "Let's make a list."

They each took turns, naming someone from their past. Edie began with her cousin's boyfriend Derek, even though they'd discussed and eliminated him previously. This time, Jake began by listing his and his wife's friends. He named them as couples instead of individually. Leo and Angela. Hunter and Susan. After he'd finished going through his former friends, he started on his former wife Marina's relatives.

By the time they were done writing the names of every single person they could think of, they'd filled several sheets of the hotel stationary.

"Wow." Sitting back in her chair, she looked at him. "I wonder if we should forward this to your FBI friend in Oklahoma City. When we talked to him, we didn't get nearly as comprehensive."

He grimaced. "I know, and part of that is my fault. I still can't believe anyone from my past had anything to do with this. I've been searching for my child for a long time, and not once did any of these people even reach out to me. How would they have found her before I did?"

"I agree." Considering him, she looked back at the paper. "Same here. I have a lot of friends in Getaway. I can't think of a single person who'd want to hurt me or take my daughter."

"Which leaves people your cousin knew."

"Maybe," she said. "But we know Derek is still in prison."

"True, but what about his friends? Is it possible your cousin might have had another boyfriend on the side?"

"Anything is possible," she replied. "But from what I understand, Gina was pretty sick for most of Laney's life. I was told she received her diagnosis when Laney was eighteen months old."

He frowned. "That would be six months after she took her."

"*If* she took her," Edie corrected. "Since she's not here to defend herself, I'd rather give her the benefit of the doubt."

"What did she tell you about Laney," he asked. "Did she claim she'd actually birthed her child?"

"She didn't actually say," Edie said. "In my defense, we all assumed she'd had the baby. In retrospect, I'm now realizing that we never saw pregnancy photos or anything like that. Of course, with Gina, that wasn't all that unusual. She barely stayed in touch with any of us in Texas."

"Yet you still went up there and took in a child after she died."

Though he'd phrased it as a statement rather than a question, she explained anyway. "I came from Idaho," she replied. "My birth parents were killed in a house fire. My parents here in Texas were their cousins. They didn't hesitate to drive up there and rescue me." To her surprise, she found herself a bit teary. She continued on, despite the rush of emotion, needing him to understand.

"I've known nothing but love my entire life. How could I not do the same for Laney?" She met his gaze. "I didn't know she'd been abducted."

Clearly frustrated, he nodded, a muscle working in his jaw. "There were Amber Alerts. I kept the website updated and tried relentlessly to keep the media interested. And yet somehow she still slipped through the cracks."

"I'm sorry." She touched his arm. "I really am. But I promise you, Laney knew nothing but love."

Before he could reply, her phone rang, startling her. Though the number looked familiar, she couldn't place it. She answered, anyway. "Hello?"

"Mommy?"

At the sound of that beloved little voice, she gasped. Heart pounding, she managed to say her daughter's name. "Laney?"

Immediately, Jake looked up and hurried over.

"Laney, where are you?" she asked, trying to keep her voice calm. "Honey, are you all right?"

"Mommy, I'm scared," Laney whispered. "The bad man is asleep, so I got his phone."

Blessing the way she'd required her daughter to memorize her phone number and address, Edie knew she had to hurry. "Do you know where you are?"

"A big house," Laney replied, sounding as if she were on the verge of tears. "Mommy, come get me. Please. I want to go home."

Biting back panic, Edie took a deep breath. "Honey, can you go outside and tell me the house number? That will help me find you."

"I can try." Laney sounded doubtful. "I think he'll wake up."

"On second thought," Edie said. "If you can get outside, I want you to run. Run as fast as you can, okay? Just keep going until you see another grown-up. Go to them and get help. Can you do that, Laney? For Mommy?"

"Umm… Okay."

"Keep the phone with you," Edie ordered. "And run. Run like the wind. Go. Now!"

But before she even finished speaking, she heard a

man's voice. "What are you doing?" he asked. "Give me that."

Then Laney screamed and the call went dead.

Edie's heart stopped. Fumbling with her phone, she went to call the number back.

"No. Wait." Jake grabbed her arm. "Let's give Rayna the number first and see if she can find out who it belongs to."

She shook her head. "We can give it to her later. I'm calling back. If that man hurt my Laney..." Her voice shook.

Two deep breaths and she punched redial. The call rang twice, before someone picked up and disconnected. "He doesn't want it to go to voicemail," she said. "I'm going to keep calling."

"In the meantime, let's get the number to Rayna." Jake took her phone and jotted down the digits on the hotel pad. "Here you go." He handed the cell back to her. "Let me call Rayna. If she doesn't answer, I'll keep trying."

"You do that." A fierce determination gave her strength. "I've heard my baby's voice. I'm calling back until either he answers or I hear it again."

Jake sat down on his bed and called Rayna. He kept his back to Edie, pitching his voice low while he spoke. Either he'd gotten through, or he was leaving the sheriff a voicemail.

Edie didn't listen. Right now, she didn't care.

She hit redial once more. This time, the call went directly to voicemail. Whoever owned the phone must have erased their voice message, letting a robotic one replace it and then turned the phone off so they didn't have to hear it ring.

Unable to help herself, she spoke into the phone when directed to at the sound of the beep. "Answer your phone," she said, her voice low and furious. "My daughter is frightened and she wants her mother. Don't keep her from me, please. Let her go. Just let her go."

After punching the off button to end the call, she gave in to her wild despair. Covering her face with her hands, she wept, letting out all the rawness. Hearing Laney's voice, the instant of savage hope only to have that dashed away, had broken her.

Jake pulled her into his arms and held her, murmuring soothing words while he smoothed her hair away from her face. She turned into his chest, still sobbing. He didn't try to calm her with platitudes or empty promises, simply kept his arms tight around her and let her cry it out.

When the tears finally stopped, he handed her a tissue and courteously looked away while she blew her nose. For whatever reason, this made her smile. "I'm a mess," she told him.

"I'm not going to argue," he replied, a slight smile curving his mouth. "But I get it. What happened just now would have destroyed anyone."

At that, the tears started up again. Instead of giving in, she blinked them away, swiping at her eyes with the backs of her hands.

"We're going to find her, you know," he promised. "We're so close. You have to believe that."

The certainty of his words had her lifting her chin. "I do," she replied. "It's just taking too damn long."

He placed a kiss on her temple. "Yes. It is."

His phone rang. "It's Rayna," he said. "Let me put the call on speaker."

"Hey, guys!" The sheriff sounded upbeat. "Edie, I can't express how glad I am that you were able to speak to Laney. That's actual proof she's alive and unharmed."

For the first time, Edie realize Rayna hadn't always considered that a possibility. Humbling. Shocking, even. But then again, she wouldn't have wanted to know.

Rayna chatted a few more minutes, her tone upbeat and positive. She told them to keep the faith, that they would likely get a break in the case soon and to try and stay calm.

Though Edie promised she would, she struggled with the urge to hurl the phone into the wall, smashing it, then stomping on it for good measure. Clearly, she now had anger issues on top of everything else.

She went to Jake that night, not because she wanted sex, but because she needed to be held.

As they were getting ready to try and get some sleep, she didn't even bother pulling down the covers from the bed closest to the bathroom. Instead, once she'd finished her evening toiletries, she simply slipped into his bed and curled up next to him.

To her relief, he seemed to sense what she needed, because he pulled her close without any attempt at seduction. After a few minutes of absorbing his body's warmth, she began have second thoughts.

She turned at the exact same moment he did.

"What?" he managed once she'd made it clear what she wanted.

Grabbing a condom, he slipped it on over his arousal before coming back to her and giving her a long, passionate kiss. He entered her easily since they were both ready. They made love, this time not rushed, but with the slow ease that familiarity sometimes brings.

I could get used to this, Edie thought. More than the sex, but this man.

She could love this man. She might even already be more than halfway there.

Her heart stopped. Sheer foolishness.

Then he kissed her again and she let herself get lost in him.

They fell asleep wrapped in each other's arms. He woke her, sometime before three, and entered her from behind. Though sleepy, just the touch of his fully aroused body made her instantly ready.

They came together, swift and sudden and strong. He stayed with her, even after the tremors quit shaking them. She smiled when he kissed her shoulder and murmured something that sounded an awful lot like endearments. She fell asleep with him still inside her.

When she woke next, his side of the bed was empty. She sat up, realized he was in the shower and lay back down. Today, she told herself. Today would be the day they found Laney. That was the only thing that mattered.

After, maybe the rest would fall into place.

Her phone chimed, indicating a text. She glanced at the screen and froze. It was from *him*—the man who'd taken Laney.

If you want to see your daughter, you can. But only if you come alone.

She frowned. Maybe she could get him to give up some information.

Who is this?

Your adopted daughter's father.

Not sure how to take that, she stared at her phone. In the other room, the shower still ran. She debated walking in on Jake and showing him the text but decided to wait. She wanted to see how far this could go.

No, you're not. I've met Laney's birth father. And you're not him.

Instead of debating this point, the anonymous person texted her another question.

Do you want to see her or not? If so, follow my instructions and you will. But only if you come alone. And leave the police out of it. If I see anyone else, and even catch a glimpse of a police car, I promise you'll never see your girl again.

When she didn't immediately type back, he sent a single sentence that chilled her blood.

She won't stop crying. She needs you. If you don't do as I say, you're abandoning your daughter when she needs you the most. You can be with her. Comfort her. And help her adjust.

Heart pounding, she wasn't sure how to respond or what to do. But she really had two options. Take a chance and see what Laney's abductor wanted, or show Jake and end up in the dark without her daughter. Again.

What do you want me to do?

Trouble. Jake stood under the hot shower and willed it to make him feel better. His insides twisted. What a complicated mess this had become. For so long now, nothing had mattered except finding his daughter. Now… There were so many other things to consider.

He thought about Edie yet again, how she'd felt when he'd entered her, and how he'd realized he was where he belonged. In her arms. With her. And he'd known in that moment that he wanted things to stay that way, consequences be damned.

Not possible. Again, trouble. Like her, he needed to keep his attention where it belonged—on finding Laney. How the hell they'd deal with the mess of their complicated relationship after had to be secondary.

When Jake finished his shower, he dried off and got dressed. Debating slipping in between the sheets and joining Edie, he smiled. His body reacted to the thought of her smooth skin and sweet curves.

Emerging from the bathroom, he stared at the empty bed, puzzled. She wasn't there.

Despite having just emerged from the bathroom, he turned and checked it anyway. Nope.

"Edie?" he called out.

She didn't answer. Of course not. She wasn't there.

Despite knowing better, he made a circle of the entire hotel room just in case. Refusing to be alarmed just yet, he checked his stuff that he'd dumped on the nightstand, relieved to find his truck keys were still there. Which meant she hadn't gone off on some wild search of her own without him.

But then where the hell was she?

Remembering this place advertised a free continental breakfast, he guessed maybe she'd gone down there to either eat or make a couple of plates to bring back up to the room. That would be something she'd definitely do, but wouldn't she have left some sort of note?

He grabbed his phone and called her. Her phone began ringing from inside her duffle bag on the other bed.

She'd left her phone. Oddly enough, this gave him some relief. Edie wouldn't have gone anywhere without that. She must have run down to the lobby to check out the food.

Jake decided to go down and surprise her.

Whistling, he left the room, walked to the elevator, and rode it down to the ground floor. The room where they served the breakfast had several people in it already eating. The array of breakfast goods had been set up on a long table at one end of the room.

He scanned the faces. No Edie. Disbelieving, he looked again. Muttering a curse, he hurried to the front desk and asked the bored desk clerk if she'd seen anyone matching Edie's description.

"Oh yeah," the young woman replied. "She came down here maybe fifteen minutes ago. She seemed in a hurry."

"Where did she go?"

"Out the door." She pointed. "I have no idea where she went after that."

"Thank you." Though he had his keys, he went out

to check that his truck was still parked where he'd left it the day before.

Glancing around, he tried to figure out if she might have walked somewhere. With free breakfast and coffee at the hotel, going for food didn't make any sense. Maybe Edie had just wanted some exercise, so she'd gone for a walk.

The instant that thought occurred to him, he discarded it. In all the time he and Edie had been traveling together—which admittedly wasn't that long—she'd never shown a propensity for taking off on walks in unfamiliar places. And he suspected that if she had, she would have at least left him a note.

Then where could she have gotten off to? Puzzled and growing increasingly more worried, he decided to drive up and down the area surrounding the hotel. Who knows, maybe her emotions had gotten the better of her and she'd had to get outside.

He made two complete circles around the hotel before it occurred to him that she might have tried to set off for the nearest upscale neighborhood. Why she would want to do something like that without him, he didn't know, but she had to have gone somewhere, and that was the only thing that made even a tiny bit of sense.

Except she'd left her cell phone. Even if that had been an accident, he couldn't imagine anyone going off somewhere on foot without a way to call for help.

Even so, he drove around the closest residential areas, looking for her. Nada. Zip. Nothing.

Frustrated, he went back to the hotel, parked and took the elevator up to their room. Inserting his key card into the door, he hoped against hope that when it opened, he'd find Edie inside.

But she wasn't.

He checked the entire room, aware he was being obsessive, but he wasn't sure what else to do. He grabbed her cell from inside her bag, but since he didn't know the password, he couldn't unlock it.

Finally, he trooped back down to the lobby and asked to speak with the manager.

After Jake explained the entire situation, including who he was and what he needed, the man nodded. "I'll just need some identification. I want to make a few calls to verify that you are who you say."

"I can appreciate that." Handing over his driver's license, Jake also showed the manager a screenshot of his website. "My story was also featured on that *One Hour* show the other night."

At that, the man narrowed his eyes and studied him. "I saw the commercials for that, though I didn't actually catch the show. Let me call a local police officer who comes by here for breakfast a lot and see what he says."

Jake nodded. "Go right ahead."

He waited near the front desk while the manager disappeared into the back to make his phone call. He wondered if he should alert Rayna but decided to wait and see what the camera footage revealed. Edie disappearing like this made absolutely no sense.

"Come on to the back with me, and we'll take a look at the security footage."

Trying to curb his impatience, Jake waited while the man fiddled around with a computer.

"Here we go," the manager said.

"Any idea what time you need to look at?"

Since he'd gotten into the shower at seven and Edie had been asleep in the bed, Jake said from 7:00 a.m. on.

Things were pretty quiet at first. A few guests arrived in the lobby and headed for the breakfast buffet. Some employees walked in and headed to the back to get ready to start their shifts.

And then Edie emerged from the elevators, head down, making a beeline for the front door.

"There." Jake pointed. "That's her. Do you have a camera feed outside?"

"We do," the manager confirmed. "At least on the portico area. If she went beyond that, like out into the parking lot, we're out of luck."

At Jake's urging, they pulled up the outside camera. Focused on the front entrance, it showed Edie emerging and getting into a black vehicle.

Muttering a curse, Jake leaned forward. "Is there any way to enlarge the picture? I need to see what kind of car that is."

The manager shook his head. "I'm sorry, there's not. It's a very basic security camera. This is all we're going to get."

Jake watched it again a second time. Then a third. Finally, he thanked the man for his time. "Please don't erase any of that. I have a feeling the police are going to be asking to see it."

He went back to his room and called Rayna. Once he'd filled her in on what had happened, he took several deep breaths, trying not to give in to panic.

"That definitely doesn't sound like Edie," Rayna said, her voice thoughtful. "Are you sure she didn't leave a note?"

"I've checked everywhere. There's nothing."

"Yet you say she didn't take her phone?" Rayna asked.

"It's here in her duffle," he responded. "That bothers me more than her not leaving a note."

"Sounds like whoever she was meeting wanted to make sure she wasn't tracked. Since you have the phone, can you look at text messages or recent phone calls and tell me what you find?"

"I would if I could," Jake replied. "But I don't know the password to unlock it."

"Why don't you work on that?" Rayna suggested. "Meanwhile, I'm going to call my contact with Houston PD."

After ending the call, Jake grabbed Edie's phone and carried it over to the desk. He sat down and pressed the on button. It asked for a four-digit PIN.

He thought for a moment and then googled the address of Edie's bakery. The street number was 2250. He typed that into the phone.

Nope.

Next he tried her house number, which he had stored in the map app on his phone. Another dead end.

Just in case, he tried a few random series of numbers: 1234; 5678. None of those worked.

Okay. Something personal. What about Laney's birthday? Edie had said she celebrated it October 1. He typed in 1001. That wasn't it either.

Trying not to give in to frustration, he typed in the day Edie had said Laney's adoption had been finalized: 0928.

Instantly, the log-in screen cleared and he had access.

First, he checked phone calls, just in case Laney had

called Edie again. But while there had been a flurry of activity the previous day, she hadn't made or received any calls since they'd gotten up that morning.

Next, text messages. The first thing he saw was a random phone number that, for some reason, looked familiar. He opened the texts. What he saw made his blood run cold.

She'd gone off with Laney's abductor. And she hadn't let Jake know.

Numb, he read and reread the text exchange. What immediately stood out to him and struck him as the oddest is that this man, whoever he was, claimed to be Laney's real father.

Why would he be under that delusion? While Jake and Marina had experienced a few rocky patches, when Marina had learned she was pregnant with their baby, she'd been ecstatic. And Jake had shared her joy. They'd done it all together. The maternity photo shoot, the birthing classes and the decorating of the nursery.

Putting the now painful memories out of his head, Jake read the texts again. This guy had warned Edie to come alone and, predictably, warned her to keep the police out of it.

Edie had given the man her location. If he'd been surprised to learn they were so close, he didn't reveal it in a text. He'd actually stated he wasn't too far away, which meant they'd been right to focus on the area near the Galleria.

She'd been ordered to leave her phone, go down to the lobby and out the front door, where he'd be waiting for her.

Jake supposed he shouldn't be surprised that she'd obeyed every direction to the letter. After all, she'd been promised that she could be with her daughter and told her Laney had been crying and needed her. Edie wouldn't have been able to say no to that.

While Jake couldn't exactly blame her, it bothered him that she hadn't trusted him enough to at least leave some sort of note. Something, anything, just to let Jake know where she'd gone and why. While he acknowledged the fact that he would have tried to talk her out of it if she'd told him before going, she could have at least filled him in on her plan after via a note or even a text left unsent on her phone.

Just in case he got lucky, he tried calling the number that had sent the texts, the same number from which Laney had called Edie. The call went directly to a recording that claimed the number was no longer in service.

Damn it. Seething with a combination of anger and terror, he dialed Rayna again and revealed what he'd learned. She made him read her the text line by line.

When he'd finished, Rayna swore. "Why would she do that? We're closing in on him, and now she's given him another hostage."

"I don't think she looked at it that way," he said. "All she could see was his promise that she could be with her daughter."

"And he dangled the perfect carrot by saying Laney was crying and needed her." Rayna sighed. "That would be hard for any mother to resist."

"What do we do now?" Jake wanted to know. "I'm sure Houston PD will want to go over the hotel tapes. Beyond that, what's their plan of action?"

"That's what I'm going to need to find out. I promise I'll keep you posted."

After Rayna ended the call, only the fact that he refused to damage other people's property kept Jake from putting his fist through the wall.

Chapter 13

When she'd walked outside, the humid night air made Edie's skin feel clammy. The sight of the black Mercedes sedan almost caused her determined stride to falter. This was it. No phone, no protection, no Jake or Rayna. Just her and the man who'd abducted her daughter.

Only the knowledge that she'd be seeing Laney again kept her moving forward. This was wrong. Every instinct, every ounce of self-preservation she possessed screamed at her, warning she was making a horrible mistake.

Nonetheless, she made herself continue. Laney mattered more than her own personal safety. Laney mattered more than anything else.

Hands shaking, she reached for the rear door handle, as she'd been instructed to do. Opening it, she slid inside the back leather seat.

And found it empty. Laney wasn't there.

"Where's my daughter?" she demanded, panicking. "You promised I could see my girl."

"And you will," the man in the driver's seat replied. There was some kind of plastic shield in between the front seat and back, so she couldn't have gotten to him even if she'd wanted to. He wore an Astros baseball cap pulled low and a protective, disposable mask over his mouth and nose. Because of that, she couldn't tell much about his features.

Right now, she told herself, none of that mattered. He'd promised to take her to her daughter. She knew full well that she'd put herself in danger. She could picture Jake or Rayna's reaction once they learned what she'd done. She couldn't blame them.

But she'd do it again. Without question. She'd go to hell and back if she could get to Laney.

"When?" she asked. "You said she needed me. I know she does. I'm her mother."

His chuckle chilled her blood. "She's been crying for you nonstop. But that's not the only reason I wanted you."

Wanted her. Hoping the inherent threat of his choice of words meant nothing, she swallowed. "Really? Then please, enlighten me. Why else would you text me and get me to meet you?"

"To eliminate a threat?" Though he phrased it as a question, a sliver of violence edged his tone. "Has it ever occurred to you or your boyfriend that I might be tired of you two?"

Though his words made her shiver, she kept her chin up. When she'd gone away to Dallas to culinary school, she'd felt like a fish out of water. She'd learned then that projecting an air of confidence worked wonders. She'd need to tap into that now.

"Don't lie to me," she said. "The police are going to keep looking for you anyway. Even more, now that you have me. Give me the truth."

"I already have." He sighed, an exasperated sound. "Plus, the girl won't stop crying. She wants you. I want her happy. If she can't be happy without you, then I'll give her what she wants."

The girl. Unsure what to make of that, Edie stayed silent, though her heart ached knowing her daughter had been crying for her.

"Did you leave your phone like I told you?" he asked, his tone once again hard.

"Yes." She hadn't even considered defying him. Not with her daughter's safety at sake.

With a sudden jerk of the wheel, he pulled over onto the shoulder, sending her heart rate into overdrive. "I'm going to check. Once I've ascertained that you're telling the truth, we'll continue. But first, there's a blindfold on the seat next to you. Put it on. I don't want you to see me yet, or where we're going."

Though she did as she was told, she knew this wasn't good. She hated not being able to see. Her skin crawled, and she had to work on controlling her breathing so she didn't go into a full-scale panic attack. Clearly, he never intended for her to leave. At least not alive.

But then, she had no intention of staying. Not for one moment longer than she had to. One she'd gotten to Laney, she had to figure out a way for them to escape.

When the car door opened and he crawled into the back seat with her, she braced herself. Being blindfolded made her more vulnerable than she cared to be.

He searched her quickly with a professional detachment that suggested he'd done such a thing numerous times before. Though relieved he didn't try anything sexual, his thoroughness creeped her out.

"Very good," he finally said, something in his tone suggesting he might be smiling. "Be sure and keep the blindfold on until I tell you it's all right to remove it."

She gathered up her nerve. "Do you have a name? I need something to call you."

Instead of immediately answering, he sat silent for so long that she began to fear retaliation. "You can call me Mark," he finally said, his voice flat.

Real name or false, at least it was something. She nodded and murmured a quiet thank-you. "My name is Edie." She'd read somewhere that in these kinds of situations, it was best not to let your captor regard you impersonally.

"I know what your name is," he snapped.

When he got out of the back and went into the front, closing the door behind him, she exhaled with relief. So far, so good.

As he shifted into Drive and they pulled back onto the road, the vehicle's movement made her nauseous. She swallowed and clutched blindly for the door handle. Being unable to see anything at all made her feel queasy, likely with motion sickness.

"I need you to lie down on the seat now," he ordered. "I can't risk my neighbors or their security cameras catching a glimpse of you."

Quickly, she did as she'd been told. She really hoped she didn't puke. Between this and her raw nerves, it felt like she might expel the contents of her stomach at any moment.

A few minutes later, they coasted to a stop. She sighed with relief, anticipation making her nerves jangle. It sounded like Mark punched something like a code into a control box. When a second later she heard the sounds of metal gates opening, she knew she'd guessed right.

Gated community. Check. She and Jake had been so close. They'd seen several in the area around the Galleria Mall.

Thinking of Jake, she knew she needed to find a way to get a message to him. No doubt her disappearance had put him out of his mind with fear. She'd been too spooked to even leave a note. She'd known if she didn't get away while he'd been in the shower, he'd try to stop her.

Guilt on top of nerves made her feel even worse. She took a deep breath, pushing everything from her mind but her little girl. First things first. She had to get to Laney. Then she'd figure out a way for them both to escape.

Once the gates clanged open, they moved forward again.

"Stay down," Mark ordered. "Do not sit up until I say it's okay."

She did as he asked, even though the movement made her feel sicker. She hoped they'd arrive soon, because if this kept up too much longer, she'd ruin the leather interior of his fancy car.

Finally, they turned into what she guessed had to be a driveway. They stopped, apparently waiting for his garage door to go up before they pulled in.

He killed the ignition, and she heard the sound of

the garage closing. Once it hit the floor, Mark told her it was okay to remove her blindfold.

Immediately she did, blinking despite the relative dimness. They were in fact inside a garage, as she'd guessed. She swallowed rapidly several times, hoping to settle her stomach.

"Is Laney inside?" she asked.

"Yes." Still he made no move to exit the car. Despite her eagerness, she was afraid to make a move without his say-so.

"Is she...is she alone?" she asked, because no one would leave a five-year-old on their own inside a house.

"She is," he replied. "But she's definitely not conscious. I've given her a mild sedative to keep her calm. It knocks her out."

Trying not to panic took every ounce of self-control she possessed. She had a ton of questions, like what kind of sedative? How long does she stay out? What steps are you taking to make sure she stays safe when she wakes? While all those were credible questions, she had a feeling Mark wouldn't welcome them.

In fact, right now he stared straight ahead, both hands on the steering wheel with the ignition off, apparently lost in thought. Inside his dark garage.

They sat there so long her skin began to crawl. Was he having second thoughts, regretting bringing her here, wherever here was?

"Can I see my daughter now?" she finally asked. "Please."

He swiveled to face her and then slowly removed his face mask. With it off, he looked ordinary, like any other man she might meet on the street. "You may," he replied, his tone mocking. "But be aware, if you give me any trouble, I'll be sedating you, too."

"I won't," she assured him, struggling not to show her revulsion. "I just want to see Laney."

"Come on, then." He stepped out of the car, motioning at her to do the same.

When she did, she realized her legs were surprisingly unsteady. He started to lead the way but then apparently realized his vulnerability with her behind him, because he stepped aside and motioned at her to go past him.

Swallowing nervously, she opened the door into the house. She stepped inside a luxurious kitchen, all white and gray, with stainless steel appliances. Unsure where to go from there, she stopped and waited for him to direct her.

"She's in her room at the top of the stairs," he said, pointing. "That way."

She pushed past him, stepping into the foyer where a massive sweeping staircase dominated the area.

"Upstairs to the right," he directed. "Her room is the one with the door closed."

Nodding, she began climbing the stairs, her heart hammering so hard it felt about to burst through her chest. He followed, two steps behind her.

When she finally reached the closed door, she stopped to catch her breath. Her hands trembled as she reached for the knob.

"Go on," he urged, his voice harsh. "You might as well see her even if she won't know you're here."

"Oh, she'll know," she murmured under her breath. She and Laney shared a connection. They always had, from the very first day Edie had scooped her up into her arms. No matter how many drugs this monster had pumped into her, on some level Laney would realize her mother had come to protect her.

She opened the door. The room was dark, curtains drawn. Behind her, Mark flicked on the switch, flooding the room with light.

An elaborate bed with a frilly white canopy dominated the room. And there, curled up under a pink-and-purple comforter pulled up to her chin, was Laney. She looked so tiny, so vulnerable, so…unconscious.

Edie's heart stuttered. She rushed over, calling her daughter's name. "Mommy is here, Laney girl. Mommy is here."

Laney didn't even stir. Crouching down next to the bed, Edie took in her girl's pale and clammy skin and her shallow breathing. She smoothed a lock of hair away from Laney's forehead and placed a gentle kiss on her cheek.

No reaction.

"How much did you give her?" she demanded, turning and glaring at Mark over her shoulder.

He stared back, clearly unconcerned. "I gave her the same amount I always do. She'll be out for hours, but when she wakes up again, she'll be fine."

"You always do? How often are you drugging up my daughter?"

"As often as necessary. I told you, I don't like to listen to her wailing and carrying on. Hopefully, now that you're here, she'll stop, and I won't have to knock her out."

Jaw clenched, she eyed him. "How long does it take to wear off?"

He shrugged. "It depends. Usually when I give her

this much, she's out for around eight hours. And I dosed her up right before I came to pick you up."

Which meant it would be awhile. Likely the rest of the day.

"How can you be sure what you're giving her is safe?"

He assessed her with his dead stare. "I'm a physician," he finally answered. "I know what I'm doing."

Since she had no choice but to believe him, she nodded. "Okay." She'd need to be careful, because the last thing she wanted was him sedating her. How could she watch over Laney if she, too, was unconscious? They'd both be far too vulnerable to this evil man. "Thank you for letting me know."

Instead of acknowledging her words, he simply stared at her. He looked younger than she'd expected, maybe early forties, with patrician features and thin lips.

"There's a bathroom right there," he told her, pointing. "So far, she's refused to take a bath, but maybe she will for you."

Which meant Laney hadn't bathed since she'd been abducted.

"Leave," Edie ordered, surprised at her audacity but beyond caring. "Close the door behind you."

He shrugged and did as she asked.

Alone with Laney, Edie got onto the bed and gently gathered her baby in her arms. She held her close, rocking her and singing one of her favorite songs in a low voice.

She sat there for hours, or so it seemed, though she completely lost track of time. At one point, she fell asleep with Laney's cheek against her chest.

Every so often, she'd check to make sure Laney was still breathing.

Once, she got up to use the bathroom. When she returned, she realized Laney had actually changed her position and appeared to be stirring.

Hope and anger simmered inside of her. That man would not be drugging her daughter again. In fact, as soon as Laney came to and regained her strength, Edie planned to work hard on a plan to get them out of there.

She couldn't help but wish she'd been able to stash her phone somewhere.

Laney whimpered and began thrashing, tangling the sheets around her slight body.

"Shhh. It's all right. Mama's here," Edie said, attempting to soothe her. While she wasn't sure if the words registered, or maybe the sound of her voice, Laney instantly quieted.

Soon, she told herself. Soon her girl would open her eyes and realize her mommy had come to save her.

Jake didn't know what to do with himself now that Edie had placed herself in danger. He felt responsible, even guilty, but in reality he'd been in the shower, and she was a grown woman, capable of making her own decisions. Even if he considered them poor ones.

But hell. He had to admit that had their situations been reversed, he'd likely have done the same thing. Laney was five years old, scared and defenseless against a man who'd deluded himself into believing he had a claim to her. At least now she wouldn't be alone. She'd have the comfort of her mother to console her, protect her and keep her safe.

But who would protect Edie?

Rayna called again, adding Jake into a conference call with the Houston detective in charge of the case.

"Have you had any luck tracking who that cell phone number belongs to?" Jake asked, drumming his fingers on the desk in impatience.

"It appears to be a single-use phone," Detective Miller said. "Purchased at a local Walmart for cash. They sell a lot of those, apparently. On the date that particular one was purchased, they sold thirty-seven. We have asked to review security camera footage, and I have an officer on the way over there to do that."

Refusing to feel defeated, Jake asked for the location of the store. "I'm not going to interfere in the investigation," he promised. "I actually want to drive around the neighborhoods close to that store."

While they all knew that could be a colossal waste of time, no one said so. Detective Miller read off the address, Jake wrote it down, and they all promised to keep each other posted.

Then, because doing something felt infinitely better than sitting around worrying, Jake headed out to his truck. He took Edie's phone along with him, just in case she or Laney managed to get a call out again.

Naturally, he didn't expect to find Edie standing outside someone's house, frantically attempting to wave him down. He wasn't sure what he expected, actually.

Something. Anything. Just the slightest hint toward where she and Laney were being held.

He'd spent four long years worrying about his daughter. The fear hadn't faded over time; rather, it had sharpened as he'd struggled not to give into a fatalistic acceptance. He'd been reminded on numerous occasions how conventional wisdom held that after so long missing, Noel was likely dead. He'd refused to believe that, refused to give up hope.

Nor would he this time.

Especially since he not only had to worry about his little girl, but about the woman she believed to be her mother. The woman whom he'd also come to care about. Maybe even could love.

Back at the hotel, he did another search of the room, unable to accept that Edie wouldn't have left him a hint, some sort of note. Anything.

But just like before, he found nothing.

Pulling out her phone, he typed in her password and reread the text messages. He understood why she hadn't been able to leave him a hint. She'd been told almost nothing other than to walk outside and get in a waiting car. Her bravery astounded him. She had to have been terrified and grasping at straws, desperate to see her daughter again.

Though conventional wisdom told him to leave it to the police, he'd heard that before. Hell, he'd *been* the police.

His phone rang. Rayna. "I think we might have a lead," she said. "There's a gated community north of the Galleria. Someone who lives there called in a report. Said one of their neighbors, a single man who keeps to himself and no one knows very well, was seen driving with a young girl in the passenger seat of his black Mercedes. The woman who called said the tinted windows made it difficult to get a good look at the child, which is why she didn't report it initially. But since the local news ran that story, she reconsidered."

"Hotel security footage showed Edie got into a black

vehicle." Jake pushed to his feet. "How far away is this neighborhood?" he asked.

"Unmarked units are on their way there right now," Rayna replied. "The FBI is assisting. Jake, I need you to stay out of their way. You don't want to jeopardize this."

How many times in his own career had he issued those very same orders? Yet this was different. Not only was he trained law enforcement, but the only person he completely trusted with Edie and Laney's safety was himself. And maybe Rayna, but she wasn't here.

"Look, either you give me the location, or I go out and find it myself," Jake told her. "No way am I hanging around this hotel room waiting for news."

Rayna sighed. "I knew you were going to say that. But Jake, you can't go barging in there. They don't know who you are. Even if you tell them, you're a civilian now. They can't permit you to place yourself in harm's way."

"I just want to be there," he lied. "I don't intend to step on anyone's toes." In fact, he knew he had two choices. Announce himself to whoever was in charge and volunteer his assistance or go in on his own, unannounced, and risk getting shot.

"I'm going to let them know to expect you," she said. "Once I have, I'll text you the address. I promise."

While he didn't know Rayna well, he could tell she was a woman of her word. "I'll be expecting your text."

Shoving his phone into his pocket, he took Edie's, too. He grabbed his truck keys and headed out. When he'd been driving around earlier, he'd driven past a gated community. While he felt sure there were more than one in the area, he might as well drive out to that one just in case. If he saw a few unmarked but obvious police vehicles, he'd know he'd gone to the right place. Nothing like being right on the scene.

Pulling up to the neighborhood, he saw the gates were closed. Since he couldn't very well ram them—at least not yet—he'd either need to wait for someone to arrive or to leave.

Five minutes passed with no cars and no text from Rayna. He was just about to call her back when the text came through.

They want you to stay away. They're assembling a task force and aren't on the scene yet. They're also working on obtaining the gate code. It's the community right off Petunia Street.

Which meant he was there. He double-checked the street sign.

Deciding to park his truck in the ungated neighborhood across the street and go on foot, he was just about to back out when a car pulled up to the gate to exit.

As soon as the vehicle breezed past him, he drove through the now slowly closing gate.

Inside, he took a minute to consider his good fortune. Now what? Until law enforcement arrived, he had no idea which house it might be. All of them were elaborate and large, set well back from the street with curving driveways and manicured lawns.

He dialed Rayna. "Do you happen to know the actual address?"

"That is the one thing I cannot give you," Rayna told him. "I'm sorry, but I can't let you jeopardize the investigation."

"I might be their only hope," he argued. "The longer they're in there with him, the more danger they're in."

"You don't know that," Rayna countered. "Let's give the professionals time."

"To do what? If their plan is to surround the place and make demands, he's just as likely to hurt Edie or Laney. You know as well as I do that forcing a hostage situation rarely works."

Rayna sighed. "I'm sure they'll send a professional negotiator. They know what they're doing."

"And I have the element of surprise on my side. I can get in, take the guy down and free Edie and Laney without any bloodshed."

"We don't even know for sure that this is the right guy, the right house, the right kid," Rayna said. "They're checking various resident's security cameras at this point. I'm sorry, Jake. You're going to need to hold off. Until we're a hundred percent sure, you can't just go barging in there."

"But—" he protested.

"No. End of discussion." And then Rayna hung up.

Staring at his phone in disbelief, he wanted to hurl it at the truck window. Naturally, he did not. Instead, he tried to figure out another way to get the information he needed.

Might as well get started.

Parking in front of one of the mini mansions, he started scrolling through his contacts who worked in law enforcement. He'd begin with those who were with the FBI.

Numerous unproductive phone calls later, Jake's stomach growled. Glancing at the clock, he realized over an hour had passed since he'd parked. If it wasn't so difficult getting in and out of the neighborhood, he'd leave and grab something to eat. With Edie disappearing, he'd skipped breakfast and lunch.

Desperate, he texted Rayna, this time with a single word. Please?

She didn't text back.

Since he'd parked with a view of the entrance, he figured he'd see when law enforcement arrived. The fact that they hadn't yet worried him. Lack of urgency usually meant they didn't have their ducks in a row. Possibly the intel could be faulty, or they were busy trying to obtain a search warrant or some such other bureaucratic nonsense.

Impatient, he considered driving around the neighborhood just in case. But since he didn't want to lose sight of the entrance, he decided to stay put.

He made a few more calls. Two of them went directly to voicemail. The third didn't answer at all.

Once again, he tried Rayna, this time calling.

She answered immediately. "Jake, you need to settle down. They're working on this as quickly as they can. There's nothing else I can do from my end."

"Yes, there is," he said. "Give me the address."

She sat silent. "Not today," she finally answered. "We've got to give them time. If they're not making a move by tomorrow, I'll consider it."

"Tomorrow?" He couldn't believe what he was hearing. "Edie could be in danger."

"Judging by the text messages you read me, it doesn't sound like she is. This guy apparently is trying to make them all one big, happy family."

Frustrated, he bit back a retort. None of this was

Rayna's fault. She'd gone above and beyond, attempting to help and coordinate everything long distance.

Now though, he no longer had a reason to remain parked near the front gate.

Shifting into Drive, he cruised slowly around the neighborhood. To his surprise, there were only three streets. Petunia, the main one, made a complete circle. In between that, Gardenia Street. And off to one side, Gardenia Court.

He'd bet nothing in the entire enclave sold for less than one million dollars.

After he'd made several complete circles, checking every driveway for a black Mercedes, he returned to his original parking spot. He couldn't help but wonder if any of the residents had noticed an unfamiliar pickup cruising their streets and scoping out their driveways. If so, he could likely expect a visit from one of Houston's finest.

Which might not be a bad thing at all. At least one of them might be able to fill him in on the details of the ongoing investigation.

Needing to stretch his legs, Jake got out, locked his truck and went for a walk. On foot, he might notice details he'd overlooked while driving. And possibly, he might come across some of the residents outside in their yards. Striking up a casual conversation might reveal information that could help him with his search.

But either everyone was at work or shopping or parked in front of their television sets. Despite the decent weather, he didn't encounter one single person outside of their home. Not one. Not even yard services or landscape companies. The perfect houses with manicured yards had begun to feel like a movie set. Beautiful false fronts with no actual substance behind them.

Admitting defeat, he finally walked back to his truck. Once inside, he started the engine and sighed.

Now what? Did he truly plan to sit parked here, in the hopes that black Mercedes just might drive by?

Chapter 14

"Mama?" Laney's plaintive voice woke Edie from her light doze. Her daughter still lay snuggled up in her mother's arms, but now her eyes were open.

"Mommy's here," Edie said, kissing Laney's forehead. "I found you."

Struggling to sit up, Laney blinked several times, as if trying to clear the fog from her brain. "I'm thirsty," she said. "And I need to go to the bathroom."

"Come on." She took her daughter's hand, helping her out of the bed and making sure she could stand. No way was she letting Laney out of her sight now.

Once Laney had finished up and washed her hands, Edie grabbed one of the plastic cups that had been stacked on the counter. "Let's get you some water."

Gaze locked on her mother's face, Laney drank eagerly, taking great gulps until she'd drained the entire cup.

"Do you want some more?" Edie asked, aware she needed to make everything seem as normal as possible for her little girl right now.

Laney shook her head. "I want to go home."

The mingled hope and heartbreak in her childish voice nearly broke Edie's heart. "We will, sweetheart," she promised. "As soon as I can figure out a way to get away from Mark."

At the name, Laney's expression shut down. "The bad man," she said.

That sentence felt like a punch to the gut. "Has he..." Edie took a deep breath and tried again. "Has he... hurt you?"

"No. If he tried, I would kick him." The fierceness in Laney's voice mingled with the innocence in her gaze told Edie what she'd wanted to know.

Still, she needed to be sure. "Then why do you say he's a bad man?" she asked.

"He took me away from my friends," Laney said. "And you. He threw me into his car, Mama. I didn't want to go with him, I promise."

"I know you didn't, honey." Eyeing her daughter's lank hair, Edie gestured toward the tub. "How about you take a bath? I'll run it for you."

Laney glanced toward the closed door. "Only he can't come in. He took the locks away."

Now Edie understood why Laney had refused to take a bath or shower. "I get it," she replied. "I won't let him in. Would you rather take a shower? It's quicker."

Appearing uncertain, Laney bit her lip. "Will you stay right here?"

"Of course. I won't let him in."

"Okay." Laney hopped from foot to foot. The familiar and sweet movement made Edie's throat ache. "Then I think I want a shower."

"Let me find soap and shampoo," Edie said. She opened the glass shower door, finding an unwrapped bar of soap and a large bottle of baby shampoo inside. Large, fluffy towels and washcloths hung on bars nearby. "It looks like you're all set."

Solemn-faced, Laney nodded but made no move to get undressed. Clean clothes would be another issue, Edie realized. Unless Mark had purchased new things for Laney to wear.

"Honey, do you have any other shirts or pants here?" she asked.

Instead of answering, Laney pointed at a dresser with drawers. Edie crossed the room and pulled the top one open. Two brand new packets of little girl panties and two more of socks were in there. Feeling queasy but aware she couldn't let any of that show, Edie got out some underwear before moving on to the next drawer.

Shirts, dresses and pants. In a wide variety of sizes. Since clearly Mark had no idea what would fit her, he'd gotten a range. She had to admit that was good thinking, even if she despised the thought of him dressing her little girl.

"Here we go," Edie said, keeping her tone bright, as if she found it all perfectly normal. "Let's go with a T-shirt and jeans."

Watching her mom closely, Laney nodded. "Okay."

Edie carried the clothing back into the bathroom and placed it on the counter. Then she turned on the shower, getting it to the perfect temperature, before she turned and helped Laney undress.

Right before she stepped into the shower, Laney

turned and looked up at her mother. "Mommy, that man keeps saying he's my real daddy. Is he?"

"No, sweetheart. Now, why don't you get clean? I'll stand here and guard the bathroom door."

Laney finished the shower without incident. Edie helped her wrap a towel around her hair and then handed her another to dry off.

Once she'd helped her daughter get dressed and combed through her wet hair, she looked around in case there might be a blow dryer stashed somewhere. There was not. "Air drying it is," she said, keeping her voice cheerful. "Now we need to try and find something to eat. It's got to be around dinner time."

Again, Laney's expression clouded over. "I don't want to eat with *him*."

"I get it." Edie pulled her in for a quick hug. "I don't either. But we have to eat so we can be strong. We need to do that so we're ready when it comes time to escape."

"Will we?" Laney wanted to know. "Escape? I don't think that man is gonna let us."

"We're not going to tell him." Taking her daughter's hand, Edie opened the bedroom door and led the way to the staircase. "Right now, let me see what he has in the kitchen and see about making us food."

"I want fried chicken," Laney said, perking up. "Can we have that, Mommy?"

"We'll see."

Down the stairs they went and into a fancy, shiny gourmet kitchen. Mark didn't make an appearance, though Edie guessed he had to be around somewhere. She knew he wouldn't allow them to be out of the bedroom without ensuring they couldn't escape.

Or would he?

Walking toward the back door, she saw an alarm control panel on the wall. The display read ARMED. Which meant sirens would likely start shrieking the second she opened the exit door.

Almost tempted to do so anyway, just in case the alarm had been set to notify the police, she decided against it since she feared repercussions from her captor.

When she turned around, Mark stood watching her, his arms crossed. Laney had shrunk back against one wall, as if by doing so she could make herself invisible.

"I wouldn't if I were you," he said, smiling slightly. "Since we're all going to be one happy family together, I thought I'd show you around the kitchen. If you'll make a list of what groceries you require, I can order them and have them delivered."

Nonplussed, she stared at him for a moment. Laney ran to her, hiding behind her legs and quivering with fear. "It's all right, honey," she told her daughter. "Mark's not going to hurt you. You don't have to be afraid."

Laney wasn't buying it. She shook her head emphatically, keeping her grip on Edie's jeans. Judging by the sniffling sounds she made, she was about to break out into tears any moment.

Mark's thunderous expression revealed how he felt about that.

"Give her time," Edie urged, afraid he might rethink his decision to reunite her with her girl. "She only just woke up a little bit ago."

"Fine." Glaring at both of them, he turned to leave the room. "Don't forget to make a list." He paused. "By the way, I'll be expecting you to cook and clean while you're here. You know, all the things the woman of the household should do."

What the...? With difficulty, she bit back her instinctive retort and managed to nod. Only once he'd left the kitchen did she exhale.

"Is he gone?" Laney peeked out from behind Edie's legs.

"Yes." Edie took her daughter's hand. "You don't have to be so afraid. Mama's here now. I won't let anything bad happen to you, I promise."

Laney nodded. "Mama, when can we go home?"

Crouching down and pulling her daughter close, Edie hugged her. She inhaled the clean scent of her little girl's hair, both grateful she'd found her and worried about what the next steps should be.

Suddenly, Laney stiffed. Looking up, Edie realized their captor had returned to the kitchen.

"Do you have that list?" he asked.

"Not yet," she replied. "I'll get to work on that soon."

"Soon?" He glanced from her to the small child cowering away from him in Edie's arms. "We need to talk."

Stomach sinking, Edie nodded. "Let me just get Laney situated in her room, okay?"

"No. She needs to stay. What I have to say concerns her, so she should hear it." Gesturing toward the kitchen table, he pointed toward a chair. "Sit. Both of you."

Edie tried to move that direction, but Laney clinging to her made that difficult. "Honey, it's going to be all right," she promised, hoping she was telling the truth. "Why don't you sit down so we can listen to what Mark has to say?"

"Daddy," Mark corrected, his voice sharp. "She should call me Daddy."

Both Edie and Laney froze. Eyeing him, Edie tried to formulate some sort of response and couldn't.

Laney, however, tugged at the hem of Edie's shirt. "Mama," she whispered. "Tell him he's not."

"I am!" Mark roared. "You just don't remember."

Cowering once again, Laney hid her face in the back of Edie's leg.

"You're scaring her," Edie said, keeping her tone level. She could only hope this didn't set him off. Though she wasn't sure how, she thought his instability might actually be something she could use against him.

Shooting her a disgusted look, Mark once again pointed toward the table and chairs. "Sit. Don't make me tell you again."

Swallowing, Edie pried her daughter away from her leg and moved her toward a chair. Once she'd gotten Laney situated, she took the seat next to her, waiting for their captor to spew whatever nonsense he had planned. She could only try her best to appear interested and engaged. She knew she needed to keep him calm.

Once they were both settled, he pulled out a chair and straddled it. "This is all a very good thing for both of you," he commented, waving his hand vaguely. "I've seen where you were living in that podunk little town. You work at a bakery, for Pete's sake. Laney attends *public* school." He spoke the word with great distaste.

"Here in Houston, with me, neither of you will want for anything. You," he said, pointing at Edie, "won't have to work outside the house. As long as you keep things clean and prepare good, healthy meals, that is."

Welcome back to the fifties, Edie thought, though she kept her mouth shut.

"And Laney," he said, "will have access to the best private school in Harris County."

Though Edie knew better than to poke the snake, she had to ask. "What will you be doing? While Laney is in school and I'm dusting and vacuuming, that is. Do you have a job?"

Expression both haughty and incredulous, he looked at her as if he found her question ridiculous. "You don't know who I am?" he asked, his voice disbelieving. "You haven't seen any of my ads on television?"

She shook her head. "We're not from around here, remember?"

"I'm a doctor," he said. "A highly sought-after and world-renowned plastic surgeon. People come to me from all over the state. I'm also very active in charitable organizations and am well respected here in the community."

Until they learn you've kidnapped a young girl and then her adoptive mother. Edie kept those thoughts to herself.

"What was your connection to that house in Conroe?" she asked, genuinely curious. "The one that exploded."

"It's one of my numerous rental properties," he explained. "I have so many that I formed my own property management company."

Since he sounded so pleased with himself, she tried to look impressed. "You're wealthy, then?"

Instead of answering, he simply smirked.

Laney put her head down on her arms, effectively hiding her face from him. Edie reached over and smoothed her daughter's hair. "It's going to be all right," she said.

"Damn straight, it is," Mark interjected. "What I need you to take care of first is teaching my own daughter not to be afraid of me."

Dare she ask? Or would doing so anger him, since her question might poke holes in his delusionary world. She decided to play it safe and pretend like she knew why he considered himself to be Laney's real birth father.

"I'll get to work on that right away," she said.

Laney raised her head in disbelief. Edie shot her a look, warning her not to protest.

"And get me that grocery list," Mark demanded. "I've got some patients I need to see tomorrow, so all of this minor stuff I need to get out of the way today."

"Will do," Edie replied.

He would go to work? And leave them there, alone? Did he intend to drug them both so they couldn't leave? Or would there be someone else working with him who'd come in to act as guard?

She'd ask Laney what she knew as soon as they were alone. Then she could make her plans accordingly.

Loathe to leave and have to figure out how to get through the gate again, Jake knew he couldn't park in his truck overnight. He'd need food and a restroom, for starters.

Damn it. Frustrated, he glanced at the gate. Nothing happening there.

As he looked back toward the street, he saw an older woman marching down her lawn toward him. Finally! A person.

"Excuse me," she said loudly, tapping on his driver's side window. "Young man, you can't park here."

Pressing the button to lower the window, he gave her his best, hopefully charming, smile. "My apologies, ma'am. I got a bit lost and I'm calling around trying to figure out which house to go to."

She narrowed her eyes. "Are you here to do work for someone? I don't see any lawn equipment or tools in your truck. And you people usually have some sort of signage on the side of your vehicle."

You people. Keeping his smile in place, Jake shook his head. "I'm visiting someone," he said. "One of your neighbors called the police department in response to an Amber Alert. I'm here to investigate that."

"What?" Clearly intrigued, she cocked her head. "Which neighbor?"

"That's what I'm trying to figure out. I think someone got their wires crossed. And now I can't get anyone to answer the phone." Which wasn't entirely true. He'd spoken to multiple people. But everyone he'd talked to had no idea what was going on.

"I'm looking for a single man," he said. "He lives alone. One of your neighbors claimed she saw him driving a black Mercedes with a young girl inside."

"The doctor?" She shook her head. "I rather doubt that. There's no way he'd abduct anyone."

Now they were getting somewhere.

"This doctor, does he drive a black Mercedes?"

"Well, yes. But…" Clearly reluctant, she eyed him. He sat quietly and waited.

Finally, she appeared to reach a decision. "Take a left on Gardenia. It's the next street, the one in the middle. Look for the largest house on the block. It sits up on a small hill. You can't miss it."

"Thank you so much," he told her. "You've helped me out more than you'll ever know."

Narrowing her eyes once again, she tilted her head and pursed her lips. "I only hope you won't do anything to make me regret helping you."

And then, without waiting for a response, she turned and went back the way she'd came.

He put the shifter into Drive and headed to scope out the house.

Once he'd turned onto Gardenia, he immediately knew what house the elderly woman meant. While every home in this particular subdivision was upscale and luxurious, this one stood out. In his multiple drives around, he'd noticed a wide variety of architecture ranging from pillared colonial to ultramodern, with the occasional rustic farmhouse in between. The only thing they all had in common was their sheer size, and the fact that when they'd been built, clearly no expense had been spared.

But this house, the doctor's, had taken things to the next level.

This home had been built to replicate the White House, home of the president of the United States of America. The people's house replicated here in Houston, Texas.

The sheer audacity of such a thing didn't escape him. Wanting to double-check, just in case his memory deceived him, Jake pulled out his phone and did a quick internet image search. He wasn't wrong. This doctor, whoever he was, apparently had a huge ego.

And likely also had Laney and Edie, holding them prisoner inside.

Not wanting to alert anyone, Jake continued driving. At the end of the block, he made a U-turn and then parked. Obviously, he couldn't just walk up and ring the doorbell. And houses like this always had an alarm system and surveillance cameras, which would alert the doctor to Jake's presence long before he could break in.

His cell phone rang. Rayna.

"Any news?" he asked.

"Some," she replied. "They're trying to get a judge to sign off on a search warrant. This is apparently a little more difficult because this guy is some prominent surgeon. He's friends with a lot of movers and shakers and is very well respected in the Houston upper crust."

He almost told her about the guy's house but knew she wouldn't be happy to know he'd found it.

"I get that," he said instead. "But if we have credible evidence he has Laney—and now Edie, too—that should be enough to convince a judge."

"You'd think so, wouldn't you?" Rayna sounded glum. "But I've been told one nosy neighbor isn't enough evidence. Honestly, I think the judge is one of this guy's golfing buddies. I wouldn't be surprised if he didn't call him and give him a heads-up."

Alarmed, Jake glanced down the street. "Wouldn't that be illegal?"

Rayna gave a wry chuckle. "Come on now, Jake. You know how this good ole boy thing works. The two of them are probably good friends with the chief of police. Now, I don't know that for certain," she clarified, "but the way this has been going, nothing would surprise me."

Unfortunately, he knew how the system worked. He didn't like it one bit, but he'd seen proof of this almost his entire life.

"He's not going to get away with this. If this doctor is holding Edie and Laney captive, we're going to rescue them."

"Yes, we are." Rayna sighed again. "But it looks like it might take a bit longer than usual. Just hang in there, okay?"

Incensed, Jake clenched his teeth. Somehow, he managed to keep his voice level when he responded. "All right. Keep me posted." He ended the call, aware he probably hadn't fooled the sheriff at all. But she didn't know he'd located this doctor's house. All he needed to do was come up with a plan to get inside.

In the end, he decided to take a direct approach. He drove back and parked directly in front. Getting out of his truck, he grabbed a blue file folder and a pen and strode confidently up to the front door.

One of those video doorbells had been installed, so he went ahead and rang it.

No one answered. Which either meant no one was home, or they were trying to pretend they weren't.

He pressed it again. "Pest control," he said, just in case someone might be watching him on video. "I have an appointment to treat your house and yard."

Though he waited, no one spoke. "All right, then. I'm going to get to work."

Turning, he went back out to his truck. While he didn't have any real pest control equipment, he figured most people never looked too closely. And since one of the odd jobs he'd taken frequently over the years had been working as a painter, he did have a pretty nice spray-painting rig in the bed that in a pinch could pass for something a pest control technician would use.

He retrieved that from the truck and strode back up to the house. The fact that the paint tank had nothing in it wouldn't show unless someone grabbed it. Since Jake planned to go around the entire perimeter and scope out the house, he didn't think this doctor fellow would be coming out to inspect his work.

At least he hoped not.

Starting in the front, Jake made a show of pretending to spray around the foundation. He stepped around bushes, being careful not to trample any landscape, and tried his best to see inside windows without being too obvious.

Most of the windows on the front side that faced west had blinds closed to ward off the afternoon sun. He could only hope that wasn't the case with the other windows.

When he reached the gate to the backyard, he reached to open it, wondering if he'd find it locked. To his surprise, it wasn't. The gate opened easily, and he stepped into a backyard that looked like something out of a magazine.

A large pool dominated the lushly landscaped area. In addition to a hot tub with a cabana nearby, there was an outdoor kitchen and bar area. Well maintained tropical plants and brightly colored flowers ringed teak patio furniture and lounge chairs. The large yard even had a good-sized grassy area on the other side of the pool.

Jake forced his attention away from all of that and back to the house. He'd started with his pretend spraying of the foundation, aware he'd be coming up on the main living area right before the covered patio. The double French doors no doubt led to the kitchen, and with the sun shining on the other side of the house, he had high hopes of being able to see inside.

A little surprised no one had confronted him yet, he continued moving slowly toward the back patio. About halfway there, he nearly stepped into a small ant mound. He used the metal nozzle to stir things up, all the while pretending to pump chemicals out.

It occurred to him he might try the back door and see if it was locked. He also couldn't help but wonder if he had the right house. Because it would stand to reason if this was the place where Laney and Edie were being held, their captor would be a lot more paranoid about intruders.

Unless he didn't know. But since Jake had counted no less than five exterior security cameras so far, he sincerely doubted that.

Just as he stepped out onto the patio, the back door opened. Jake froze, bracing himself.

But as quickly as it had opened, the door closed.

Which meant someone inside the house was not only aware of his presence but actively watching him.

Now what? Reflecting grimly at how that question seemed to come up a lot these past few days, Jake bent over and continued his pseudo pest control treatment.

A sound behind him made him straighten up and start to turn.

"Don't move," a man's voice said. A second later, Jake felt the barrel of some kind of gun press against his back. "Raise your hands and walk toward the house or I'll drop you right where you stand."

Despite the way the dialogue sounded like it had

come from a bad detective movie, Jake did as he was told, dropping his painting equipment onto the grass. Clearly, he'd come to the right house. And now Laney and Edie's abductor planned to make sure he didn't rescue them.

Still, how many captives did the guy intend to have? From what he'd texted Edie, he'd brought her into his place to fulfill some sort of fantasy of the perfect little family. That and to make Laney happier.

But bringing Jake inside wouldn't serve any purpose. Which mean this doctor mostly likely intended to find out what Jake knew before killing him and disposing of his body.

Shaking his head at his own bad movie internal dialogue, Jake continued toward the house with the guy right behind him, weapon digging into Jake's shirt.

Several possible scenarios occurred to him. He could turn and strike, using the painting rig as a weapon to help drop the guy. The only thing wrong with that idea is that the man would likely be able to squeeze off a shot, and at this close range, the consequences would be deadly.

As Jake reached for the doorknob, his captor spoke again, just two words. Jake's full name. "Jake Cassin."

When Jake paused, about to turn and ask how, the man prodded him with the pistol.

"Inside."

They stepped into a large kitchen, all white and fancy. Not sure what to do next, Jake stopped. "How do you know my name?" he asked, hands still raised.

"Turn around," the guy ordered. "Slowly."

As Jake complied, he braced himself for something, though he wasn't sure what.

Holding the gun still pointed at Jake, a tall, wiry man with aristocratic features and dark hair stared. "Well?" he demanded. "Don't you recognize me?"

"You look familiar," Jake hedged, wondering what this guy might do if he said no. All he knew about him was that he was a doctor. What kind, he had no idea. Had Jake or maybe Marina been his patient at some point in the past? Or had he been Noel's pediatrician?

"I have a really bad memory," Jake lied. "Who are you, and what's your connection to me?"

"Not to you," the man said. "I'm Dr. Mark Renard. And I'm Noel's actual birth father."

Whatever Jake had expected him to say, it hadn't been that.

"I don't follow," he said, cautiously. "My wife Marina and I—"

"No. Marina and *I*. Not you. Marina told me you and she tried and tried to get pregnant. She came to me crying, begging me to help her. So I did."

Stunned, Jake tried to think. "How did you know Marina?"

"I was her plastic surgeon."

"Her what?" He hadn't even known his wife had once had plastic surgery.

"Before she met you. She and I dated, too, after I'd completed all her work. She started with breast implants, then liposuction, a tummy tuck and finally rhinoplasty—that's a nose job."

Marina had never mentioned any of this. And Jake and she had been married two years before she got pregnant with Noel.

Some of his shock must have shown in his face.

Dr. Renard laughed, a malicious sound. "You didn't know?"

"I had no idea," Jake said.

"Once she got pregnant, having accomplished what she'd set out to do, Marina and I went our separate ways. She struggled with postpartum depression for months after Noel was born and reached out again."

Jake felt as if he'd stepped into an alternate reality. While he'd known Marina had been weepy and moody after the birth of their daughter, every time he'd tried to talk to her about it, she'd claimed to be fine.

"Marina was going to leave you," the doctor said. "Right before Noel was abducted. In fact, the reason she delayed alerting the authorities about her disappearance was because she'd thought I'd come to get her."

Not sure how much of all this to believe, Jake simply nodded. "What do you want with me?" he asked.

"You shouldn't have come snooping around here," Dr. Renard said. "Because, now, you have to die. But I do respect how long you looked for Noel after she went missing. I'm going to let you meet her before I kill you."

Chapter 15

With Laney helping, Edie had just about finished making the requested grocery list when Mark had rushed into the kitchen. A quick glance at his reddened complexion, tight jaw and narrowed eyes revealed his anger. Since Edie had known she'd done nothing to set him off, she could only hope it wasn't related to her or Laney.

As soon as he'd entered the room, Laney had immediately ducked behind her mother.

"Take her to her room," he'd ordered, pointing at Laney. "Both of you go, now. Don't come out until I tell you to."

Edie decided it was best not to argue. "Here's the groceries we need," she'd said, shoving the list at him before reaching for her daughter's hand. "Come on, honey. Let's go."

Laney hadn't resisted. In fact, she'd pulled Edie along as if they couldn't move fast enough. As they'd hurried toward the stairs, Edie had caught a glimpse of movement outside. A person, maybe a man. The police? But she hadn't dared stop to look. She'd figured she'd do that from an upstairs window, where Mark couldn't see.

Heart pounding, she'd kept her grip on her daughter's hand as they'd rushed up the steps. When they'd reached the landing at the top, instead of turning toward Laney's room, she'd hurried across where a series of floor-to-ceiling windows overlooked the backyard. But unfortunately, because of the covered patio, she hadn't been able to see directly below them, only out toward the pool and the grassy area beyond.

"Mommy," Laney had cried out, clearly frightened. Immediately, Edie had changed course, heading toward her daughter and moving them both inside the bedroom. She'd closed to door behind them.

They'd both stood silent for a few moments, trying to catch their breath. Downstairs, Edie swore she heard the peculiar chime the alarm system made whenever a door was opened. Which meant Mark must have gone outside.

"Who was that?" Laney whispered, her eyes huge. "The man in the yard? Who was he?"

"You saw him, too?"

Laney nodded. "Is he coming to help us?"

"I don't know." Answering honestly, Edie could only hope. "He might have been a worker, here to cut the grass or take care of the pool."

"Oh." Laney's face fell. "Then why are we supposed to hide?"

Good point, Edie thought. "I'm guessing Mark doesn't want to take a chance on anyone knowing we're inside. It sounded like he might have gone out. Let me check," she said. "Wait here."

Opening the bedroom door, Edie moved to the landing. As she did, the chimes sounded again, indicating another door opening.

Heart pounding, she waited, ready to bolt back to Laney's room if necessary. She heard voices coming from the kitchen, too low for her to make out the words.

Dare she? Why not? If she was careful, Mark would never know.

As she crept down the stairs, hoping to get closer so she could hear what was said, she realized who Mark was talking to. Jake. Somehow, Jake had found them. And now it sounded as if he'd been taken prisoner, too.

She'd need to help him. But how? She wasn't even sure how to help Laney and herself. Still, she had to try. Maybe working together, they could somehow take down Mark and escape.

Quietly moving closer to the bottom of the stairs, she peeked around the corner. Mark faced Jake, pointing a gun at him.

Her heart sank. Neither man saw her, and she took care to move back so they wouldn't.

"You shouldn't have come snooping around here," Mark told Jake. "Because now, you have to die. But I do respect how long you looked for Noel after she went missing. I'm going to let you meet her before I kill you."

Crud. Edie backed away, hurrying soundlessly up the stairs. When she rejoined her daughter in the bedroom, she knew she had to put together some sort of plan. She couldn't let Mark kill Jake. Nor could she endanger her daughter.

"Mommy?" Laney tugged at her arm. "What's wrong? What's going on?"

Edie crouched down, looking her daughter in the eye. Though Laney was only five, Edie had always spoken to her like an adult. "A friend of mine is here to help us. But Mark has a gun. We all need to be extremely careful, okay?"

Solemn-faced, Laney nodded. "Is Mark going to shoot us?"

"I hope not." Then, as her little girl's face crumpled, Laney kissed her cheek. "I want you to be brave, sweetheart. You've done so well so far. But now I want you to promise me you'll do whatever I tell you to do, with no questions. If I say run, you are to run. As fast and as far away as you can."

"But I don't want to leave you," Laney protested.

"I will find you." Crouching down, Edie touched her nose to her daughter's. "I'll always find you." She took a deep breath. "Now, let's go downstairs. Stay behind me."

As they descended, Edie could still hear Mark and Jake talking. Mostly Mark, since Jake clearly knew better than to argue. When Laney started to ask, Edie put her finger against her lips to warn her to be quiet. Laney's eyes grew huge, but she nodded to show she understood.

Edie still wasn't sure what to do. She knew she needed to use the element of surprise to her advantage. Beyond that, she had several choices, all of them dangerous. She could rush Mark from behind and try to knock the pistol away. Or come in low, slamming into the back of his legs to make him fall. If she could figure out a way to coordinate something with Jake, they might actually have a chance.

Once they reached the landing, she pointed to the bottom step. "Wait here," she mouthed. Though Laney's frown revealed her feelings about that, she promptly sat and crossed her arms.

Edie straightened her shoulders, took a deep breath, and entered the kitchen. Mark continued to talk, ranting about Jake and how he'd followed Jake's progress in his search for Laney, finally tracking her down to the grimy little West Texas town.

"I beat you to her," Mark bragged. "We both arrived the same day, but I grabbed her before you could even meet her."

Jake saw her first. His gaze met her, one swift glance, before he looked away. Since Mark stood with his back to her, he didn't seem to be aware of her presence.

Until Jake looked at her again and gave a quick nod.

It all happened at once. Keeping the gun aimed at Jake, Mark partly swiveled to see what Jake saw. Edie leaped forward, going in low, hoping if she knocked her nemesis off balance, Jake could get the weapon away from him.

She slammed into Mark's legs, right behind the knee, sending him staggering. Jake rushed him from the other side.

The gun went off. Then Jake knocked it out of Mark's hands, and it clattered away. Edie dove for it at the same time as Mark.

From the bottom of the stairs, Laney screamed.

Edie tried to shout out to her daughter, to tell her to

run, but all that came out was a grunt as Mark's elbow connected with her throat. Then Jake grabbed the man, slamming him into the wall, then the floor.

Scrabbling to her feet, Edie rose, trying to breathe.

There was blood. Lots of it, bright red and spattering on the floor, wall and the pristine white cabinets. Whose, she couldn't tell. Hopefully, it wasn't Jake's.

"Go," Jake ordered, still grappling with the smaller man. "Run!"

Seeing her chance, she sprinted toward Laney, still cowering at the bottom of the stairs. Edie grabbed her by the hand, and they ran for the front door. She didn't want to leave Jake, but they'd always agreed the first priority had to be Laney. His Noel.

Outside, green grass had never looked so good. Since Laney's shorter legs couldn't keep up, Edie scooped her into her arms and ran with her child on her hip.

Heart pounding, fueled by adrenaline, Edie kept going, only glancing back once.

No one emerged from the house to chase them or shoot them.

They ran down the long drive, onto the sidewalk and toward the house next door, a modern farmhouse complete with a metal roof. Stepping onto the expansive front porch, Edie pounded on the door, shouting for help.

Finally, someone answered, opening up just a crack. "Call 911!" Edie said, setting Laney down and swaying as she doubled over, trying to catch her breath. "A man's been shot next door where we were being held hostage."

"Which house?" the woman asked.

Finger shaking, Edie pointed next door.

Luckily, the neighbor believed them. A middle-aged woman with short salt-and-pepper hair and a kind face ushered them inside while she dialed 911.

The dispatcher apparently made her stay on the line, because she kept her phone cradled between her ear and shoulder while getting out a plate of chocolate chip cookies and pouring two glasses of milk. She also mentioned Edie and her daughter, letting the dispatcher know they were safe with her.

Finally, she ended the call. "Sit," she said, smiling a gentle smile. "Milk and cookies makes everything better. The police are on the way and EMS has also been sent. Do you know how bad the gunshot wound is?"

"No." Edie grimaced. "I don't even know who was shot." She could only hope and pray it hadn't been Jake. "My friend Jake Cassin came to rescue us. He was fighting the other guy when the gun went off."

"The man who lives there is a doctor," the woman said. "I've lived next door to him for a couple of years, but he's not a very friendly sort of neighbor."

Edie nodded. "He said he was a famous plastic surgeon. I'm still not sure why he abducted my daughter."

The woman patted her hand. "I'm sure you'll find out soon enough. Right now, just be grateful you're safe."

Edie nodded and thanked her. "I'm Edie and this is my daughter, Laney."

"I'm Grace. Please, sit. Eat."

Laney had already helped herself to a couple of cookies and was munching contentedly, though she appeared to have shut down. She wasn't talking, just focused on the sweet treats, ignoring both her mother and Grace.

One thing, however, gave Edie hope. The pinched look around her daughter's mouth and eyes, while not completely gone, had lessoned significantly. Maybe since this had happened so quickly, her child wouldn't have long-lasting trauma from all of this. She'd make sure to get Laney in therapy, but first, she had to get them back home.

Right now, she couldn't stop worrying about Jake. Was he hurt? Had he been shot? Was he okay? He'd become more than a friend to her, despite the short time they'd known each other. He had to be okay. After all, he hadn't met Laney yet.

When she heard the sound of sirens drawing closer, her heart rate sped up again. Glancing at the older woman now sitting with her daughter, she hesitated.

"Go," Grace said. "Laney and I can keep each other company while you check on your friend."

"No!" Laney jumped to her feet so quickly she knocked over the chair. "Mommy, don't leave me." Rushing over, she locked her arms around Edie's leg.

"I won't, sweetheart," Edie promised, her heart breaking as she looked over her shoulder at Grace.

Immediately understanding, Grace nodded. "How about you give one hand to your mommy and let me take the other? Then we can go outside and talk to the nice policemen."

"Okay." Laney peeked around at her with a solemn look. "We can do that."

Outside, the noise and the flashing lights had drawn others from their homes. Neighbors gathered in small groups, watching from across the street and from several houses away on both sides. An ambulance and a fire truck, along with three police cars, had parked in front of the house next door. For the first time, Edie got a good look at the place, shocked to realize it was a replica of the White House.

Paramedics were unloading a stretcher, getting it ready to carry into the house. Edie could only hope it wouldn't be Jake they'd load up on it. Despite the police presence, she couldn't help but wonder what she'd do if Mark ran out the door toward them.

Panicked, she glanced at Grace.

"I think you're safe now," the older woman said, clearly understanding. "Let's go check on your friend."

Edie took a deep breath and nodded.

With Laney in between them, the two women walked across the lawn and up the hill toward the monstrosity of a house next door.

Where was Jake? Why hadn't he come outside? Every instinct Edie possessed urged her to go and find him, to make sure he wasn't hurt and to let him know she and Laney had escaped.

Except there was no way she would ever take her child back into that place. Especially since there was blood everywhere from someone being shot. That someone better not have been Jake.

One of the police officers spotted Edie, Laney and Grace as they neared the front steps and hurried over. "I'm sorry, but I'm going to have to ask you to step back," he told them. "This is an active police investigation."

"I'm aware," Edie replied. "I'm the one who escaped and had Grace here call 911."

At her words, his expression changed. Now, he

looked more closely at Laney. "She's the one from the Amber Alert?" he asked. "Laney Beswick?"

"Yes." Edie nodded. "Laney Beswick. And I'm her mother, Edie."

"We need to take your statement," he said.

"And I'll give it," she promised. "As soon as I find out if Jake Cassin is all right." She kept a hold of Laney's hand, wondering how to best go around him. "He came and helped us escape. If not for him, my daughter and I would still be trapped inside with that awful man."

Feeling as if she'd explained herself enough, she moved to go past him.

"I can't let you go in there," the officer began, stepping in front of her in an attempt to block her progress.

"Young man," Grace interjected, her tone stern. "This woman has been through enough. For heaven's sake, let her check on her friend."

Looking from one woman to the other, he finally capitulated. "Come with me," he said. "I can't allow you back inside, as it's an active crime scene, but I can tell you the homeowner is unconscious. I will get an update on your friend. What did you say his name is?"

"Jake Cassin." Just then, the paramedics emerged carrying someone in a stretcher. Her breath caught. She hadn't even noticed them going inside. "Is that…?"

Before the policeman could answer, someone called her name. She knew that voice. "Jake!"

And then he came out the front door, rushing to her and gathering her into his arms. One quick, fierce hug, a press of his mouth on her cheek, and he released her.

Relief made her sway. "You're bleeding," she said, feeling helpless. "Were you shot?"

"No," he answered, his gaze going immediately to Laney. "It's not my blood."

Relieved, she nodded. Aware of the importance of this moment, one he'd waited four long years for, she kept her voice calm. "Laney, this is my friend Jake. I know he'd really like to meet you."

Immediately timid again, Laney hid her face in Edie's pants leg. "Okay," she replied, her voice muffled.

Edie met Jake's gaze and nodded. Her chest ached with a complicated mixture of love and relief and pain. "Go ahead."

With a slight incline of his head, he thanked her. Turning his attention to the frightened little girl watching him with huge eyes, he crouched down and solemnly held out his hand for her to shake.

"Hi, Laney. My name is Jake Cassin. I'm very pleased to finally meet you."

After he'd known for sure that Edie and Noel had escaped, Jake had slammed the doctor's head into the tile floor, hard. Once, twice, until the other man finally went still. It wasn't until that moment that Jake had noticed the blood.

At first, he'd wondered if he'd been shot, and the adrenaline had kept him from feeling any pain. But then he noticed the large bleeding wound on the other man's pants and realized Dr. Renard had accidentally shot himself. Poetic justice.

Even better, the wide-open front door had proven that Edie and Laney had escaped. They were safe. They all were. Finally.

The sound of sirens outside had made his knees go weak with relief. Help was on the way. Police and ambulance, most likely. He had gotten to his feet and stood over the unconscious man until flashing lights let him know they'd arrived. When the EMTs and the police pulled up and rushed through the open front door, Jake had stood with his hands up and led them into the kitchen.

While the EMTs attended the unconscious doctor, Jake had talked fast, explaining who he was and what had happened. One of the policemen had seemed familiar with the entire case and said he'd recognized Jake from the news. When Jake had told him Edie and Laney had escaped, the man nodded.

"I think I saw them next door," he said.

When Jake turned to go look for himself, the man had stopped him. "Don't go far. We'll definitely need to take your statement."

"I'll be right outside," Jake had promised. "Wherever they are."

"Go." The officer had waved him away. "At least you know for sure that their abductor won't be escaping. You're all safe."

Right then, Jake's phone rang. Rayna. He'd have to talk to her later. Sending the call to voicemail, he made his way outside to look for Edie and Laney.

There. Not next door, but right on the front lawn.

The instant he caught sight of Edie standing with an older woman and a small child in between them, Jake felt a rush of love so strong he nearly staggered. At last, his daughter, now four years older than she'd been the last time he'd held her, protected by the woman he now realized he loved.

For one heartbeat, then two, he couldn't move. Now that he finally had the chance to see his little girl's precious face, he didn't want to blow it and scare her. She'd been through so much already. They all had.

Then he took a deep breath and hurried over to face his future.

"Edie!" he called.

The relief and joy shining in her beautiful blue eyes when she saw him lightened his heart. He pulled her into his arms for a quick hug, kissed her cheek and then crouched down to finally meet his long-lost daughter.

Epilogue

One Month Later

Now that the media attention had finally died down, Jake, Edie and Laney were able to settle into their new routine. Dr. Mark Renard survived his accidental, self-inflicted gunshot wound and the concussion caused by Jake knocking him out. His practice, however, did not survive the loss of his license to practice medicine or the negative publicity his actions had brought him.

Though in jail awaiting trial, he'd hired a top criminal attorney and had expressed confidently to anyone who would listen that he would fight this, but with the way Laney, Edie and Jake's story had been splashed across the news, public sympathy was against him, and it seemed likely he'd be looking at some jail time. Edie and Jake both planned to testify, though they were insisting on a recorded interview only for Laney, since they didn't want her in court or to ever have to see her captor's face again.

Both Jake and Dr. Renard had been ordered to take a DNA test, in order for the courts to ascertain who actually was Laney's birth father. They were currently awaiting the results. While he wanted to know, Jake realized as far as his feelings for Laney went, her DNA didn't matter. He'd love her no matter whose daughter she turned out to be. In his heart, she'd always be his.

The town of Getaway had welcomed Jake with open arms. Used to living in the big city or bustling suburbs, the friendliness of the small West Texas town had felt like a salve on his wounded soul. For so long, he'd been adrift, the only thing anchoring him to this earth had been his search for his missing daughter. The irony of all of it didn't escape him, but he truly believed fate had brought him here to Edie and Laney.

He'd decided to stay. Truthfully, he'd decided this long before he'd acknowledged his growing love for Edie. He'd known he couldn't swoop in and rip his daughter away from the only life she'd ever known. Since now that he'd finally found her, if he wanted to be a part of her life, he'd have to make Getaway his home.

The days after their return had settled into a predictable routine. After four years of living such a nomadic existence, Jake had used the time to decompress. He and Edie had grown closer, though neither of them had attempted to put a label on their relationship. At first, Laney hadn't been exactly receptive to her mother's new friend, but who could blame her. Jake hadn't pushed. He'd been friendly, and gradually little Laney had begun to acknowledge him with the occasional smile. She'd even initiated brief conversations, which made his heart sing.

"Time," Edie had counseled. "She just needs time. Her therapist says she's doing remarkably well after everything she's been through."

Both Edie and Laney attended therapy together. Jake admired the way Laney used every means necessary to help her daughter heal.

"I don't like any of this," Edie told him, when he'd stopped by her bakery after she'd dropped Laney off at school.

Laney no longer rode the bus, which had been a mutual decision by her and her mother. Neither of them were taking any chances these days.

"Kids are going to talk and she'll have questions. I'm not sure how to even begin to answer them."

Jake planted a quick kiss on her delectable lips before taking a bite of the donut she'd handed him. As usual, the sugary perfection melted in his mouth. "Just tell her the truth. She's old enough to understand."

"But I don't know what the truth is," she protested, the spots of color in her cheeks making her skin appear to glow. "How are we supposed to deal with it if the DNA test comes back with that awful doctor as her birth father? Will that give him some rights to her?"

"I don't know the answer to that, but no matter what happens, we'll manage," Jake said, meaning it. "All that matters is this. Regardless, you're her mother, who loves her and will always be there for her. She needs to know that you're never going to leave her side."

Though he'd assured her numerous times that he'd never even attempt to take Laney from her, he also knew she never got tired of hearing it. She and Laney both still needed a lot of reassurance after the horrific events a couple months ago. Laney no longer had nightmares, and while she still acted out in school, the episodes were growing more and more infrequent.

"I tell her every morning and every night that I'll always be with her." Edie's blue eyes flew to his. "What about you, Jake? How does this DNA test affect your plans for the future?"

Aware he needed to choose his words with care, he could only speak from the heart. "No matter whose genes she carries, I'll love her just the same. And if the DNA test shows she's mine, I'll continue to respect your decision when and how to tell her who I am."

So far, they'd agreed not to say anything to Laney. Little by little, Edie had allowed Jake to become a part of both her life and Edie's. He'd made no secret of his growing feelings for her, and while Edie never said anything definitive, he felt quite sure she felt the same way.

Edie swallowed, her color high. "I take it you're planning on sticking around, then?"

He smiled, love for her making his heart swell. "I am. As a matter of fact, I have news. Rayna has offered me a job with the sheriff's department. You might be looking at the next deputy in Getaway."

"Might?" she asked, having picked up on his choice of words. "You haven't accepted yet?"

"I couldn't until I discussed this with you," he said, watching her closely. "I need to make sure you're okay with having me around all the time."

This made her smile, her bright blue eyes sparkling. "You know I am. My parents, however..."

Pretending to be wounded, he frowned. "Are you saying they don't like me?"

"I think the only reason they haven't hopped back into their RV and gone back on the road is because they want to keep an eye on you," she said. "They're still worried you might try and take their granddaughter away."

"How about we take them out to dinner tonight and tell them my news? Once they learn I'm taking a job here in town, maybe they'll understand that I'm not going anywhere."

"That's a great idea," she said. Then she leaned over the counter and pulled him close for a long, passionate kiss. By the time they broke apart, they were both breathing heavily.

Expression dazed, she shook her head. "If you only knew what your kiss does to me..."

"Believe me, I do. Since yours does the same to me."

She rewarded him with a dazzling smile. "I kind of like having you around, Jake Cassin. I'm glad you decided to stay."

As if there'd ever been any doubt, at least on his part. He kissed her again and went to tell Rayna he accepted her job offer. After he'd left the sheriff's office, he stopped by the post office in town, where he'd rented a box to pick up his mail.

When he saw the envelope from the DNA testing company, his heart stuttered. Though he wanted to rip into the envelope immediately, he knew this was something he wanted to share with Edie. Since they were having dinner with her parents that evening, he figured they'd open it together beforehand. He decided to surprise her and tucked the envelope into his back pocket.

That afternoon, Edie called him to let him know Laney had gotten into her car after school crying. Some of her classmates had apparently heard their parents talking and were teasing her about not knowing who her daddy might be.

"It's time," Edie told him, sending his heart into overdrive. "We need to talk to her. I've rescheduled dinner with my parents to Friday night. Can you come over? I'll cook."

"Of course," he managed. "Truthfully, I'm a little bit nervous. This is so huge, so important, and I don't want to mess it up."

"You won't," she reassured him, her warm voice allaying his fears. "And you won't be alone. We'll be doing it together. She's only five, so there's no need for complicated explanations. She'll likely ask for those later, once she's older. For now, we'll just stick to the simple truth. She already knows she's adopted. I've always told her that Mommy chose her. We'll just build on that."

Throat tight, he agreed. His worries almost made him regret not opening the DNA test results, but once again, he told himself this was something he wanted to share with Edie.

For the rest of the afternoon, he was a mess as he hashed out various scenarios in his mind. Since he hadn't yet started work, he settled on perusing real estate listings, looking for a place to rent. Once he started his job with the sheriff's department, he'd have a steady income and would need something better than staying at the Landshark Motel.

There weren't a lot of apartments in Getaway, but he located a unit in a fourplex for rent and made an appointment to take a look at it. Though small, it had been renovated, it looked clean, and best of all, it wasn't too far from Edie's house. He went ahead and filled out an application, paid the deposit, and after the landlord verified his upcoming employment with Rayna, he was given the okay to move in on the first of the month, which was in two days.

Back at the motel, he realized he needed to be at Edie's in an hour. He took a shower and shaved, put on his newest pair of jeans and boots, and a button-down western shirt instead of his usual tee. Then, judging himself presentable, he stopped by a store called Serenity's on Main Street to pick up some flowers.

Inside, the owner herself greeted him. With a brightly colored scarf over her long and wild hair and her flowing floral skirt, she reminded him of a cheerful aging hippy.

"I'm Serenity," she said, her multiple bracelets jingling as she shook his hand. "Have a look around and let me know if you need anything. Though you have the aura of a man in the market for flowers, so I'll get started on making up a special arrangement just for you."

She drifted away without waiting for an answer, leaving him staring after her.

Lucky guess, he thought, but then he noticed the sign stating she was a psychic and advertising readings for a small fee. He shook his head and began wandering around the shop. It was an eclectic mix of rocks and crystals, paranormal books and, of course, flowers.

"Here you are." Serenity reappeared carrying a bright and cheerful arrangement of tulips. "These are her favorites," she said. He started to ask who she meant but decided not to.

"How much do I owe you?" he asked instead.

"Wait. I almost forgot something," she replied, hurrying off to another room. A moment later, she emerged carrying a smaller arrangement, this one made up of carnations and baby's breath. "This is for Laney. This small gesture will cheer her up, I promise."

He started. "How did you know?"

His question made her laugh. "Folks around these parts are used to me," she told him. "You'll understand once you've been here awhile."

Again, he asked for her price, getting out his wallet. She named a completely reasonable sum, and he paid her, adding an extra ten dollars because he knew it wasn't enough.

Smiling, she accepted his cash. "Good luck tonight," she said. "Not that you need it."

Back at his truck, he loaded the flowers carefully into the passenger seat, using the seat belt to keep them in place. Then he drove to Edie's and parked in front.

Heart pounding, he stared at the flowers before making himself get them out. Heading for the front door, he rang the bell, holding both arrangements carefully.

A moment later, Edie opened the door. Her eyes widened as she took in the bouquet. "Thank you," she exclaimed, taking it from him and smiling. "Tulips are my favorite. How did you know?"

Then before he could answer, she shook her head. "Serenity told you, didn't she?"

"She did," he replied, holding up the smaller arrangement for her to see. "I also brought this for Laney."

"Oh, she'll be thrilled. Come on in." Ushering him inside, she led the way to the kitchen.

Laney sat at the table coloring something. She looked up when they entered, taking in the colorful tulips before glancing at Jake.

"Hi, Mr. Jake." Her usual bubbly countenance had been replaced with a glum quietness that broke his heart.

He smiled and walked over to her, placing her flowers in front of her. "I brought these for you," he said. "I thought they might cheer you up."

"For me?" she said, her incredulous voice matching her surprised expression. "Mommy, look!"

"I saw," Edie replied. "Jake brought us both flowers. Now what do you say, honey?"

"Thank you," Laney said dutifully. Then she jumped up and wrapped her little arms around Jake in a quick hug. "You're right," she said, once she released him. "Pretty flowers do cheer me up." She sat back down, picked up a crayon and resumed coloring.

"Dinner's almost ready," Edie said, happiness radiating from her.

He offered to help, but she shooed him away. He stood for a moment just watching her, his heart full. She moved with a sensual grace, her long blonde hair swaying.

"Come see what I'm coloring," Laney ordered, flashing him a tentative smile.

"Okay." Since this was one of the first times she'd initiated conversation with him, Jake pulled out the chair next to her and lowered himself into it. He leaned over, noticing she'd started working on a unicorn, though instead of the usual pinks and purples, she'd chosen black and gray. "Why no bright colors?" he asked, though he suspected he knew.

"The other unicorns made fun of this one," she told him, picking up a dark brown crayon and adding that to the mix. "They took away his happiness and he changed to this."

Jake met Edie's gaze. Immediately, she joined them, taking a seat on her daughter's other side.

"Tell Jake what happened in school today." Voice gentle, Edie smoothed Laney's hair away from her face.

Laney shook her head, her lips pursed tightly together. "They said mean stuff, and they were wrong."

"What did they say?" Jake asked.

"That I have two daddies. I don't have any daddy, right, Mom?" Without waiting for confirmation, Edie grabbed the black crayon and began adding great slashes of darkness to her already grim picture.

"Everyone has a father," Edie began. "You remember how I told you Mommy went and got you after your first mother died?"

Laney nodded vigorously. "And then you adopted me."

"Exactly. Well, you also have a first father."

"I do?" Laney frowned. "Who?"

Watching, Jake wondered if they could see his heart pounding, since it felt about to burst from his chest. "I'm hoping it's me," he said.

Laney eyed him, considering, and then nodded. "That would be nice," she said, and went back to coloring.

Unsure what to do now, Jake watched her.

"I could use some help with this salad," Edie said. He got up and walked over to her.

"Well done." She kissed him on the cheek, her voice low, almost a whisper. "I'm sure she'll have more questions, but we'll answer them as they come up."

"This came today," he said, taking the envelope from his back pocket and smoothing it out on the kitchen counter. "I waited to open it so we could do it together."

Blue eyes wide, she nodded. Fumbling around in one of her junk drawers, she pulled out a silver letter opener and handed it to him.

They stood hip to hip while he opened the envelope. Hands shaking, he extracted the single slip of paper and unfolded it.

The words typed on the paper made his throat tighten. "It's me," he whispered, blinking away tears. "I'm her father."

"I knew it," Edie said, her voice fierce. She pulled him close and kissed him, right there in her kitchen in front of Laney. "It always had to be you."

Blinking hard so he wouldn't break down, he kissed her back. "Should we tell her?"

"Of course." Hand in hand, they turned.

Laney, who'd been watching them with interest, frowned.

"Why did you kiss him, Mommy?" she asked.

"Because we've got good news," Edie answered. "Remember when we had to swab the inside of your cheek and mail it away?"

Laney nodded.

"Well, that test was to say who is your birth father," Edie said. "We got it back today."

"You did?" Laney looked from one to the other. "What did it say?"

Edie squeezed Jake's hand, clearly wanting him to be the one to speak the truth out loud. Still holding on tight to her, he cleared his throat, hoping his voice didn't fail him. "It says it's me," he managed, wiping at his eyes.

"You're crying," Laney said, clearly concerned. She jumped up and went to him, wrapping her little arms around his leg and giving him a quick hug. "Why are you crying? Aren't you happy?"

Her hug nearly undid him. That simple gesture of trust from his daughter made him want to weep in earnest. Somehow, he managed to control himself. Crouching down to Laney's level, he wiped at his eyes again and held out his arms. "They're happy tears," he told her. "Though if it's okay, I'd like another hug."

She gave him one as if it was the most natural thing in the world and then returned to her chair to resume coloring.

"Come here," Edie told him.

Awkwardly, Jake got to his feet, still wiping at his streaming eyes. Edie held him, wordless, giving him time to process his emotions. He thanked his lucky stars that he'd found this woman, their daughter, this family. Truly, he had been blessed.

When he finally had his unruly emotions under control, he stepped away, embarrassed. Edie smiled at him, her gentle face full of love.

"Are y'all ready to eat?" she asked, her voice as bright as her eyes. "We don't want dinner to get cold, now do we?"

"I'm ready," Laney chimed in, though she didn't look up from her coloring book.

"I'm ready, too," Jake replied.

Edie handed him the salad bowl, and he carried it to the table. When he got there, he saw Laney had started coloring a different picture, and this time, she'd used all the colors of the rainbow.

* * * * *

*Don't miss out on other exciting suspenseful
reads from Karen Whiddon:*

Saved by the Texas Cowboy
Secret Alaskan Hideaway
Protected by the Texas Rancher
The Spy Switch
Finding the Rancher's Son
Texas Rancher's Hidden Danger
The Widow's Bodyguard

*Available now wherever
Harlequin Romantic Suspense
books and ebooks are sold!*

COMING NEXT MONTH FROM

ⓗ HARLEQUIN
ROMANTIC SUSPENSE

#2247 PROTECTING COLTON'S SECRET DAUGHTERS
The Coltons of New York • by Lisa Childs

FBI special agent Cash Colton divorced his wife, Valentina, to keep her away from his dangerous job. But when his latest investigation brings him back to her and their—surprise!—twin toddler daughters, he'll reckon with a serial killer out for vengeance...and protect the family caught in the crosshairs.

#2248 THE COWBOY NEXT DOOR
The Scarecrow Murders • by Carla Cassidy

Joe Masterson would do anything to keep his young daughter safe, even give up his life and identity. But keeping his beautiful neighbor Lizzy Maxwell in the dark about his witness protection status threatens their fledgling attraction. Until the criminal he sent to jail escapes and vows retribution...

#2249 DEADLY VEGAS ESCAPADE
Honor Bound • by Anna J. Stewart

With no memory of his identity or past, army investigator Riordan Malloy must rely on the kind woman who rescued him from a sinking car. But Darcy Ford isn't sure if the handsome man she's helping—and falling in love with—is on the run from danger...or a murderer on the run from the law.

#2250 DOWN TO THE WIRE
The Touré Security Group • by Patricia Sargeant

Not many people get the jump on cybersecurity expert Malachi Touré, but Dr. Grace Blackwell isn't a run-of-the-mill hacker. She's convinced Malachi's latest client stole her valuable research. He'll help the beautiful researcher uncover the truth...and spend passionate nights in her arms. But is Grace the victim...or the villain?

Get 3 FREE REWARDS!

We'll send you 2 FREE Books plus a FREE Mystery Gift.

FREE Value Over **$20**

Both the **Harlequin Intrigue®** and **Harlequin® Romantic Suspense** series feature compelling novels filled with heart-racing action-packed romance that will keep you on the edge of your seat.

YES! Please send me 2 FREE novels from the Harlequin Intrigue or Harlequin Romantic Suspense series and my FREE gift (gift is worth about $10 retail). After receiving them, if I don't wish to receive any more books, I can return the shipping statement marked "cancel." If I don't cancel, I will receive 6 brand-new Harlequin Intrigue Larger-Print books every month and be billed just $6.49 each in the U.S. or $6.99 each in Canada, a savings of at least 13% off the cover price, or 4 brand-new Harlequin Romantic Suspense books every month and be billed just $5.49 each in the U.S. or $6.24 each in Canada, a savings of at least 12% off the cover price. It's quite a bargain! Shipping and handling is just 50¢ per book in the U.S. and $1.25 per book in Canada.* I understand that accepting the 2 free books and gift places me under no obligation to buy anything. I can always return a shipment and cancel at any time by calling the number below. The free books and gift are mine to keep no matter what I decide.

Choose one: ☐ **Harlequin Intrigue Larger-Print** (199/399 BPA GRMX)   ☐ **Harlequin Romantic Suspense** (240/340 BPA GRMX)   ☐ **Or Try Both!** (199/399 & 240/340 BPA GRQD)

Name (please print)

Address   Apt. #

City   State/Province   Zip/Postal Code

Email: Please check this box ☐ if you would like to receive newsletters and promotional emails from Harlequin Enterprises ULC and its affiliates. You can unsubscribe anytime.

Mail to the Harlequin Reader Service:
IN U.S.A.: P.O. Box 1341, Buffalo, NY 14240-8531
IN CANADA: P.O. Box 603, Fort Erie, Ontario L2A 5X3

Want to try 2 free books from another series? Call 1-800-873-8635 or visit www.ReaderService.com.

*Terms and prices subject to change without notice. Prices do not include sales taxes, which will be charged (if applicable) based on your state or country of residence. Canadian residents will be charged applicable taxes. Offer not valid in Quebec. This offer is limited to one order per household. Books received may not be as shown. Not valid for current subscribers to the Harlequin Intrigue or Harlequin Romantic Suspense series. All orders subject to approval. Credit or debit balances in a customer's account(s) may be offset by any other outstanding balance owed by or to the customer. Please allow 4 to 6 weeks for delivery. Offer available while quantities last.

Your Privacy—Your information is being collected by Harlequin Enterprises ULC, operating as Harlequin Reader Service. For a complete summary of the information we collect, how we use this information and to whom it is disclosed, please visit our privacy notice located at corporate.harlequin.com/privacy-notice. From time to time we may also exchange your personal information with reputable third parties. If you wish to opt out of this sharing of your personal information, please visit readerservice.com/consumerschoice or call 1-800-873-8635. **Notice to California Residents**—Under California law, you have specific rights to control and access your data. For more information on these rights and how to exercise them, visit corporate.harlequin.com/california-privacy.

HIHRS23

HARLEQUIN
PLUS

Try the best multimedia subscription service for romance readers like you!

Read, Watch and Play.

Experience the easiest way to get the romance content you crave.

Start your **FREE TRIAL** at
www.harlequinplus.com/freetrial.